★

"It's hard to find a better book about the Southwest..."

—*The Poisoned Pen*

"One of the finest examples of this tenet that I've ever run across... I'll add this one to my shortlist of best first mysteries."

—*Deadly Pleasures*

"Ms. Martin knows her borderlands, and she has created a picture of the barren, remote countryside with skill."

—*Dallas Morning News*

"...an intricate plot and well-paced mystery."

—*Chattanooga Times*

"...the story is believable and well-developed... a standout."

—*Contra-Costa Times*

"Martin gives her readers the heat and beauty of the desert...the mix of people and cultures, politics and superstition that marks Texana's corner of the world as something special."

—*Alfred Hitchcock Mystery Magazine*

★

Previously published Worldwide Mystery title by
ALLANA MARTIN

DEATH OF A HEALING WOMAN

ALLANA MARTIN

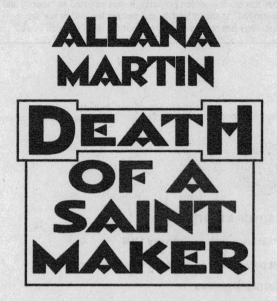

DEATH OF A SAINT MAKER

WORLDWIDE.

TORONTO • NEW YORK • LONDON
AMSTERDAM • PARIS • SYDNEY • HAMBURG
STOCKHOLM • ATHENS • TOKYO • MILAN
MADRID • WARSAW • BUDAPEST • AUCKLAND

In memory of my parents

DEATH OF A SAINT MAKER

A Worldwide Mystery/February 1999

First published by St. Martin's Press, Incorporated.

ISBN 0-373-26299-X

Acknowledgment

Many thanks to the United States Customs Service for information used in this book.

Tell me how you die and I will tell you who you are.
— Octavio Paz, *The Labyrinth of Solitude*

ONE

I SAW THE GRIN, the wink, and the nudge that passed between the two Border Patrol agents lounging by the door. Before I could react a wide paw reached from beneath the table, and Pat Aply screamed and jumped away as it swiped at her ankle.

Pleased with her quarry's reaction, Phobe scooted out from under the table, leaped to the top of the bread rack, flattening four loaves, and climbed onto the shelf above, where she plopped down on top of the highest stack of boot-cut jeans, aimed her black-tipped ears in the direction of the satisfactory noise, and stared down with round, unblinking eyes at the spectacle of a large human being running down the aisle.

"That awful wild animal," Pat shouted at me across the length of the trading post. "I can't think why you keep it."

I rolled my eyes at the Border Patrol agents snickering into their Dr Peppers.

Fully grown and already named, the bobcat had been handed over to my husband Clay, a veterinarian, by a glum father and his three tearful little boys when, in the midst of a rabies outbreak, the mother of the family had refused to let the animal remain in the house. Given a bobcat's love of gnawing all manner of things, I thought the woman must have been waiting for an excuse to get rid of Phobe.

When the youngest child had sobbed, "Please don't kill Phobe," my husband, too tenderhearted for his own good, had promised to give her a home. The bobcat, perched on the examination table at the time, had made a chirping noise and then bumped Clay's chin with the top of her head, a typical bobcat greeting, he had told me, as pleased as if he were another bobcat.

Over the sixteen years of our marriage, we have given a home to a succession of abandoned pets and wild animal babies. Clay's office, a custom-built trailer behind the trading post, is small. The majority of his work is with large animals on the ranches. Since he's often away on calls, and Phobe likes company and needs the space, she spends her days with me.

My name is Texana Jones. I own and run a wood-frame trading post near the end of Ranch Road 170 where the Rio Grande cuts a thin blue boundary between Texas and Mexico. I sell gas, groceries, and ranch supplies to *fronterizos* and to tourists making the scenic drive up from Big Bend National Park. The three-thousand-square-foot trading post provides Phobe with ample room to run, dark places to hide, tables and shelves to climb, and a variety of items to gnaw—all inventory, and thus deductible. The sale table was covered with merchandise discounted because of tooth and claw damage.

For now, Phobe had sheathed her claws and slumped against the wall, eyes closed, purring contentedly. Pat, unaware she had lost Phobe's attention, and watching over her shoulder for a possible rear attack, bumped into the display of votive candles and knocked three of the popular Lucky Lottery variety to the floor. She stepped over the broken glass and kept coming, her yellow half-size dress ballooning around her, the rubber thongs on her feet flapping against the floor. She halted directly in front of the register. In conversation, she had a habit of standing close and thrusting her face forward. Thwarted by the counter between us, she leaned across as far as she could, her chin raised, and her tight eyes fastened on my face in disapproval.

"Phobe won't hurt you," I said, trying to placate the

woman. "She wanted you to chase her and tickle her tummy. It's a game she played with her previous owner's kids."

"I can't think why responsible parents would let that wild animal around their children," Pat said.

"I can think of ten impossible things before breakfast," I snapped.

"Oh, someone got up on the wrong side of the bed this morning," she drawled.

I heard the Border Patrol agents choking back their laughter and regretted allowing the woman's irritating manner to provoke me. Suppressing my temper, I snatched up the dust pan from beneath the counter, grabbed the broom from where it leaned against the wall, and went to sweep up the glass. I brushed the shards and chunks of wax into the dustpan and carried it back to the garbage can and dumped the contents.

Had it been only twenty-four hours since the Aplys' RV had rolled in and Pat Aply had marched through the double doors of the trading post, her small husband Boyce following behind like a Hyundai in tow?

Her first words had been tactless: "I can't think why anyone would want to live miles from nowhere in this godforsaken country."

Not that I love humanity less, but I enjoy the emptiness of our section of the borderland. Although I disagreed with Pat's opinion, I couldn't argue with her facts. Presidio County is the southwestern-most county in Texas. It's three thousand, eight hundred and ninety-two square miles of some of the loneliest acreage in the country, stretches of the Chihuahuan desert backed by two-thousand-foot-high rimrock called *Tierra Vieja*, the Old Earth. I marveled at the Aplys' presence here. Spring, late fall, and winter make up our scant tourist season, mostly a few hearty desertlovers who want to say they made the drive to El Polvo at

the end of the river road. The normal triple-digit heat of
our summers keeps us visitor-free June through September.
And a blistering drought, now in its third year, had dwin-
dled the visitor count even more, which made the Aplys'
arrival in mid-July an oddity. What had brought them to
our remote stretch of the river road? My mistake had been
in voicing the question aloud on the day of their arrival.

Boyce, Pat had explained, was a professor of photojour-
nalism at the University of Texas. While she had talked,
the subject of her discourse had stood chewing his lower
lip and surveying my collection of fossils and Indian artifacts displayed in a large glass case against one wall. Un-
derpaid and unappreciated—Pat's words—he spent summers making ends meet by conducting tours of Big Bend
Ranch State Natural Area for small numbers of people willing to pay sizable fees for his guidance in taking nature
photographs. Boyce had heard about the new RV hookups
at the trading post and, being between tours, had decided
to drive up and spend a few days seeing the area and looking over the possibility of bringing tourists here.

During Pat's monologue, she had frequently turned to her
husband, saying, "Isn't that so, Boyce?"

Consistently ignoring his wife, Boyce had spoken only
one sentence. "You know," he had said, looking at me,
"it's illegal for some of this pottery you've got here to be
brought out of Mexico."

I had shrugged, not bothering to explain that while it
might be illegal for my customers from the other side to
bring artifacts out of Mexico, it wasn't illegal for me to
accept them in trade for food and supplies. Not to mention
the question of how one explains to a man or woman trying
to feed a family that an Indian pot is valuable for its own
sake and perhaps ought to be left in place. In my estimation,
as long as I kept the items here and didn't sell them away

from the border where they belonged, it was no one's business how I came by the artifacts.

After that first conversation, I hadn't seen much of Boyce. Pat, on the other hand, had spent much of her time in the trading post, reading the magazines and inspecting the merchandise. So thorough had been her inspection, I thought of suggesting she take inventory while she was at it. Her nosiness seemed limitless. She had made pointed remarks about how much she'd like to see our private quarters, which run across the back of the building in a series of long, narrow rooms where comfort rather than decor dominates. I had ignored her hints.

"Where's Boyce this morning?" I asked.

"Gone looking for sites to photograph," she said, looking past me to the doors that opened onto the hall of our quarters. "That's kind of an enclosed dogtrot, isn't it?" she said, trying again. Then abruptly, "I need a map of Chihuahua State."

I didn't have to tell her where the maps were. I followed her to the glass-topped counter where the samples were displayed. I stock state highway maps, U.S. geological survey maps, and special travel maps of northern Mexico produced in both Mexico and the U.S. Assuming it was one of the latter she wanted, I reached for a copy of each and put them on the counter.

"Not those," she said. "I want that one."

She pointed to an NOAA sectional aeronautical chart for the El Paso region, a reliable guide not only for pilots flying small private planes, since it shows elevations and landing strips on ranches on both sides of the river, but the best guide available for anyone wanting to drive the backcountry of northern Mexico.

"If you're going to the other side," I said, handing her the map, "I advise against taking the RV." I had visions of the brown-and-white vehicle mired in sand or nose-down in a hole on some cratered back road.

I looked up at the sound of change jingling in a pocket. The agents waited at the counter to pay for their drinks. I excused myself to Pat, who was busy unfolding the map, and went to the register. As I took their money, I heard the double front doors swing open. Glancing up, I saw a black-haired man in faded shirt, worn jeans, and tennis shoes come in. As his dark eyes found the agents' backs, he stopped short, spun around, and disappeared the way he had come. I knew he wouldn't return until he saw the Border Patrol's green 4 x 4 drive away. Half of my customers are Mexicans living in the scattered villages and ranchos across the Rio Grande—*the other side,* as residents of either bank of the river refer to the opposite bank. The Border Patrol seldom bother my customers because they know most of them are headed back across the river. We *fronterizos* slip back and forth at will, but Mexican nationals without green cards and headed north to find work don't show themselves this close to the border in daylight. They slip across by night and get as far away from the river as they can during the hours of darkness.

The quick escape of the man in the doorway had been an instinctive action. Citizens of Mexico loathe and fear their own police, from the blue-uniformed traffic cop to the plainclothes Federal Judicial Police officer. It's not only the fabricating of offenses in order to put the bite on detainees that frightens and intimidates, but the amazingly quick confessions the police in Mexico extract by torture. One refined method involves the use of hot chile peppers and carbonated water forced up the nose. The pain is said to be excruciating.

In Mexico, not only criminals, but victims and eyewitnesses flee the scene of any crime or accident. Otherwise, they could be detained indefinitely, or until sufficient money changes hands. There's the apocryphal story of the man struck by a car and crawling away from the scene because he has a week's pay in cash in his pocket. The incident has been placed in Mexico City, Chihuahua, Juarez—an urban myth that illustrates a harsh reality. The man in the doorway of the trading post had bolted because of a well-developed instinct for self-preservation.

The agents left, and I turned my attention back to Pat Aply. She had taken the map to the table by the coffee-maker, spread it out, and was busy helping herself to coffee and a package of powdered donuts.

"Would you mind taking those with you?" I said to her. "I have to close for a couple of hours."

She looked up, wiped the sugar from her lips with a napkin, and said, "I can't think how it can be good for business to shut up shop in midmorning." She pushed back the chair and stood, carefully folding the map. "But then, I guess you don't get all that many customers."

I rang up her purchases and stood waiting.

She sighed elaborately, collected her things, and walked over to the register where she put them down to feel in the pocket of her dress for a wad of crumpled bills.

"I could watch the store for you," she offered as she counted out the bills and pushed them at me.

I picked up the money, sorted the ones so Washington's face aimed the same way on all nine. "Thanks, but my customers will either wait or come back later. Border time is flexible."

I gave her change and she dropped it into her pocket, but instead of taking her purchases and going, she picked up a wood carving near the register.

"Looks like a leopard. Where'd it come from?" she asked, holding the piece up to inspect the bottom.

"Isn't it beautiful?" I said. "It's a jaguar. *El tigre* they'd call it in Mexico and Central America. I've sold several of the wood-carver's works. He has made horses, burros, and eagles. I liked the jaguar so much, I bought it for myself.''

The statue, carved from a single piece of dark, satiny wood, stood twelve by ten inches. From the base, a thick limb rose and divided. On the broad lower limb, the wild cat half crouched, looking wary, intelligent, and dangerous.

Pat set the statue down, and I locked the register and shut off the gas pumps. Still she didn't leave.

"I thought jaguars lived in South America," she said. Where'd this wood-carver see one?" she asked.

"I think there are a few surviving in the south of Chiapas." I kept it short, hoping she'd take the hint and go. Instead, she asked a question.

"Where are you going, that you have to close? Presidio?"

I looked at the plain, puffy face, the slumped shoulders, and thin gray hair moving in the breeze from the ceiling fans and I realized that behind the presumption and self-assertion, Pat Aply was acutely lonely. I thought of how her husband had ignored her comments as if from long-standing habit, and I felt guilty at my impatience with her pushiness.

"I'm going to the dedication of a chapel across the river," I said. "It's at a place called Ruined Walls. Would you like to come with me? The villagers won't mind one more guest. If you can be ready in ten minutes?"

She scooped up her purchases. "I'll wait for you by the RV." She held up the coffee. "Can you give me a refund on this? I won't have time to drink it, now."

Careful with pennies, I thought as I disposed of the coffee, returned her fifty cents, and escorted her to the door. Turning the lock behind her, I flipped the Open sign to Closed. Ten minutes later I went out the back door to my pickup. I wore a wide-brimmed hat as protection against the intense sunlight, a brushed cotton tunic in white over a sage-green, ankle-length skirt, and flat shoes for walking. The full measure of the heat, rising up from the seared ground and bearing down from the shimmering, empty sky, left me feeling short of breath.

As soon as I started the pickup, I put the air-conditioner on full blast then drove around to the RV area where the Aplys' vehicle was the lone occupant.

Pat stood waiting by the RV as promised. Her concession to dressing for the occasion had been to change the thongs for tennis shoes and put on a bizarre straw hat. The crown had been fashioned as a green felt frog with bulging eyes, its webbed feet flopping over the brim. To complete the ensemble, a camera dangled by a cord around her neck. Pat climbed into the pickup. As she fastened her seat belt, she glanced up and caught me staring at her hat.

"Tacky, isn't it?" she said, grinning.

"It's unique," I said weakly.

"It's damned ugly. But it's a great conversation-starter with strangers." She reached up and patted the top of the felt frog's head. "I love my froggy."

I kept my mouth shut and drove out of the RV lot and onto the blacktop. Just as I started to accelerate, Pat twisted around to look behind us, did a double-take, and clutched my arm.

"There's a man running after us," she said.

I glanced in the rearview mirror before stopping. Carl Sebastien, a squatter for the past three months in an abandoned, nearly roofless adobe in the foothills behind the trading post, was waving his arms and mouthing words as he trotted after the pickup.

I stopped and backed to meet him, rolling down my window.

"He looks mad," Pat hissed in my ear as Carl stretched one arm out to lean against the pickup, his breath coming in gasps.

I waited for him to tell me what was wrong. Carl is one of those people for whom something is always wrong, and for whom the petty problems of daily living grow to insurmountable obstacles.

As soon as he caught his breath, he said, "Where's Clay? I knocked at the office and got no answer. That dog of Pete's has killed my goats. I want Clay to put that dog down. He's dangerous."

"Clay isn't here," I told him. "Did you actually see the dog kill your goats?"

"No, but that dog's a pit bull. The only pit bull around here. Everybody knows those dogs are vicious. I've seen him plenty of times roaming around my place. I want him put down."

New to the area, Carl, like so many with a little land and a lot of ignorance about livestock, assumed you put the animals out and they took care of themselves. Carl's sickly goats were half-starved and looking for a place to die. The pathetic creatures had likely succumbed to heatstroke or stomach worms.

"Clay can't put the dog down on just your word," I said firmly. "Not without proof." I dug in my pocket and pulled out a key, handing it to Carl. "This is for the back door. "Put one—and only *one*," I emphasized, "of the dead goats in the walk-in freezer. When Clay gets back, he'll look—"

"For what?" Carl threw up his hands. "To tell me it's dead? I'm going to see Rosales about this."

"To determine what killed it," I said, finishing my sentence. I eased my foot onto the accelerator. "I'll be home in a couple of hours. I'll drive you over to Pete's place. It's too hot for you to walk."

I speeded up and watched Carl's figure dwindle in the rearview mirror as we headed northwest. Too late I wished

I'd reminded him to wrap the dead animal in something before depositing it in the freezer.

As we passed through the scattered grouping of flat-topped adobes and sagging trailers that make up tiny El Polvo, I waved at the only person out in the midmorning heat. Irene Pick waved back as she rounded the corner of the schoolhouse and went up the front steps. I wondered if she found the two-room adobe cooler than the teacherage behind it.

Two miles beyond the town I pulled off the road. The pickup bumped up the rough riverbank, shocks squeaking in protest, then dipped into the cut of the river crossing. Perpetually diminished above and below El Paso by dams and irrigation, the river that reaches us is anything but grand. The shallow water barely dampened the tires as we drove into Mexico.

TWO

"DO THOSE MOUNTAINS have a name?" Pat asked.

"The farthest are the Sierra de Pilares, the nearest the
Sierra Bonita. The ranges run northwest to southeast, one
after another all along the river," I told her as we drove
out of the drought-narrowed green belt of drooping salt cedars and onto the dirt road that was visible against the pale
soil only because the repeated passage of vehicles had
worked the scree into rough ridges of natural curbing on
either side.

The road followed the curve of the riverbed for a half
mile until it veered across the cracked alkali flats toward
Canyon Oscuro, a narrow valley of yellow alluvial clays
hemmed in by the wind-eroded hoodoos high above.
Ahead, our destination shown blindingly white against the
brown of the parched land.

"That's the chapel," I told Pat. "It was in use in 1874
when the river flooded and cut a new channel. When the
waters receded, the ruined walls were all that was left to
mark the site of the village. Last year our local priest found
out about the chapel and got interested in restoring it. He
took up collections all along the river, arranged for an *adob-
ero—*"

"What's that?"

"Someone who knows adobe. We watched the old man
who did the chapel feel the clay with his hands. Then he
mixed it with a little water and cut it with a hoe to determine whether it could be used for brickmaking. As I was
saying, the priest arranged for the adobe work and per-

suaded the families of the closest village to adopt the chapel for Mass.''

A bored look on her face, Pat hit the search button on the radio and listened to the hissing search down the digits.

"There's no signal strong enough to lock onto," I told her.

She punched the radio off. "Like I said, miles from nowhere. How do you stand it?"

"Familiarity shrinks the distance."

"And the isolation?"

I shrugged. "Solitude can be habit-forming."

"Sounds awful," she said, slumping against the seat and staring ahead. She didn't care where we were going, I realized. She cared only that she was not alone.

I parked in a cluster of five dust-coated pickups, two saddle horses, and three burros, two hitched to small wagons. Uncharacteristically, no one paid any attention to our arrival. The thirty or so people, mostly women and children and a few old men, stood near the front of the small, whitewashed chapel staring at the double doors of solid wood and chattering amongst themselves. One small boy stood on top of a boulder—where obviously someone had lifted him—his hands shading his eyes as he watched the far horizon to the south.

As Pat and I got out, the boy gave an excited shout, jumped up and down, and pointed.

Every eye turned in the direction he wagged his finger. I glimpsed a plume of dust far away, and then a glint of sun on glass. It was a vehicle moving fast across the desert. The people murmured and looked relieved. One old man, erect and slim, with the bowlegged walk of a cowboy and a face lined by a lifetime of exposure to the desert sun, came forward to greet me, smiling in welcome. We shook hands, and I introduced Pat to Hector Cruz, mayor of the village of Providencia, the tiny community up canyon that eked out a subsistence living by raising goats and growing corn and beans, dependent for survival on the envelopes of cash sent back by the men of the village who worked in the U.S. As Hector shook hands with Pat, he professed in his courtly way his immense joy that she would be sharing in the celebration of the dedication of the chapel. I smiled and glanced around trying to pinpoint where the muffled, persistent barking was coming from.

"What's making all the noise?" Pat asked bluntly.

"Lady," Hector said, "there's a dog locked in the chapel. We're waiting for the priest with the key."

"I hate dogs," Pat remarked. "Noisy, dirty animals. My husband loves dogs. He's always wanted one, but I put my foot down."

Hector smiled graciously, but his eyes held a puzzled look at the self-centered pointlessness of Pat's comment.

"The poor animal sounds frantic," I said. "How did the dog get locked in?"

He shook his head. "No one knows. The doors have been kept locked except when work was going on. The *santero* should have been here to let us in. It was he who had the final work to complete, the placement of the statue of the Virgin of Guadalupe. He insisted on doing it himself. He didn't want anyone to see it until the Mass. I gave him my key. The priest has the other."

Uninterested in our conversation, perhaps because we spoke in the border mix of Spanish and English, Pat had wandered toward the group of women and children, camera in hand. Concerned that she might offend them by taking their pictures without asking permission, I excused myself to Hector and went after her. I needn't have bothered.

The children had spied her hat and, enchanted, had surrounded her, jumping up and down and begging to see the great green frog. Good-naturedly, she removed the straw hat and placed it on the head of the youngest child, a smiling toddler of five or six. As the other children closed in to touch the felt frog, Pat snapped their picture. The camera was a Polaroid, and in a moment she handed the photograph to the children, who enthusiastically clamored for more.

While Pat obliged and entertained the children, their mothers and grandmothers watched the growing dust cloud hurtle toward us. In anticipation of minor disaster, I clamped a hand over my nose and mouth just as the white Bronco wheeled up and braked fast, sending gritty dust flying. The brown fog enveloped us, blinding and choking everyone. Father Jack Raff's arrival typified his personality: abrupt and well-meaning, but short-sighted of the consequences. And fair-minded enough not to spare himself the inconvenience of his own actions. Rather than sit and wait for the dust to settle, Father Jack hopped out and joined us, coughing and laughing at his own foolishness.

The six-foot, red-bearded priest wore his vestments over blue jeans, and carried a Mass kit containing chalice, altar breads, wine and water in one hand, a briefcase with Sacramentary and extra vestments in the other. The heavy dust settled quickly, and the coughing group parted to let the priest through. Hector moved to his side and walked with him down the dirt path, their feet raising puffs of dust with each step, to the door of the chapel.

"Isidro should be here," I heard Father Jack say over the incessant barking of the dog. He handed Hector the Mass kit and briefcase, and lifted the white chasuble to dig in the tight pocket of his jeans for a key.

He fitted it into the lock and turned it. Abruptly the barking ceased. Hector put down the briefcase to free a hand to push one side of the door inward while Father Jack pushed the other side.

A snow-white pit bull, his muzzle red-streaked and frothy, paused for an instant in the doorway. The women gasped and crossed themselves. Mothers grabbed their children, lifted them into their arms, and moved away. Hector grasped Father Jack's arm and jerked the priest away from the door.

The dog bolted for freedom, leaping the two shallow steps and darting straight toward me. I felt someone grab my shirt, and I was yanked backward as the dog charged past, running flat-out toward the border.

"Gringo," I said under my breath.

Pat had released her grip on my shirt and was standing close beside me.

"I've seen that dog around your place," she said.

I composed my face and said only that I had, too.

We both turned our attention back to the chapel. I saw two black-clad women hurry inside, no doubt to do a quick cleanup after the dog. Father Jack was picking up his Mass kit from where the mayor had dropped it when the dog bounded out the doors. Hector looked around as if he'd lost something, but couldn't remember what. Everyone else waited politely for the priest to enter the chapel first.

"Ay-eee!"

The high-pitched wail hung in the still air as the women ran from the chapel.

"The *santero* is dead," one cried. "The *nagual* has killed the *santero*," the other said, pawing at Hector's arm.

Hector tried in vain to calm the women. Father Jack stepped around them and went inside. The women with children stayed put. Five of the older villagers followed the priest, Pat and I right behind them.

The chapel's interior was shadowy and cool. The pews that would later provide seating for worshipers had yet to be made, and the narrow, twelve-by-twenty space was empty except for a homemade screen that stood just behind the stone altar. The emptiness made the damage done by the dog obvious. Dark paw prints marred the adobe bricks of the floor, and rust-colored streaks discolored the walls and showed where he had scratched in his frenzied attempts to get out.

While most of us stood staring, stunned at the damage, Father Jack moved purposefully toward the screen and stepped behind it.

We heard a cry of "God!" that sounded equal parts anguish, curse, and prayer. The priest staggered backward. He reached for the screen for support and toppled it.

Hector ran forward, then stopped short as he got a close look at what the screen had hidden. The women huddled together and stayed back.

Morbid curiosity carried me forward, something I soon regretted. The *santero* had fallen in the narrow space between the altar and the wall, his legs and arms tumbled haphazardly. One of the heavy leather sandals had slipped off his foot, exposing thick callused skin—formed from a lifetime of walking to every destination. His body, short and thick in life, appeared even more compressed in death. He was dressed as I had always seen him, in white cotton pants and a smock shirt, which partially disguised his hunchback.

Now the smock and white pants were splotched pink, and blood had spread in a wide pool around the wood-carver. But it was the horrific injuries to his face that made me turn away.

Someone bumped me and pushed past Hector. I turned back and watched as Pat bent over to press her fingertips against the wood-carver's neck for a pulse. Her hand came away with clotted blood sticking to it. She lifted an edge of the smock and wiped off the blood.

"No pulse," she said. "His heart beat a long time after those dog bites, though. Died of circulatory collapse or shock, probably."

"You are a doctor, lady?" Hector asked.

"A nurse," Pat said. She stared dispassionately at the

wounds on the face of the wood-carver, adding, "If he'd lived, he'd have been blind."

I shuddered, shutting my eyes against the sight, but the terrible image of the torn flesh and crushed bone remained all too vivid in my mind.

My eyes flew open when I heard the click of a shutter.

Camera in hand, Pat stooped over the dead man. She registered my shock at her ghoulishness, but made no comment.

"Lady, that's an excellent idea," Hector said. "We'll need a record to show that the dog killed the *santero*. Otherwise the authorities might come here, a thing I should wish to avoid at all costs."

As the camera spit out the print, he held out his hand. Pat hesitated, then surrendered the picture to him.

"What's that word you used?" Pat said. *"Santero?"*

"It means saint maker," Hector said.

"I get it," Pat said. "The Saint Maker makes saints."

There was a loud groan from the priest.

"Are you all right, Father Jack?" I asked, bending over to touch his shoulder where he sat on the floor, head in hands.

Even as I spoke, Pat fished in the wide pocket of her dress and brought out a flask.

"Give him a swig of this. If it's shock, it'll help. If it's his heart, it can't hurt."

"I thought liquor wasn't good for shock," I said.

Father Jack opened his eyes, raised his colorless face, and stretched out his hand for the flask. Pat passed it to Hector, who twisted off the cap, turned, and put it in the priest's hand.

Father Jack lifted it to his lips and drank. Two quick swallows and he choked, spewing out the liquid. I smelled vinegar and looked questioningly at Pat.

She said, "It's my own desert mix to prevent dehydration. Equal parts vinegar, sugar, and water. Sugar is good for shock.''

In spite of the grim circumstances, I couldn't help laughing.

Father Jack rose to his feet, wiped his face with his hands, straightened his chasuble, and said, "That stuff tasted like bad salad dressing. Kept me from passing out and for that I'm grateful. We've got a lot to do. You'll have to forgive my weakness. Never could stand the sight of blood, even as a kid." He looked around blankly, adding, "Where's my briefcase?"

Hector looked puzzled, then remembered and said, "I put it down when we opened the doors, I think."

I offered to get the briefcase.

Outside, I discovered that the burros, horses, wagons, pickups, and people had vanished except for one rusted green Ford, circa 1969, with two men, both older than Hector, sitting inside, and one small brown horse with the shiny coat of a well-cared-for animal, the reins of his bridle looped over a creosote bush. The horse, I knew, belonged to Hector and was his proudest possession, friend, and companion. The pickup, I guessed, had been left as transport for the body.

The Mexicans had a saying: *When there is trouble brewing, stay inside*. The women had gone home, to shut themselves in against the woes they expected the death of the Saint Maker would bring. They feared witchcraft—the woman had called the dog a *nagual*, a witch that takes animal form. Or trouble could arrive in the more demonic form of the authorities—the state or federal police that Hector so dreaded.

At the moment, what I most dreaded was telling Pete Rosales that his favorite dog had killed a man. This made my worry over Carl Sebastien's goats negligible.

Pushing such concerns to the back of my mind, I looked

around for the briefcase and found it leaning against the wall of the chapel. I picked it up, and carried it inside to Father Jack.

"Was he a Catholic, then?" Father Jack was asking Hector.

"As much as any man in Mexico is Catholic, I guess," came the honest answer. I had never known Hector to tell a lie, but he was adroit at avoiding the more blunt truths.

"Well, I dare say I've buried worse than skeptics," Father Jack said. "You let me know when you need me, Hector, and I'll be here. Ah, here's my briefcase."

He took the case from me, set it on the altar, opened it, reached in, and brought out his own flask, from which he screwed off the top. I could smell the rich whiskey scent even over the musty odor of the blood on the floor.

He offered the flask to Hector, who took a healthy swallow, then to me. It was good whiskey. I should know. I'd sold him the bottle from my private stock when he'd asked for something better than the cheaper brand I keep for customers of modest income. I sipped, felt better for it, and gave the flask back to Father Jack. He held it out toward Pat, who tilted it so far back she must have drained it.

We looked everywhere but at the body.

"The *santero* was a good man," Hector said, his usual reticence relaxed perhaps by the whiskey, perhaps by the shock of the death of the Saint Maker.

"In the short time he has been among us," he continued, "he has done much. When he wasn't working in the church, he would sit in the shade of a mesquite and carve animals, tiny human figures, and tops for the children to play with. The little ones loved him. And so did the women. He carved *santos* for them to put on the family altars."

"Well, then," the priest said, collecting his belongings to make the point that he was ready to go, "we'll give Isidro a fine funeral. What was his full name, anyway?"

Hector shrugged. "We knew him only as Isidro the *Santero*."

"Well, he'll have a fine funeral," the priest said again. "It's the least we can do for the man who made this." He half turned and gestured toward the statue of the Virgin of Guadalupe.

The life-size Indian Virgin, mother-protectress of Mexico, symbol behind which Father Hidalgo's ragged army of Indians and mestizos marched in 1810, stood on a *sillar* block pedestal set into a niche against the wall behind the altar and to the left of the crucifix. In the dim light she looked as if she might reach out and breathe life into the dead man at her feet.

The Saint Maker had put all his skill and love into the wood, as well as something of the Virgin's true heritage. While her face showed the traditional compassion and passivity, it also reflected the darker attributes of Tonantzin, the Aztec goddess on whose hilltop sanctuary the Virgin of Guadalupe had appeared to the young Indian convert Juan Diego. At the feet of the statue, the *santero* had carved a single rose, a symbol of the miraculous sign the skeptical archbishop had demanded as proof of Juan Diego's vision. The boy had gathered roses blooming miraculously in the dry hills and carried them back to the bishop in his serape to find the image of Our Lady herself imprinted on the cloth. Even the Spanish friars had been suspicious of the speed with which the devotion to the Virgin of Guadalupe had spread, for in Aztec, Tonantzin means "the Mother of God." Thus did the undercurrent from another world and time wash into the present. The Virgin's ancestry was full of ambiguities, but no more so, it seemed to me, than the death of the man who had so lovingly carved her statue.

"Isidro's death is regrettable," Father Jack said, breaking both the silence and the hold the statue seemed to have on us.

His words prompted me to speak out. "How can we be sure the dog killed him?"

"The animal had blood dripping from its mouth," Father Jack said.

"Look at the Saint Maker's hands," I said. "They're unmarked. If the dog attacked him, why didn't he try to protect himself with his hands? He had powerful hands and arms. Couldn't he have strangled the dog? Wouldn't he have tried?"

Hector knelt beside the body and gently lifted first one, then the other of the dead man's hands, turning them to examine both the backs and the palms. He pushed up the loose sleeves of the smock, revealing the *santero*'s heavily muscled arms.

"Unmarked," he stated, rising stiffly to his feet. A puzzled expression on his face, he looked at the priest. "If the dog attacked him, surely he would have defended himself. Surely his hands would have been bitten and scratched."

"Maybe when the dog jumped him, he had a heart attack," Father Jack said. "Or maybe he fell and hit his head. We can't know what happened." And he glared at me as if to say, "And we don't want to." I appreciated that everyone preferred the dog as villain because it meant not bringing in the authorities, but the truth seemed important.

"What about the chapel key?"

Father Jack said, "What about it?"

"If he locked himself in," I said, "the key should be here somewhere."

Hector knelt again and performed the disagreeable task of searching the Saint Maker's pockets.

"Is it there?" Father Jack asked.

Hector shook his head and stood back up. "We'll have to look for it on the floor. Hector's shrewd eyes darted around the chapel. "The *santero*'s bag of tools should be here, too. I don't see it."

"No reason the door had to be locked when he died," Father Jack said firmly. "Somebody could have found him already dead, taken the poor man's tools, locked the door from the outside, and taken the key with him."

A look of relief settled on Hector's face. "This could easily be true. Let's us hope the person who took the tools will put them to good use, if only to sell them to buy shoes for his children. The *santero* has no more need for the things of this world."

"He got what he was looking for," said a somber voice.

We jumped as if the voice of God had spoken instead of one of the three old women, who until that moment had remained in the background, content with observing.

"This is a saying we have," Hector hastily explained, "when somebody dies violently. Death must have meaning, so we say how you die tells what you are."

Father Jack merely mumbled a vague "You don't say," and asked Hector what he wanted to do about the body.

"There are two men waiting outside in a pickup," I told them. "The rest have gone."

"We will take care of things here, Padre," Hector said. "The women will prepare the body and we will bury him as one of our own, even though he lived among us only a short time."

"Tomorrow?" Father Jack said.

"In this heat, it would be best," Hector said.

"Did he have family?" Father Jack asked.

Hector shrugged.

We stood silent, as if fearful of taking any action. Hector moved first, going to summon the men from the pickup, and Father Jack followed him. Through the open door, I watched as he got into his Bronco and drove away. The three women shook their heads when I asked if they needed any help. I started toward the door, assuming Pat would follow.

Click. I turned around at the sound, but she was already stepping away from the body. She caught up with me. As we walked to the door together, the camera rolled out a print and Pat slipped it into her pocket. At the door, we passed the two old men from the pickup coming in. Hector, walking behind them, stopped to speak with us.

"This shocking death, please, forget it happened," Hector begged. He added that he hoped Pat would visit Providencia and meet all the good people on a happier day. Then he went sadly in to supervise the removal of the body.

"You were very cool," I told Pat as we padded through the dust to the pickup, "about feeling for a pulse. I didn't have the presence of mind to even think of it."

"I used to work the emergency room. That's how I supported Boyce while he got his doctorate."

That explained the air of confidence. And the assertiveness.

In the pickup we found her frog hat where someone had placed it on the seat.

"The kid could have kept it," Pat said. "I still have the pattern." As she cinched the seat belt around her girth, she added, "Let's get out of here."

That fervid comment was the last remark she made all the way back to the trading post. And just as well. I had a number of things to think about. Was I wrong in my interpretation of the lack of marks on the body? Could the dog have killed the Saint Maker? If not, had he have been killed for the contents of his tool bag? Why else was it missing? And what did Pat want with a picture of the body?

As we turned into the RV lot, I thought after taking Pat to the scene of a death the least I could do was invite her in for iced tea. Amazingly, the woman who had spent so much of her time trying to get a look at my living quarters, said, "No, thanks."

I pulled up beside her RV.

"I see Boyce is back," I said, noticing the small, blue pickup he used for his photographic excursions, and that was towed behind the RV when not in use. "It's good you won't be alone. By the way, please don't tell anyone, except Boyce of course, about the dog just yet. I want to tell the owner first."

"Sure," she said, getting out. Poised on the step of the RV, she looked back at me. Before she turned away and stepped inside, I caught a glimpse of such suspicion and doubt on her face that I wondered what she thought I'd done.

THREE

FROM THE BACK of the trading post I could see through to the front. Carl Sebastien stared in, hands cupped over his eyes, nose pressing against the glass, anger and impatience evident in every line of his angular body. As soon as I turned the lock, he charged in, fists clenching and unclenching, and stopped in front of me. For a moment we glared at each other, then he dropped his eyes. A bad sign, I thought, if he intended to confront Pete Rosales. My old friend would have no respect for a man who backed down. To Pete, such a man was not to be trusted.

"I did what you said," Carl told me. "Put the goat in the freezer. Here's your key. Now what? When's Clay getting back? Are we gonna see Pete now? How soon can—"

I raised my hand. "One thing at a time," I said. "First I change clothes. Then we'll go and see Pete." I looked at his melancholy expression, noted the color of his skin—waxy beneath the yellowish stubble of several days' growth of blond beard—took in the trembling hands, and diagnosed low blood sugar.

"Have you eaten today?" I asked him.

He shook his head.

"Get yourself some cheese crackers and something to drink," I ordered him, walking toward the back. "No diet anything," I added over my shoulder as I passed through to the living quarters. "You need sugar."

When I emerged ten minutes later in jeans, shirt, and boots, he sat at the table by the cold wood stove, gulping down a Coke. One crushed can, three crumpled cellophane wrappers, and a few crumbs littered the tabletop as proof of his hunger. He unfolded his thin height from the chair, his face showing more color, his manner more calm.

"Put it on my account," he told me, tossing the two empty cans into the garbage bin and leaving the paper trash where it was.

"I will," I said, wondering if I would ever collect. In the three months since Carl had settled in our community he had run up bills with me for everything from canned goods to shoes and clothes, and with Everett Barron, who brings the mail and lottery tickets, bouncing the forty-eight miles down FM 2810 from Marfa and then twelve miles farther to El Polvo. I suspected Carl would have to pick the six winning numbers before he could pay either of us.

I locked up the trading post once more, stopping by Clay's trailer to pick up a choke lead for the dog. Since Carl's only mode of transportation is his feet, we took my pickup. I had a pistol in the holster on my belt in case we ran into a rattler, though the ground temperature this time of day made it unlikely that we would see one. The porch thermometer read 114 degrees. Anything above ninety sends the pit viper seeking deep shade. But I carried the pistol, just in case. In the borderland it's considered unfriendly to pass a rattlesnake without stopping to kill it because if you don't, it may be your neighbor it bites.

The rickety footbridge that led to the Rosaleses' *rancho* was two miles south, where the brown hills that guard the river step back a foot or two to let the thin soil support a scrub and grass cover fit only for goats. The soft sand of the river bottom made fording difficult, so at the narrowest point Pete had built a footbridge. I parked beneath the shade of an immense mesquite, and we walked across the rickety structure one at a time to lessen its sway and sag, gripping the rope rail as if its frayed hemp gave real support. Once we were both on the other side, I stopped to offer Carl advice.

"As the owner of the dead goats, you're the injured party. Pete will expect you to do the talking. I'll translate."

I didn't explain the reason Carl should let me translate. Pete understood more English than he spoke, but he conducted business only in Spanish, particularly with outsiders, and for this Carl's high school Spanish was woefully inadequate. If communication was only knowing the words, Carl would have been okay, but his formal Spanish had little in common with the sloppy, everyday speech of the borderland, a speedball mix of English, Spanish, and sometimes a hybrid of both Spanish and English syllables in the same word.

"If we want Pete to cooperate, we have to be polite, patient, and firm," I told Carl. "It would be best if he would agree to let us take the dog back and lock him up until Clay gets home, examines the goat carcass, and a decision is made. Whatever you do, don't say anything to Pete about putting the dog to sleep. Time enough for that if it has to happen."

Carl grunted and lunged down the dirt path. I let him go. This entire exercise, I decided, was likely to be a wasted gesture. Carl's patience was as thin as his body. The heat soon forced Carl to slow his pace. Three hundred feet brought us to our destination.

Pete and his wife Zeferina lived in a two-room, mud-plastered adobe with a raised porch shading the front. Several fifty-five gallon drums of water, hauled from the well in El Polvo, lined the porch. A rusty trailer a few feet away housed one of Pete's sons, Jaime, and his wife Rosa. On the far side of the bare-soil yard was the shell of a school bus that served as living quarters for whichever of Pete's many other children might be visiting. Since the most recent nosedive of the peso against the dollar, most of Pete's grown children had moved north to find work, leaving the grandchildren behind under Zeferina's care. A broad summer sleeping platform made of sotol stalks had been erected in the yard to handle the overflow of little ones. Adjacent to the adobe was an arbor that served as dining room and kitchen. Parked nearby was Pete's proudest possession, an ancient John Deere tractor. Whenever the large Rosales clan needed transportation, Pete used the tractor to pull a much-dented cattle trailer in which the family rode. No local fiesta had officially begun until the Rosales family arrived, laughing and waving from the trailer.

As we approached the adobe, scattering the few scraggly chickens pecking dismally in the narrow belt of shade next to the house, Zeferina appeared in the doorway, a sweet smile on her round face, her long hair tied back neatly.

"Pete is in the dog compound," she said, her eyes on Carl's face. In Mexico the house is the domain of the woman, and the street or the outdoors, the male domain. Seldom do the two mix, thus Zeferina's assumption that Carl's business was with her husband, and mine with her.

"Carl wants to speak with Pete," I explained, "but his Spanish is a little rusty. I came along as interpreter."

Beside me, Carl made a bristling motion, puffed out his chest, and said, "I don't need no help." He stalked away, disappearing around the back of the house. In seconds, we heard the barking of many dogs.

"Is there a difficulty," Zeferina asked me.

"For Carl, maybe." I said, wondering how long Pete would tolerate his rudeness.

Because of the heat, and the number of grandchildren in the house, Zeferina invited me to join her at the wooden table under the arbor. Her bare feet were as tough as saddle leather and she seemed not to notice the burning ground as we walked, yet I could feel the heat through the soles of my boots. We sat on a bench and asked after each other's health and inquired about family. In a few minutes, a child of twelve came out of the house carrying a wooden cup carefully in one hand. The girl ducked her head and looked away when I greeted her by name as she held out the cup of goat's milk. Behind her, in the doorway of the adobe, several more children of varying ages, including two older girls carrying babies, huddled to watch their sister serve me. Their clothes were hand-me-downs, patched many times, but clean.

I drank the milk, knowing it would hurt Zeferina if I suggested she keep it for the babies. A precious commodity at any time, the liquid was more so during the drought, since to keep a goat in milk in this heat meant the expense of supplementing its feed.

The child had returned to the house with the empty cup when the shouting broke out.

"¡Vete a la chingada!" Pete yelled, a sentiment equivalent to "go to hell." Carl, I judged, had not been tactful.

Instantly, the children in the doorway vanished into the darkness of the house. Zeferina sat still and silent, her back erect. I stood up, walked to the corner, and peered around in time to see a red-faced Carl retreating from Pete's clenched fist. He made it safely to the gate of the dog compound and headed for the river.

I sighed, stepped back to the arbor, and told Zeferina I needed to speak with Pete about Gringo. Her eyes widened.

"Do you know where Gringo is?" I asked her.

"He's under our bed," she said in a low voice. "He came home a while ago and ran under the bed. He had blood on him. Pete talked him out, gave him water, and looked for wounds, but when we cleaned off the blood, the dog had no wounds. As soon as we stopped patting him, the dog ran back under the bed. Pete told me to let him stay."

"I'd better talk to Pete," I said.

She nodded her head, stood, and went toward the adobe. On reluctant feet, I went to see my old friend.

Pete Rosales had been four grades ahead of me in the El Polvo school that taught grades one through eight. Pete had dropped out at age twelve to go to work, as did most of the students from this side of the river. Childhood ends early in the borderland.

Pete loves three things—equally, as far as I can tell, since he has many of each—and those are children, goats, and dogs. The dog compound is bigger than the house, a bare-earth square twenty-by-forty feet, fenced with chicken wire, and with a sotol arbor in the middle to provide shade. Beneath this arbor, Pete sat cross-legged, a battered straw hat on his head, his arms around two of the baker's dozen of mutts that surrounded him, squirming and wriggling and wagging their tails and licking Pete's face. Each pet had a name, and Pete never forgot a dog's name or confused one with another, as he sometimes did with his equally numerous grandchildren.

"*¡Hola, Pete!*" I called to him.

He scrambled to his feet, shaking off the dogs as he rose, grinned broadly, and started toward the compound gate, crooning to the dogs as he went, calling them his sanchos, a word that can be used to mean both orphaned kid goats and baby animals. Pete closed the gate behind him, and the dogs whined and pawed at the wire, begging to be allowed out.

Our conversation began with the polite formalities of good neighbors in the borderland. We shook hands, and I asked, "*¿Que pasa, amigo?*"

"We're about droughted-out here," he said, shaking his head. "You had any rain?"

Weather is a benign subject, showing good will. Desert dwellers talk rain obsessively—how much, how little, how close, how far.

I said, "Not even a hint of a drop."

He nodded sympathetically. "Drought's killing everything. We're eating the weakened goats already.'' He gestured toward a clothesline beyond the dog compound where three goat skins had been draped to dry. ''It's that or watch them die.''

''You know your credit is good for all the feed you need.''

''*Gracias.* I think I can hold out till fall. Then we'll see. I'm trying to save enough goats to start again if this dry spell ever ends.'' He shook his head. ''They're saying it could last a couple of more years.''

We stood silent in contemplation of the lengthening drought and our own helplessness in the face of nature's whimsy.

Done with conversational openers, Pete cocked his head and narrowed his eyes. ''What's up with this Carl Sebastien, anyway? He ain't boss of nothing and he acts like he's boss of everything. Trying to tell me my Gringo killed his goats.''

''Pete, something happened this morning—''

''Gringo never killed no goats,'' Pete said vehemently. ''That dog nursed on a nanny goat. He thinks he is a goat.''

''Pete,'' I said almost pleadingly, ''It's more than dead goats. We found the Saint Maker dead this morning in the chapel at Ruined Walls. Gringo was locked in with the body when we got there. Hector Cruz and Father Jack think the dog killed him.''

Pete looked stunned for a moment, then he rallied. ''I don't care if the Archbishop of Chihuahua says so, Gringo never killed nobody. He's a pure pet.''

Pete is short, with a runty voice to match his small stature, but I have never known him to be without a kind of boisterous dignity that reflects the good will basic to his nature. His quiet words, and the head up and shoulders back stance he assumed as he spoke, would have warned even a stranger to go carefully.

I said gently, "When the chapel doors were unlocked, Gringo ran for home. I'd already promised Carl I'd bring him to see you about his goats, and since he was waiting when I got home I let him come along. He doesn't know about the Saint Maker. I wanted to warn you so you could get Gringo locked up before somebody gets a notion to shoot him."

The tight shoulders relaxed slightly and I could see by the expression in Pete's eyes that he had moved past stubborn resistance to reasoned consideration.

For the second time that morning, I heard a shrill cry, but this one was a child's voice raised in terror and panic.

Pete cried, "¡Alejandro!" and took off in the direction of the river, his feet pounding the earth.

Though I'm taller and very fit and started right behind him, Pete quickly outdistanced me. By the time I reached the outer edge of the trees along the bank, Pete was squatting on the ground, supporting the boy's shoulders with one arm and whipping out his pocket knife with his free hand to slit the boy's pants leg. Around them, the frightened, varicolored goats shifted nervously.

"¡Ay, me pico la vibora!" the child wailed, and I reached for my pistol.

Two of the goat dogs found the rattler before I did, coiled in the sand shaded by the low brush, its head raised, poised to strike again. I aimed, fired, and the snake's broad head burst apart, the long, thick body behind it completing the striking motion signaled by the brain in the instant the bullet hit. The crack of the shot sent the goats scattering wildly. The dogs leaped to attack the pit viper's writhing body, biting and shaking it.

I turned back to see Pete sucking blood from the bite wound he had enlarged with his knife, spitting it out, and repeating the process. Using his kerchief and the boy's T-shirt, he had tied two tourniquets, one just above the bite, the second higher up. He loosened the higher one for thirty seconds, tied it, loosened the lower one, then massaged the boy's thigh in the direction of the wound. Blood gushed from the cut, cleansing it of venom. Scenting the blood, the dogs dropped the dead snake and whimpered nervously. Alejandro stared at the sky and wept silently. After half a minute, Pete tied the lower tourniquet, and loosened the higher again. Like the sucking of the wound, the process was repeated several times.

Just when I thought the boy could stand no more, Pete lifted his youngest son in his arms. Blood dripped down the boy's left leg. Pete walked slowly in order not to jar the child. I hurried ahead to alert Zeferina.

She met us halfway—probably alerted by the shot—and scooped the child into her arms, at the same time ordering Pete to kill a goat so the boy could drink a cup of its warm blood to strengthen him. I followed her through the low door of the adobe, where she placed the boy on the bed. The other children gathered around, but were careful not to get in the way. One of the older girls had slit a *nopalito* to use as a poultice. She handed it to Zeferina, who washed the wound with bleach water then placed the moist side of the cactus pad firmly against the cut flesh and wrapped it tightly with a cloth. She untied the tourniquets and the child gave a shuddering sigh and relaxed. Zeferina sent the other children away, sat down on the bed, and stroked her son's forehead.

I gladly would have driven Alejandro the 130-odd miles to the hospital, but I knew Zeferina and Pete would refuse. Pete had been snake-bitten when he was boy, as had more than one of his older sons, and the treatment was the same, now as then. Medical doctors would frown on the whole procedure—tying off and cutting the wound to let it bleed—as dangerous and useless. Pete believed in the folk remedy that had saved his life, saved his sons. One did not argue

against experience. I prayed that this was one of those times
when the snake had made a warning strike, not injecting
venom.

Except for the boy's steady breathing and Zeferina's re-
assuring murmurs, the room was quiet. Pete came in, carrying a cup, and I could smell the hot, sweet scent of the
goat's blood, though I hadn't even heard its plaintive cry
as its throat was cut. Zeferina raised the boy up so he could
drink in small sips.

As he finished the last drop, Pete said, "That's good, my
son." There was a scraping sound, and Gringo wriggled
out from under the low bed to sit at Pete's feet whimpering.

Pete rested his hand on the dog's head, and his eyes met
mine. "Do me a favor, Texana," Pete said, "and take the
dog back with you. He'll be safer on the other side."

I nodded, pulling out the choke lead from my pocket and
giving it to Pete, who put it on Gringo.

FOUR

CARL HADN'T WAITED at the pickup for me. The crazy fool had started walking.

"He'll get heatstroke," I said to Pete as he lifted Gringo onto the seat of the pickup.

"Good," Pete said. He gave the dog a pat on the head, told him to be good, and slammed the door.

When I opened the driver's door, Gringo growled and I froze.

"Get in, Texana," Pete said impatiently. "He won't hurt you. Poor Gringo."

I eased in, sat back gingerly, and started the motor. The dog whimpered.

"He's not used to riding in a pickup," Pete said. I pulled away slowly, and Gringo watched Pete through the rear window until we rounded a curve and lost sight of him. Gringo whimpered, turned around, sat on his haunches, and leaned hard against me. I could feel the animal trembling.

Halfway to the trading post, we caught up to Carl. Red-faced, his shirt black with sweat, flecks of foam forming at the corners of his mouth from dehydration, he was barely limping along.

I stopped, and Carl turned around, relief evident on his face. Until he saw the dog. We resumed the journey with Carl riding in the back end.

I parked near the small kennel Clay has next to the trailer. I had to lift Gringo out and carry him into the enclosure. I fed and watered him, scratching his hard head before shutting the gate. How I hoped when Clay got home there'd be some way he could prove Gringo didn't kill the Saint Maker. I wanted Pete to be right.

I heard the gush of water as Carl turned on the hose and sprayed his face and head to cool himself down. First sensible thing he'd done. I waited until he was through, then rewrapped the hose and checked to be certain he'd cut the water off completely.

"Hey, Texana," Carl shouted, "I think somebody broke into your place."

"What?" I ran across to see if Carl knew what he was talking about.

The back door sagged open, the wood around the lock splintered and broken where it had been jimmied.

"Phobe," I yelled. I yanked the door and ran inside and through to the front, calling her name until I heard an answering *fr-rrr-o* from behind me. She stood in the hall of our private quarters. I knelt beside her and thoroughly examined her for injuries. As far as I could tell, she was unharmed, but I wouldn't be happy until Clay had a look at her for internal injuries. Whoever had broken in might have aimed a kick at a friendly bobcat.

Only then did I take time to look around. Things had been disturbed. Shifted and lifted slightly was the best way to describe it. But at least there was no damage, no wanton destruction. The register was closed. I rang up No Sale. It popped open. The money was all there.

"S' everything all right?"

I jumped at the sound. Carl had walked up behind me.

"It all seems okay, including Phobe. I guess when I have time to check over the stock, I'll find out what was taken. A couple of times before, kids have broken in, but always through a window. Mostly they eat all the ice cream, and take candy and petty cash. I'll ask Pat Aply if she saw anything. I can't imagine someone doing all this damage without the Aplys hearing it."

"Who are the Aplys?" Carl asked.

"The people in the RV."

"There was an RV out there when I put the goat in the freezer, but it's not there now."

I strode around the counter, marched to the front door—it hadn't been jimmied—unlocked it, and went to the end of the porch to look at the RV lot on the far side of the trading post.

I stared incredulously at the space where the Aplys' RV had been as if it would materialize before my eyes.

"They're gone," I gasped.

"Guess that explains why they didn't hear nothing," Carl said, pleased with his own good sense.

FIVE

SHOWING A SKILL and a willingness to help that I would never have suspected, Carl Sebastien repaired the door, using some scrap lumber from the storeroom and my tools, and reset the lock and bolt. In return, I offered to pay him for the work by putting a fair sum against what he owed me, a considerable amount since he'd bought not only supplies, but a kerosene stove, bedroll, lanterns, water barrels—in short, everything he needed to live. He'd arrived in our desert community with only a knapsack of clothes. In response to my offer, he announced he'd rather have cash. That will teach me to ask.

After he departed, I tidied the trading post, stacking the jeans, shirts, and other items of clothing the burglar had shifted, and checking the wardrobe and dresser in the bedroom of our living quarters, plus every other shelf, drawer, or box that I suspected might have been disturbed. Even my seldom-used luggage had been replaced the wrong way round on the top shelf of the walk-in closet. In the ranch supplies a couple of sacks of range cubes had been shifted and broken open.

Whatever it was the burglar had hoped to find, it had not been valuables. The antique silver-and-turquoise jewelry I had inherited from my mother lay in the wooden cache box on top of the dresser. Clay's hunting rifle stood propped against the side of the wardrobe, and his three handguns, including his great-grandfather's ivory-handled Colt .41, were in the carpenter's box beside his desk in the study. The one credit card I have but seldom use remained stuck between cloudy plastic in the billfold in the top dresser drawer, and the cash box where I keep bundles of bills and rolls of coins for the register rested undisturbed in its usual hiding place.

Last, I used the sliding ladder to reach the topmost shelves where I keep slow-moving items like portable kerosene heaters, which I couldn't imagine a burglar bothering with. As I climbed, Phobe sprang from shelf to shelf, thinking I was chasing her, and enjoying herself immensely. When she tired suddenly, she rolled on her back in front of me, and of course I had to pause and rub her belly. Five minutes of that made her sleepy, and she thudded onto the tabletop and then to the floor to retire to one of her favorite sleeping places, a spot beneath the counter on a stack of used, burlap feed bags. She seems to like the rough texture of the burlap and the rich malt smell left by the grains. When I had satisfied myself that the burglar had stolen nothing, unless it had been something insignificant—candy or a six-pack of beer or a bottle of liquor that wouldn't be accounted for until the next inventory—I performed the final chore of the day, emptying Phobe's litter box. I refilled the box and returned it to its accustomed place in the laundry room. Phobe has a pile of burlap bags there, too, where she sometimes sleeps, especially if she is stressed out by too much noise in the trading post.

That was where I found it. A scrap of yellow cloth, only a few threads, really, caught on the rough burlap near the elongated imprint of the bobcat's body. Left just where her claws might have rested. Bright yellow cloth. I pictured Phobe's paw swiping at Pat's ankle. She must have hooked the hem of Pat's embroidered dress and carried away these threads on her claws. I dropped them in the waste basket, relieved that Pat hadn't realized her dress had been snagged. What a fuss she'd have put up otherwise.

It was nine o'clock. The whole day had been nightmarish, and I felt drained of energy. Every joint in my body seemed to ache, and my head had started to throb. Like Scarlett O'Hara, I told myself, I'll think about it tomorrow. Tired as I was, I still had one more chore to do. I returned to the front and removed the cash from the register. The tapping at the door came as I reached to switch off the lights.

I looked through the window, recognized Felicia Pena and her ten-year-old daughter, Kate, and unlocked the doors to let them in.

"Sorry to bother you this late," Felicia said, pushing Kate in ahead of her, "but I saw your light and I have to get Mama Isela's candle. Kate walked down this morning, but you were closed."

I mustered up a smile and stood by the door with Felicia while Kate, a dark, round-faced child with huge eyes, hurried down the aisle to the display of votive candles. In addition to the many choices of colors, there were candles imprinted with the image of the various popular workers of miracles such as St. Martin de Porres—a favorite because, like the Mexican nation itself, he was of mixed ancestry, born of a Spanish grandee and a freed slave woman—and St. Jude, the saint of the impossible. I'd burned a few candles to him over the years.

"As soon as I drove in," Felicia said, "before I was even out of the car, Kate came running, saying I had to drive her to get the candle." She shook her head in exasperation. "Mama Isela can light all the candles she wants for Romiro to come home. That's harmless enough, I guess. Me, I know he's either dead or living with another woman and that's why the letters and money have stopped coming."

For years Romiro, Felicia's husband, had worked on a ranch in Chihuahua, but the collapse of the peso had driven the family across the border, and Romiro had found better-paying work on a ranch in north Texas. To save money, and because he did not have a green card to work legally in the United States, he had left his wife and daughter living with his grandmother, Mama Isela, in her adobe in El Polvo. Each month he had been away he had faithfully sent a letter and cash. His last visit to see his family had been during the Holy Week preceding Easter, when every Mexican yearns for his home village. The next month Romiro failed for the first time to correspond with his family. Felicia had come to the trading post to telephone the ranch. The ranch manager could tell her nothing. Romiro had not returned to his job after his Easter break. To support herself and her daughter, Felicia had taken a job cleaning rooms at a motel in Van Horn, the last major stop on Interstate 10 before the long stretch of desert going west to El Paso. Driving a twenty-year-old car repaired by a local mechanic working under a tree in his yard and using salvaged parts with an ingenuity never envisioned by the manufacturer, Felicia came home every Friday in order to spend Saturday with her daughter. She made the last thirty miles of the trip over bone-jarring ranch roads, an effort that shaved the distance she had to travel down to slightly over 100 miles. Without a green card, on every trip she chanced being picked up by the Border Patrol, processed at the nearest border crossing, and returned to Mexico. Felicia had been born in Ojinaga to a mother who had the ambition that one of her seven daughters would get an education. Felicia had finished ninth grade before her family's poverty necessitated her going to work to support herself. It was Felicia's goal to see Kate through college.

Now she called impatiently to her daughter, "What's taking you so long?"

"I don't know which one to choose," Kate answered, her light voice quavering slightly in response her mother's sharp tone.

I intervened. "You picked St. Joseph last week, I think.

Why not try the Virgin of Guadalupe?'' I suggested. The lady was on my mind because of the statue in the chapel.

Kate stood on tiptoe and with a delicate hand lifted down a candle with the image of the Virgin depicted in vivid colors on the blue glass. Holding it tightly with both hands, she came tripping back to her mother and me. I heard Felicia sigh as she pressed two dollars into my hand.

"How long will it burn?" Kate said breathlessly. Every week, after she chose a candle, she asked the same question.

"Three days," I told her. A long time for a little girl to hold a whispered prayer for a lost father in her heart.

Kate carried the candle out to the car and climbed in. Felicia, watching her, shook her head, and said, "All week long Mama Isela fills the kid up with superstitious garbage. I believe in God, mind you. And in the Virgin of Guadalupe, and the whole army of saints. What I don't believe in is ghosts, witches, and devils. Do you know why Kate wouldn't come here at dusk by herself? She's afraid to go by the school because she says she hears *La Llorona* crying, and she's afraid the weeping woman will catch her and throw her in the river. As soon as I can get a second job, I'm moving Kate to Van Horn with me, green card or no."

"Mama, are you coming?" Kate called anxiously from the car window.

I watched Felicia get into the car before I closed the doors, testing the lock to be sure it worked. Making my way to the back, I turned off the ceiling fans and the lights and went to have a shower. As I peeled off my sweat-sticky clothes, I thought about what Felicia had said.

The legend of the weeping woman was a belief that went back, some said, to pre-Conquest times, when *La Llorona* was the earth-goddess *Cihuacoatl,* but the simple story told in the villages was one of love and betrayal. A *hidalgo*—a somebody—fell in love with a peasant girl named Maria, established her in a little house, and visited her often, always in secret. Over time, Maria bore him two children. They lived happily together until the man betrayed her by marrying a wealthy young girl who was his social equal. At the wedding, Maria slipped into the church, her face hidden by a shawl, and watched her lover betray her. Afterward she ran home and in a fit of vengeful despair, threw her children in the river before drowning herself. At the gates of heaven, the Lord asked her, "Where are your children?" Ashamed, she lied, pretending not to know. "Go and find them," she was told. "You may not rest until you find them." And so she wandered eternally, the long-suffering mother, weeping for herself and for the children she murdered.

Mexican elders used the legend as a cautionary tale, telling young children not to be out after dark or *La Llorona* might get them.

Kate's grandmother had probably cautioned her in just this way. Though I had noticed Kate had become sensitive and somewhat nervous since the disappearance of her father, I had always found her to be a sensible and intelligent child. I could believe her imagining *La Llorona* was real, but would she hear noises where there were none? My guess was that she had heard a mountain lion driven down by the drought to look for water or hungry for a taste of puppy. El Polvo has 125 people and very nearly as many dogs.

That thought sent me out of the shower and into fresh clothes to check on Gringo. Had I closed the kennel gate securely? It wouldn't do much good for me to try and save Gringo from a murder charge and death sentence if he was trapped and eaten by a mountain lion, or escaped and got shot.

I had my hand on the doorknob when the telephone rang. The phone is on the far wall of our long living-dining area, a narrow, timbered great room with a galley kitchen. I picked up on the fourth ring and heard my husband's voice.

"Can you get somebody to work the trading post tomorrow? My host is inviting you to join us. Dress is casual, and be sure and bring a bathing suit. Believe me, it's worth the drive to see this place. Think you can make it?"

"After the day I've had, it sounds like a vacation. Hold on while I get the map and you can give me directions."

I put down the phone and went to the desk for the road map and a pen. The drought was killing livestock on both sides of the border, and Clay was in Mexico advising a rancher on the culling of his purebred herd.

"Okay," I told Clay. He described the route to Rancho de Sierra Vista, and I marked the map. When he finished I asked a few questions about a couple of landmarks that signaled a change of road, then it was his turn to question me.

"What's this about a bad day?"

"Nothing for you to worry about."

"I know you. If you think it's something that will worry me, you'll try to resolve it first and tell me later."

"It's nothing I can resolve, but it is too complicated to explain on the telephone. By the way, can you identify a predator kill from a photograph?"

"I can try. Depends on how good the photo is and how obvious the wounds."

Pretty obvious, I thought. "You'll get to try," I said, "when you get home." We said goodbye and I went outside to check on Gringo.

Even the darkness could not dissipate the heat, and dust hung in the air. Just walking the few yards to the kennel made me feel in need of another shower. I could see Gringo's pale form where he crouched in the corner of the enclosure. At the sight of me, he barked joyfully and wagged his stubby tail. I bent over and reached through the bars to scratch his head and ears, forgetting that it might be prudent to be more cautious. As if offering proof of his good nature, he licked my hand. I gave his head one last pat, and told him I'd see him in the morning. I tugged at the kennel gate to be sure it was locked, then turned back toward the trading post. He whined pitifully as I left, and then I heard his toenails click against the cement floor as he trotted back to his corner.

By now it was well after ten, but tired as I felt, I stopped as I often do to look at the immense sweep of the sky. The stars were brilliant, but even their creamy white light seemed to radiate heat. Standing in the thick darkness, the only sound the rush of silence, I shivered when a muffled series of sobs, like ghostly antiphons, reverberated down the river and died away.

From his corner in the kennel, Gringo howled in response.

SIX

On Saturdays, my business consists mostly of video rentals and the sale of gasoline and beer. I woke at 6:00 a.m. with Phobe sprawled and snoring on Clay's pillow. By seven, I had opened the doors, counted out two hundred dollars in bills and change and the same amount in pesos for the register, fed and exercised Gringo, and shifted hamburger patties from the freezer to the refrigerator to thaw for Felicia's and Kate's lunch. Phobe woke and padded into the kitchen, nipping me on the ankle to remind me she was hungry. I chopped up a half portion of Phobe's food log—she eats about a little over two pounds a day of horse meat supplemented with vitamins and minerals. We keep three months' supply in the freezer.

Felicia had readily agreed to my request to work at the trading post for the day, pleased at both the extra money and a day with Kate away from the cramped adobe they shared with Mama Isela.

Waiting for them to arrive, I aired the pickup's tires, checked the spare, topped up the dual tanks, and loaded everything I needed for a trip into the backcountry of Mexico, including three water bottles, two extra gas cans, a strong nylon snatch strap for towing, and chains—in the remote chance that it might rain and I would have to get across slick clay flats. I slipped ten 500-peso notes into my pocket, handy for paying *la mordida,* though the likelihood of being hassled by an official and having to pay a bribe decreased geometrically away from main highways and towns. I would be driving the back roads all the way to my destination.

Promptly at eight, Felicia and Kate drove up, both neatly dressed in starched shirts, jeans, and tennis shoes. I showed Felicia how to work the register, how to cut the gas pumps off and on from inside, and pointed out the list of videos that were due back. Because most of my customers drive fifty miles or more to reach the trading post, I check tapes out from weekend to weekend. I cautioned Felicia to stay away from the kennel and to keep Kate away, explaining that I had left enough water and food for the dog to last until Sunday when I returned.

I made one last check of my papers—copies of the car title and my birth certificate, items one should always carry when traveling in Mexico. I counted out some cash in dollars and put it in the leg wallet I wore under my jeans. I did not carry my gun. It's one thing to go armed just across the river to Pete's *rancho*. It's something else to carry a weapon deeper into Mexico. Get caught and the penalties are harsh. I didn't have enough money in the bank for that *mordida*. Satisfied I had everything, I told Felicia she was in charge.

As I drove away, mother and daughter watched from the wide porch. Kate held Phobe cradled in her arms, waving one of the bobcat's wide paws.

Turning onto the blacktop, I glanced at the empty RV lot and wondered where the Aplys had gone. Had the murder frightened Pat so much they'd pulled out? The ten-dollars-per-day charge for the RV hookup had been paid for five days in advance, so if they didn't come back it was no problem. But why the sudden departure?

I speeded up, making time while I could. Once I hit the back roads I would be lucky to average fifteen to twenty miles per hour.

In five minutes I was in Mexico, my speed reduced to a crawl as I followed the dirt track that roughly parallels the river. I stayed on this for nearly seventeen miles, until the first landmark. At the location of a boulder held back from the track by propped timbers, I turned west toward the sierras, crossing a brown and tan terrain dotted with Spanish dagger, sotol, and ocotillo. The sky was cloudless blue, the horizon limitless, the visibility twenty miles or more. Rancho de Sierra Vista lay eighteen miles ahead near the chain of irregular peaks on the western edge of my vision, but the wandering tracks I would follow added another ten miles to the trip. I figured three hours to get there.

Plenty of time to think. About whether the strange noise the night before had been a mountain lion or *La Llorona*. About what would happen to Gringo if we couldn't prove that he didn't kill the Saint Maker. About who might have broken into the trading post and why. After a few miles, I gave it all up as a puzzle with too many missing pieces and concentrated on the drive.

The further I went, the more barren the landscape. In a meager bid for survival during the long days of the drought, livestock and wildlife had stripped everything edible.

In normal years, the first rain falls in May and reaches its height in July. The scant rainstorms are isolated and heavy, causing flash floods from intense runoff. By October, the landscape would be sprinkled with wildflowers. Now the land was as bare and brown as winter, and I saw not one living creature until midmorning, shortly after I reached the fourth and last landmark Clay had mentioned, an *ejido* consisting of a general store, a boarded-up cantina, and eight tiny adobes backed by corrals of rock and sotol fencing.

I had expected to stop and ask permission to cross the *ejido* land, but when I honked, no one answered. The place appeared abandoned, though a few chickens nested on the porch of one house and a scraggy dog nursed her puppies in the shade. Probably these people had been forced out, both by the drought and the failure of the government in

Mexico City to continue its support of the collective farm system. Few of the inhabitants in rural northern Mexico, pushed from the interior by hope and government promises and waving papers given to them in the dim corridors of the Agrarian Reform Ministry, stayed on the infertile land. The harsh life proved too spare, the lure of life on the other side too great. And behind them came as many more desperate hopefuls to take their place.

Just beyond the *ejido* I made the turn off the track I had been following for the last five miles, and took a rutted trail that climbed into the hills, with a perpendicular cliff to my left and a straight drop to a narrow canyon and dry creek bed to my right. Half a mile up the trail, I found the reason for the empty houses behind me.

The funeral procession had stalled because the thin burro pulling the wagon with the wooden casket in it had collapsed and lay dying in the dust of the road beneath the implacable sun. Someone had disengaged the cart, and men and women and children together pushed and pulled the wagon slowly uphill. Behind them came a bent old man carrying a wooden cross for the grave and an old woman wrapped in the rusty black of perpetual mourning holding a garland of paper flowers. Regretting that I didn't have my gun to finish the dying animal, I pulled up and offered assistance to those I could help. In no time the casket had been loaded in the pickup's bed, the eleven children and most of the adults sitting beside it, except for the elderly man and woman, who rode in the cab with me. He introduced himself as Domingo Cano and his wife Ofrelia of Ejido de los Reyes. The casket contained the body of their youngest granddaughter, who had died, he said, of a stomach sickness.

He directed me to turn into a small, shallow field in a hollow in the mountainside, a spot where wooden crosses pierced the rocky soil seemingly at random.

I stopped, got out, and stood aside as they removed the casket and carried it to the shallow grave. As I watched them lower the small box, I wondered if Father Jack was burying the Saint Maker in such a grave at this very moment in the cemetery at Providencia.

The simple service lasted no more than fifteen minutes and was performed with the dignity and resignation of those for whom death is a familiar event. The people filed out of the cemetery, acknowledging my presence with courteous nods of the head. Three men remained to fill in the grave, erect the cross, and place the garland. The last two people to leave were the old man and the woman. They stopped to thank me again, and I resumed my journey knowing that if ever I had any trouble near here, I could count on these people for help. Respect for the dead is taken seriously in Mexico. To show irreverence is not merely rude. It is unwise. And the value of goodwill shouldn't be underestimated in a region where people are the most scarce commodity.

It took me twenty minutes to travel the next few rough and broken miles up the mountain. At the crest of the road, I stopped for my first look at Rancho de Sierra Vista. Below me spread a mountain island, a basin between the hills, much longer than it was wide and perhaps two miles across at its widest, with enough elevation to catch moisture and rich volcanic soil to hold nutrients. At its center, reflecting like a liquid mirror, a huge, natural reservoir still held water, though its wide, crusted margins showed that the drought had shrunk its reserves considerably. Cattle ranged everywhere over the trodden pastures. At the closed and narrow northern end of the valley stood a complex of buildings. The sprawling, red-roofed main house, garages, and other outbuildings rose from a stretch of dead grass, ringed by brown hills. The private landing strip seemed long enough to accommodate large aircraft, and indeed, something that looked to me exactly like a cargo plane sat on the far end of the runway, as if ready to take off into the prevailing wind.

I heard a sound, and a fist-sized rock rattled down the cliff face, sailed off a larger rock, and rolled onto the trail. I stuck my head out the window and peered up. Something on the faulted outcropping above lifted its head and stared back with mournful eyes. It was a wild burro. How did it survive? Where did it find water? Did it work its surefooted way down to the valley below and seek a route past the fencing to drink its fill in the reservoir?

The burro scrambled up the slope by a path invisible from where I watched. When he had moved out of my sight, I drove down the trail to the basin floor.

SEVEN

A VAQUERO astride a horse, a small automatic rifle cradled in one arm, waited on the other side of the locked, steel gate. He wore a Resistol hat, a powder-blue western shirt, shotgun leggings over his jeans, and tooled boots. By the quality and expense of his clothes, I judged him to be the foreman rather than a ranch hand.

As I rolled to a stop, he raised a walkie-talkie to his lips and spoke briefly, then eased the horse forward, leaned down from the saddle, unlocked the gate, and gave it a gentle push. It swung inward on well-oiled hinges, and the vaquero moved the horse across to stop the gate from closing as I drove in.

As I passed, he bowed his head in a deferential gesture at odds with the rifle and the aggressiveness in his eyes and said softly, "Buenos días, Señora Jones. El Señor awaits you."

El Señor—just like the term for God in the Spanish Mass. It could refer only to the owner, I reflected. Certainly not to my veterinarian husband. Such a foreman would consider himself more than Clay's equal in the hierarchy of power and status.

I drove slowly along a gray asphalt road, watching in the rearview mirror as the vaquero locked the gate then spurred the horse along the fenceline that stretched for miles to the west. How many times a day, and night, I wondered, did he and others like him ride the boundary?

Private landowners in Mexico had to aggressively protect the scarce and valuable wildlife—and their livestock—from poaching. Pushed by desperate poverty, the people of the *ejidos* hunted and trapped incessantly in order to feed their families. *Where* ejidatarios *go,* went the saying in Mexico, *nothing lives.* Deer, rabbits, quail, and kangaroo rats ceased to exist, as did the mountain lions, coyotes, owls, hawks, and other wildlife that preyed on such small game. Once gone, the game disappeared forever because the *ejidatarios'* goats overgrazed and destroyed the habitat. And when their own lands had been disfigured and destroyed, the collective's people were forced out into the land around them.

While I pondered the environmental disaster of Mexico's land reforms, a Jeep with two armed men pulled in behind me, following just closely enough that their presence could not be a coincidence. An armed escort. Not unexpected. The wealthy in Mexico had to be on guard against kidnapping. Only a few days earlier I had read about a filmmaker's son abducted at gunpoint from his car in Mexico City. He had been returned after his family paid an undisclosed ransom. When I reached the broad half-circle in front of the house, the Jeep made a U-turn and left me. I parked on the drive that would have accommodated twenty-five cars easily but now held only one, the ultimate 4 × 4: A Humvee.

The house made a fitting backdrop for the world's most expensive all-terrain vehicle. The building that had appeared large from the road above was baronial up close. Built of massive blocks of limestone, it had the pristine look of the homes of the very rich. And as if to emphasize that wealth can overcome even climate, palm trees in tubs lined the lower level of the terraced steps.

On the top level three people waited for me. Clay stood in between a slim man and a stout woman. As always, I felt a lifting of my heart at the sight of my husband. At slightly over six feet tall, with thick gray hair, Clay's easygoing, pleasant appearance and quick smile reveal nothing of the intense loyalties and deeply felt emotions of the inner man.

As I stepped out of the pickup, the man beside Clay advanced down the steps, stopping in front of me. We were exactly the same height.

"Welcome, Texana, welcome," he said, his dark eyes locking on mine with the full intensity of his charm. His bushy, black mustache and full brows contrasted with the slickly shaven head and forced one's focus on the strong features of his tanned face that were highlighted by the pure white of the bush shirt he wore. Jodhpurs and highly polished riding boots completed the highly individualistic image of Gordon "Ghee" Mateo Suarez, owner of one of the most successful ranches in northern Mexico, president of the major cattlemen's association in Chihuahua state, and global arms dealer. The rise of Suarez's career followed the dates of wars, revolutions, and coups that his company, ArmsNet *Norteño,* had helped equip. He had homes in Mexico City, Monterrey, and Paris. Several years ago the Associated Press had done a profile on him that had run widely in the major papers in the States, but reportedly his influence had kept the story out of Monterrey's *El Norte* and Mexico City's daily *Reforma.*

I shook hands with one of the most powerful men in Mexico. He looked down at my feet and said approvingly, "I see you know your way around a ranch—you're wearing boots instead of these dainty city shoes some of our guests show up in." He pressed my hand between both of his own like a lover. "Ready for a tour of the ranch?"

The woman advanced slowly down the steps, saying in a disapproving voice, "Ghee, you might allow our guest to come inside and relax after her long drive." She extended a plump hand to me. "I'm Eva Suarez."

She was short and dumpy, with thick black hair lacquered into an unlikely bouffant, but she looked immaculate and cool in a dress of white and blue. In comparison, I felt as dusty as the paint on my pickup. We shook hands, and I noticed the fine bones of her face beneath the layer of fatty tissue that from a distance obscured this single remnant of her beauty.

She asked me about my luggage and then turned and ordered someone behind her to get my suitcase.

The man who stalked from the shadows of the arched doorway was of medium build, in his early thirties, with drooping eyelids, and slick blue-black hair combed straight back from his forehead. He wore a white, banded-collar shirt with soft gray slacks, and a chrome-plated .45 in a shoulder holster.

Dressed like a son of the house, but treated like a servant, the gun explained the ambiguity of his position. A bodyguard, I thought, well paid to retain his loyalty.

As he walked by, his amber-colored eyes met mine in a look of such brutal sexuality that I felt violated. And yet I knew the look to be not personal but purely reflexive *machismo,* the favorite sport of the male in Mexico because it can be played in all seasons. It is an attitude born of narcissism, arrogance, and insecurity. Toward women, particularly *gringa* women, the male prerogative is to be constantly on the make. It can be as innocuous as young men strutting around the plaza, as distasteful as lewd comments made in public, as dangerous as conversation without a taint of chauvinism, as seductive and superficial as the charm behind it. As the bodyguard lifted my suitcase out from behind the front seat, my host spoke in my ear.

"My wife is right, of course. The ranch is my pride, the house hers." He turned to her. "We'll let our guest choose, Eva." The conspiratorial glance he gave me said clearly what he expected my choice to be.

I aimed for the diplomatic middle ground. "Perhaps the ranch, first, since you suggested it. But when we get back, I'd love a tour of the house."

Ghee smiled, laughed, and motioned to Clay to join us

as he led me by the elbow to the open-sided, canvas-topped Humvee. His wife stayed behind.

"It weighs three tons and it's eight feet wide, but wait till you see how the Hummer rides," Clay said, and I could tell by the enthusiasm in his tone that man and machine had bonded.

"You take the shotgun seat, Texana," Clay said as he climbed in.

"Buckle up tight so you don't fall out when we hit the really rough spots," Ghee said.

I did as I was told while staring at the dash. It looked like something out of an old Volkswagen—plain and simple, with a steering wheel of bare, black plastic.

"This is the military version," Ghee was saying, "just like the troops drive. I knew when I saw President and Mrs. Bush eating their Thanksgiving meal off the hood of one of these during Desert Storm that I had to have one. Everybody thinks Arnold Schwarzenegger was the first civilian to own one, but I had one long before he did." He laughed. "But maybe an arms dealer doesn't count as a civilian."

Ghee flipped a switch on the upper-left portion of the dash and the engine started with a decided rumble. "I've had this ranch for ten years and there are places on it I'd never seen except from helicopter until I bought the Hummer. My men patrol the far stretches of the mountains in a couple of these. It can climb anything. Wait and see."

As we drove past the runway, I turned my head and looked out the window. A C-130 with Mexican military markings was being unloaded by workers dressed in khaki uniforms, who muscled pallets of black-plastic-wrapped cargo into a large metal building. Nearby sat a helicopter and a gray executive jet.

"Those are airplane parts being unloaded," Ghee said. "I bought them from a general. Our government encourages its generals to enrich themselves through business opportunities," Ghee laughed. "Keeps them from making mischief against the civilians."

"No wonder you have guards posted," I said, thinking of the value on the open market of airplane parts. "Your people are certainly alert. The foreman met me at the gate."

"That's his job," Ghee said.

"He must have had quite a wait. I was late."

"What happened?" Ghee asked.

I explained about the funeral.

Ghee said, "¡'jidatarios! Those people are trouble, always cutting the fences to hunt. Now and then they even get bold enough to rough butcher a calf right in one of my pastures."

I was afraid to ask what happened if the guards caught the *ejidatarios*.

Ghee changed the subject. "What I want to show you first are the cattle your good husband is helping me to save from this damnable drought."

"Ghee has one of the best herds in Mexico," Clay said. "He wants to do more than produce commercial calves for the border trade."

"I intend to market the finest breeding stock in Mexico," Ghee said. "Chihuahuan cattlemen spend a lot of money in the United States each year buying superior seed stock to improve their herds. I want them to spend that money with me. Right now Brangus, Herefords, Angus, and Charolais are the most popular breeds in the state. I intend to make Rancho de Sierra Vista Beefmasters the best-selling breed. I bought my first two truckloads of heifers and bulls seven years ago at a sale in San Angelo."

As Ghee expanded on the history of his cattle and his future plans for the ranch, we followed a lane past pasture after pasture dotted with long, straight-backed, golden-red cattle.

"Beautiful animals," I said, watching the resting cows and calves as they lifted their stately heads and pulled themselves to their feet to trot after the pickup in expectation of being fed. They stopped only at the fence closing off one pasture from the next.

"The ranch runs one thousand fifty head," Ghee was saying. "I planted buffelgrass because of its natural tolerance to drought. The tops dies back, but the roots go deep." He stopped and got out.

"Look at this," he said, kicking the powdery, withered grass, sending up puffs of dust. "I hate to see my land in this condition," he said, getting back in.

At the next pasture Clay pointed out Mr. Bill's Boy, the finest sire in the bull battery. "My daughter nicknamed him Macho-Man," Ghee said.

Pasture after pasture rolled by until finally the dirt lane followed the rising land, and the ground grew bare and rocky and broken. Ghee dropped the shifter down to the DI position—what he said was low range and low gear—and we climbed at a steady, slow rate a mountain path so steep I would have been hesitant to try it on foot. I could feel the traction of first one wheel, then another as we cleared rocks that would have stopped a pickup.

"Grips like a lizard," Ghee bragged.

At the top, we stopped and got out to look back at the full length of Ghee's domain. He made a broad gesture toward the land beyond the brown hills. "In Chihuahua and Coahuila states a million head of cattle are dead because of the drought," Ghee said. "It hurts me to let go of any of my herd, but your husband recommends I cut back by twenty-five percent and I see the reason of this. I have feed flown in, but since the drought looks to be prolonged, in the future I may not be able to get hay at any price. The important thing now is keeping the land alive, able to come back from these ungrateful times." He pulled out a handkerchief and wiped his face. "The only good thing about this heat is that it cuts the breeding percentage way back so I don't have even more calves to worry about."

"What will you do?" I asked.

"The good Clay has arranged a sale of a hundred pairs to a rancher in Oklahoma."

"Because you gave him a fire-sale price for the mother cows and calves," Clay said.

Ghee shrugged. "We'll send a hundred and fifty of the heifers that didn't breed this spring and some of the bulls to slaughter," he added with audible regret. "It's the only thing I can do. The livestock market is glutted. Two years ago this calf crop would have brought in excess of four to five hundred dollars a head. Now, they'll bring less than half that. Ranchers are selling off entire herds—those who ran out of water before they ran out of grass. In that, at least, I've been lucky so far.

"Water," he continued, "means life or death in the desert. This time last year we irrigated from two deep wells. We pumped the water to a twenty-thousand-gallon holding tank. From there it was gravity-fed to eighty-six different pastures through thirty-two kilometers of pipe. We rotated the cattle regularly among the pastures and we grew various improved grasses under irrigation. It worked fine until the water table dropped and I had to stop the irrigation or face running out of water altogether." He shook his head in a gesture of disgust. "We have a saying: 'If your trouble has a remedy, why worry? If it has no remedy, why worry?' Practicing such resignation as a virtue is not for me. I prefer to take action. If that means sacrificing part of the herd, so be it. The desert demands stamina in the people who live on it as well as in the livestock."

"I like the way you speak of your land as a living thing," I told him.

Ghee faced me, smiling broadly. "I'm enchanted that

you were able to come here and see my ranch," he said. "After I heard of the disagreeable experience you had yesterday, I feared you might not feel up to making the trip."

Clay flashed me a glance of puzzlement. Whatever my host had heard, he had not mentioned it to my husband.

I said matter-of-factly, "Word passes more quickly than I drive, I see."

"I knew the old man," Ghee said somberly. "I own several of his carvings. His death is a great loss to our traditional crafts."

Clay asked, "What old man is this?"

"The one who has been working on Father Jack's pet project," I explained before saying to Ghee, "No one seems to know his last name. Perhaps you do."

"The *jorobado*," he said, using the Spanish word meaning humpback, "was a secretive man. I know he came from the South, but that is all. If it is not too painful for you to recall, I would like to hear what happened."

I repeated the story of finding the Saint Maker, including the fact that Hector and Father Jack believed a dog had been the killer. I did not identify Gringo.

Clay's expression shifted from astonishment to understanding. "Was that what you were talking about on the phone last night when you said you wanted me to evaluate a predator kill?"

"I thought it might help to be sure," I said, keeping my doubts about the cause of death to myself. "Hector worried about the state police finding out and what they might do if there was no explanation—"

Ghee said, "It's a waste of time to report crime in my country. Few are solved."

"Hector didn't intend to report anything, but he was worried, and Clay being the closest resident expert in identifying the kind of predator in livestock kills…"

"Can you really do that?" Ghee asked. "Determine what kind of animal did the killing?"

"I do it all the time for ranchers who need to know what's killing their stock—bobcat, coyote, town dogs, or eagle, for instance. Even if the kill happens to be a human, the principle's the same."

Ghee said, "Fascinating. Elaborate, please."

Clay shrugged modestly. "It's just experience and a critical eye for details. I look for pretty much the kind of things a coroner looks for on a dead body, only I'm examining a dead animal. Most predator species display a particular attack and killing procedure for various sizes of prey. An experienced coyote, for instance, when it kills a kid goat, goes for the throat. The bite compresses the trachea and suffocates the kid. When you examine the carcass, you look for injury to the larynx and trachea. Feral dogs, on the other hand, make sloppy kills."

I experienced a flashback to the Saint Maker's face and shuddered involuntarily.

Warming to the intense look of interest on Ghee's face, Clay elaborated on the topic. "The first rule is never assume anything. If the rancher says he saw a coyote slipping away from the kill, don't assume that necessarily means the coyote was the predator. Ranchers don't always know as much about these things as they think they do."

"But where do you start?" Ghee asked.

"With the kill site. I determine if the attack, kill, and feeding all took place at the same site. Before I touch the carcass, I note the position of the dead animal—sprawled, tucked into a fetal position, and so on. Is there a sign of a struggle? Of dragging? Of covering the kill with dirt and grass? I look for blood, tracks, and droppings. Then, I examine the carcass."

"Like the police at a crime scene on your American TV shows!" Ghee said. "Continue, please." I smiled to myself and thought, try and stop him. Clay's undiminished enthusiasm for his job after nearly twenty years of practice is one of the things I love about him.

He was saying, "I examine the external wounds for hemorrhage bruises, broken bones, and biting or tearing. Certain feeding behavior indicates particular predators. An eagle, for example, prunes off the ribs close to the backbone. Sometimes, the external evidence is enough. If not, I skin out the carcass and open it up to identify internal wounds—"

"A postmortem!" Ghee said.

Clay nodded. "Exactly."

"But you cannot so examine the *santero*," Ghee stated flatly. "I understand he was to be buried this morning."

"Hector has a photograph of the body," I said, looking at Clay. "A close-up of the wounds. They were mostly to his face."

"Excellent," said Ghee. "How clever of you to have taken this—"

"I didn't," I interrupted him. "A woman staying in my RV park was there. She took the photograph."

"It matters little who took it," Ghee said dismissively. "We must secure the negative and have it enlarged for Clay to examine. Could this be done?" he asked me.

I mumbled out the Aplys' names and said they had left already, never thinking to mention the camera was a Polaroid, and therefore there was no negative.

Ghee nodded and put his hand on Clay's shoulder, saying, "Would this picture be sufficient for you to know what killed the *santero*?"

"Possibly," Clay said. I was thinking Ghee hadn't been kidding when he said he liked to take action.

"Remarkable," Ghee said to Clay. "Your skills are remarkable. If ever the wildlife of this area recovers from the hunting of the *'jidatarios,* I'll know who to call on if something begins preying on my calves.''

''You're lucky not to have a predator problem,'' Clay said. ''The figures for predator losses last year in the United States came to well over four million head. We lost the most in Texas. Four thousand cattle and twenty-five thousand calves killed. Still, the landowner has to be cautious. Shoot the wrong predator, and the environmentalists and the Fish and Wildlife officials come down on you fast. You have to be smart to protect yourself and keep the rights you have. There's no room for error.''

''This is true, I know,'' Ghee said. ''Nothing angers you Americans like the killing of an endangered species. It is the chic cause of the decade. The naive—children and film stars—think they can reverse the world, make it go backwards to Eden. My daughter has this attitude. I read of a farmer in California who killed a rat with his tractor. This vermin was one on your country's endangered species list, and the farmer spent a fortune defending himself in court against his own government for the right to keep his land. In my country the government takes land for peasants, not for rats. And even as your state suffers from this drought and your ranchers are struggling to hold on, environmentalist groups are filing class action lawsuits against the citizens of I don't know how many counties to stop them using underground water. Why? To save some salamander or such thing. Or let a man get caught smuggling rare butterflies or parrots out of Mexico into the United States, and the event makes headlines and results in summit meetings between our governments.'' He shook his head. ''No, the attention of the environmentalists is the last thing any sensible landowner would welcome. Might as well invite the badges in,'' he added, laughing heartily at his own analogy about the risk of drawing police attention in his country.

''Speaking of landowners,'' I said, making a sweeping

gesture toward the long horizon of the Ghee's ranch, "you are a fortunate man to have all this."

"I was lucky to be the son of my father," Ghee said modestly. "In your country, a man may have status with titles and degrees. In mine, nothing counts but money. I inherited the family business. My grandfather, Mateo, collected money to buy weapons for Pancho Villa. My father, Felix, sold weapons to the colonels in Argentina in 1946. Your Mr. John Foster Dulles asked my father to supply arms to the rebels who overthrew Colonel Jacabo Arbenz Guzman in Guatemala. That deal made my father a major player in arms sales. He always complained your government was tardy in paying. But then, they don't want their fingerprints left on anything clandestine." He smiled, mildly amused at the subterfuge of the bureaucracy. "My father later sold arms to Batista in Cuba. After Fidel threw Batista out, we sold to Castro. Southeast Asia kept the profits rolling in during the seventies. These days, my company has clients throughout this hemisphere. I can outfit an army with everything from uniforms to Meals Ready to Eat packets. At present the surplus of cheap weapons from the old Eastern Bloc countries is undercutting the market. But the future is bright, because humankind never changes, and there will always be wars. The arsenals of the former Soviet Union are waiting for the right bidder, and the clerics in Iran can always be counted on to destabilize an area." He slapped his hands together and said, "Repeat sales are everything! Now Texana, why don't you drive us back down?"

"I hope you're not kidding, because I'd love to," I said.

Ghee smiled and waved a hand toward the driver's seat. "It's all yours."

I got behind the wheel.

"It has the feel of a Cadillac and needs a light touch," Ghee instructed me. "You'll go down in the same low range and low gear that we came up. Don't touch the brakes. They can lock up and you can start to slide. The Hummer hangs on the compression of the engine. It's all you need. One other thing," he added, "there's a slight lag between acceleration and power. Keep your foot gentle and steady."

Going down, the Hummer dipped toward its nose alarmingly, and in reaction I pushed myself back into the bucket seat until I realized we were descending as easily and steadily as we had climbed.

"How do you like it?" Ghee asked me when we reached the bottom.

"I want one," I said, ready to drive up and come down all over again. Ghee let me drive all the way back to the barns.

Two hours later, having toured the barns and working pens, the stables and riding arena, we pulled up in front of the house. Evidently waiting for us, the bodyguard approached the vehicle and as Clay and I got out the slick young man spoke to Ghee. We moved to the steps and waited for our host. Ghee joined us long enough to ask in his effusive manner if we would forgive him if he left us to attend to business.

Our forgiveness assured, he turned to go, spun around and said, "An idea. I esteemed the *santero*'s skill and mourn his death. I will offer a reward for this dog, dead or alive, as they say in the western movies." He slapped the back of one hand into the palm of the other. "Better still, I will make it dead only. The animal is obviously dangerous and may kill again."

"But there's no proof the dog killed the Saint Maker," I said.

"Half the folks on both sides of the border will be killing every dog they see trying to claim the reward," Clay said.

"You'll have to dig a pit the size of a football field to bury the bodies."

Ghee shook his head. "Not me. You will be in charge. It is the animal expert the reward seekers will have to please. I put you in charge. You must be satisfied we have the right dog, this killer dog, before any money is paid." Ghee smiled. "It is to my good friend Clay I will have the dead animals turned in." Looking pleased, he jumped back into the Humvee and with the bodyguard in the next seat, made a U-turn and sped away.

"Oh, nice," Clay said dismally.

"Worse than you know," I said, thinking of Gringo huddled against the back wall of the kennel at home.

EIGHT

I HAD TO POSTPONE telling Clay about my harboring Gringo because Eva Suarez stood at the foot of the winding staircase and welcomed me for a second time, inviting us to do as we wished—swim, read, or take siesta until the evening meal.

"This house is yours," she said, smiling. "We dine at eight. Dress is casual, Texana. My husband disdains formality when we come to the ranch. He wears nothing but his riding clothes when we are here." Adding that she would be in the kitchen overseeing the cook, she left us.

"When is lunch?" I asked Clay as we started upstairs. "I had breakfast hours ago."

"There'll be food in our room," Clay said as he led me to the bedroom in the guest wing that he had been enjoying for a week.

"It's as bland as a luxury hotel room," I said disappointedly, taking in the pale green carpet and blond furniture.

Clay laughed and sprawled in a chair near a table loaded with fruit, finger sandwiches, and bottled water. "Were you expecting ranch oak?"

I grinned at him. "Something more in line with the romantic image of our host's jodhpurs and spurs," I said. "Early Spanish mission, maybe. Or late El Cid." I looked around. "Where's my suitcase?"

"The maid will have put everything away for you."

"Well, you might have told me that on the phone. I'd have put in my best undies if I'd have known someone else would be unpacking them." I opened the closet and found my clothes on padded hangers, shoes lined up on the floor beneath. The little makeup I use had been placed on the dressing table in the adjoining bath, and my underwear folded neatly in the first drawer of the bureau.

"Have some food," Clay said. He opened a bottle of water for me and put several of the sandwiches on a plate.

I sat in the second chair by the table and eyed the plate piled high with mangoes and the stack of thick napkins nearby. I tucked a napkin tightly around my collar, unfolded another in my lap, and pronged the stem end of one of the fruits with a mango fork, cut off the sides and scooped them out. The aroma of the sticky sweet fruit filled the air and rivulets of juice ran onto the plate and dripped from the slice I lifted to my mouth. The best place to eat the oozing fruit is in the bathtub. Mango season begins in June and ends in July, and if you like them the season is entirely too short. I qualified as a mango aficionada.

I had three, and Clay ate two sandwiches, a banana, and a pear. When I had wiped my face and hands and pushed the plate aside, he said, "Now give me the details you were holding back from Ghee about what happened yesterday."

I told him everything.

"So we're giving sanctuary to a wanted animal," he said. "Maybe I'd better encourage Ghee to increase the reward."

Ignoring his kidding, I said, "I think even Hector has his doubts about how the Saint Maker died. But he's willing to ignore them."

"Can't blame Hector. If the police come into it, they'll lock up half the *ejidatarios* until someone confesses. The priest would have to pass the basket twice, at least, to buy them out of jail."

"Will you be coming home soon?" I asked, starting on my first sandwich of thinly sliced beef. The sooner he returned home, the sooner the question of what killed the goats—and maybe the Saint Maker—could be resolved.

"Not a lot more I can do here. Ghee's spared no expense

on his animals, but you can't buy rain." He leaned forward, elbows on the table, and said in an awestruck voice, "He has his own sonogram equipment for the cows."

"Sounds like he's spoiling you," I commented, leaning back and parting the curtain to look out.

Below was a tiled courtyard with a central fountain. On three sides the second floor of the house extended over the first, creating a shaded porch arranged with chairs and tables. Around the courtyard China roses bloomed in tubs and bougainvillea climbed trellises to reach for the sky. A low wall with a wrought-iron gate formed the fourth side, and beyond the blue water of a swimming pool enticed the eye. I saw a splash of water and the tight vibration of the diving board. In an instant, in the middle of the pool a sleek head popped up. The diver reached the pool's edge in a few quick strokes and hauled herself out. Dripping, waist-length black hair clung to the child's wet skin and swimsuit, and she shook herself all over like a puppy. She looked so cool and comfortable that I instantly decided to join her after a quick shower to wash off the dust of the trip.

"Who's the little girl?" I asked, turning away from the window and getting up.

"That's Inez, Ghee's youngest, and the only daughter. She's a serious, dignified kind of kid. And I'd say her father would do anything to please her. Which means we probably should, too."

"You'll have to explain that," I said.

"I came here because Ghee is an important cattleman. Now that I've been around a few days, my guess is he has other interests that make him more powerful than I'm comfortable with."

I thought about it. "You mean he's a little more organized than you bargained for."

"I don't think those planes are flying only cargo."

"So why tell me to come on down. This is no game show."

"I thought it might be smart to seem agreeably dumb. In case my guess is right. Anyway, what's it to us? He has planes. He doesn't need a poor vet and his storekeeper wife to transport anything. We can't possible be of any danger or use to him. And where else can we get room service, a pool, and be paid a hefty fee?"

NINE

THE LITTLE GIRL had abandoned the pool by the time I got there, and Clay had opted for a short nap so I swam laps alone and was dozing on a chaise longue in the shade of the cabana when he finally joined me. Thirty minutes later our host, still dressed in his riding outfit, arrived carrying an exquisite cut-glass decanter and three "horses," small glasses with tiny handles.

"You must try this," he said. His eyes twinkling with the anticipation of the pleasure that he knew awaited us, he filled the three glasses, passing one to me and one to Clay. He raised his own glass so that the light shone through the pale golden liquid. "This is a very special *anejo* tequila grown by a family at La Altena in Jalisco," he said, downing the contents of his glass in one swallow.

Though good manners made appreciation obligatory, my enthusiasm turned real at the first sip. The amber spirit smelled faintly of marmalade and tasted lightly of fruit.

"I could learn to make this a habit," Clay said, emptying his glass.

Ghee immediately poured Clay a refill. "Two keeps your outlook on life optimistic and your worries at bay," he said, raising the decanter questioningly in my direction. How could I say no?

I held out my glass, and said, "Please." Ghee beamed with pleasure and poured. "Like the grape," he told us, "the agave plant is sensitive to the earth in which it grows. Tequila, like wine, takes its flavor from the plant and earth. What the French call *goût de terroir.*"

"Showing off your languages again, Papa?"

The child had approached without our noticing and stood by the arm of Ghee's chair. Her long, silky black hair was tied back in a ponytail. Baggy shorts and an oversized T-shirt—emblazoned with a SAVE THE EARTH slogan printed over the image of the planet cupped between two hands—almost swallowed her small frame. I guessed her age at about ten.

"Texana," Ghee said, "Meet my eco-terrorist daughter, Inez, who currently prefers to be called Julia."

"After Julia Roberts," the child said. "She's smart, independent, and not afraid to stretch herself in acting roles. I admire her."

The combination of Julia's thin face and enormous smile did remind me of her namesake. "I'm happy to meet you, Julia," I said.

"My father is teasing about the terrorist bit," she explained gravely as she came around his chair to shake hands with me. "I'm an environmental activist. I'm concentrating on bats right now," she added, turning her back to me so that I could read the legend on the other side of her shirt: BATS ARE THE BEST.

"Bats are a lot of benefit to people." Julia said, "but they aren't appreciated. That tequila you're drinking—bats pollinate the agave plant. No more bats, no more tequila. Do you know that there are hundreds of bat caves on both sides of the river? Some of them on this side have been sealed up because of silly superstitions about vampire bats."

"You may preach to Mrs. Jones from your soapbox on some other occasion," her father said kindly but firmly.

She looked at her father fondly and said, "*Soapbox* is a very old-fashioned word, Papa."

"Pulpit, then," her father said. "Anyway, my little pulpiteer, you may be talking to the already converted. After all, Mrs. Jones must love and appreciate wildlife. She keeps a bobcat as a pet.'' Ghee winked at me as he said this.

"Really?'' the child said, her eyes widening in interest.

I nodded. "Her name is Phobe, and she used to live with a family that had three little boys, so she loves children.''

"I wish I could see her,'' Julia said. She danced over to her father. "May I fly Texana home, Papa?''

Much to my shock, Ghee said, "Certainly, my love. But you will have to spend the night. I don't want you making the flight back on the same day—''

"I know,'' Julia said. "Tired pilots make mistakes.''

"Now,'' her father said, "disappear until dinner. I wish to talk business.'' She kissed her father's cheek, wished us good evening, and scampered away. Ghee turned to me and said, "She won't be any trouble. Inez is a very self-sufficient child. She takes her laptop everywhere. The computer will keep her busy. You won't have to entertain her.''

"I'd be delighted to entertain her,'' I said.

"You need not worry about Inez flying you home. My daughter is a perfectionist, and piloting is an excellent pastime for perfectionists. I instructed her myself. And Mata will go with you. He's a licensed pilot as well as my personal bodyguard.''

Amber Eyes, I thought. Great. Just great. A child as a pilot and a macho-man as a copilot.

"But my pickup...'' I said faintly.

Ghee dismissed my protest with the wave of a hand. "One of my men will return it to the trading post.'' He shifted in his chair and turned to Clay. "I very much desire that you should accompany my cattle to the quarantine station at Ojinaga and oversee their care while they are there. You know how these places are. Unless someone is present to see that things are properly handled, my purebred cattle could end up in the same pens with scrub cattle carrying ticks or infected with tuberculosis.''

"One of your own men could handle that," Clay said.

Ghee shook his head vehemently. "The Ministry of Agriculture inspectors have no respect for anybody but a professional, and the *mordida,* which will be attended to." He broke off from his point to ask, "You know how the practice of the *mordida* began? No? When the first Indian convert said, 'Baptize me, Father,' and the priest held out his hand and said, 'Pay me.'"

We joined in with Ghee's delighted laughter, though the joke was old. And representative of Mexico's bitter disdain for a church inseparably tied to the Conquest. Depending on your point of view, the cynical or the wise said that Juan Diego never lived and that the church had made up the tale of the Indianized Virgin of Guadalupe to convert *Indios* rapidly and bring them under control. Those who preached this included the present-day abbot of the Basilica de Guadalupe.

Our laughter subsided, and Ghee returned to his subject. "Clay, you will be needed in Ojinaga. I ask this as a friend."

"If you put it like that, sure, I'll go," Clay said, too quickly for me to catch his eye to remind him we had a problem at home that only he could resolve.

Ghee grasped Clay's hand and shook it gratefully, then excused himself to attend to some business before dinner.

TEN

I SHUT OFF the blow dryer just as Clay stepped out of the shower. "So, how long will you be in Ojinaga?" I asked him.

"Tomorrow I do the paperwork," he said, vigorously toweling his wet hair. "Tuesday we ship. The pens can run up to twenty-eight hundred head a day, so depending on how long we have to wait, the inspection won't take long. A minute maybe for each animal. The USDA vets who work the Mexican corrals get a lot of practice. Check the number on the ear tag against the TB vaccination certificate, eyeball the animal for obvious things like wounds or ringworm, run it through the dip for ticks, and you're done. I've arranged for the cattle to rest overnight in a livestock yard in Presidio. I'll see them loaded up the next morning for the trip to Oklahoma. If everything goes without snags, I should be home for lunch on Wednesday. I'll check out the goat carcass and look over this photo of the Saint Maker. Whether that will save Gringo or not..."

"At least Pete will have an answer one way or another. I think he'll believe you. I'll have to borrow Hector's photo for you to look at. When the Aplys took off, the second picture went with them."

"Wonder why they pulled out so unexpectedly."

"I guess the murder must have spooked them."

Clay stood before the wide vanity mirror, lathered his face, and picked up his razor to shave. "I know you think I agreed to what Ghee wanted too fast—"

"No," I said, "I was just hoping you'd be able to resolve the Gringo problem as soon as possible. But I admit, asking you to go with the cattle shipment did sound rather like make-work to me.''

"Not at all. He's right about the problems at the quarantine station. The Ministry of Agriculture inspectors are supposed to ensure that all cattle are healthy, dipped, and parasite-free. In reality, the Americans do it. But the drought has caused upwards of three hundred thousand extra head of cattle to be exported from Mexico to the U.S., mostly packer cows. The stations are overwhelmed. When the gates are rushed, sometimes tick-infested or tuberculosis-diseased animals slip by. I think Ghee knows his animals will be okay, but he has put time and money into buying and breeding the best, so some anxiety is natural. And he can afford my time.''

While he had been talking, I had finished applying mascara. My skin has a naturally tan hue, a throwback to Mediterranean ancestors on my father's side, and the only other makeup I wear is a touch of powder to take off the shine. It's my good luck to have thick, naturally wavy hair. A touch of the curling iron to turn the sides back and lift the crown, and I was done.

I turned away from the mirror and went to slip on my peach-colored shirtwaist dress. I eased my feet into a pair of beige pumps. I habitually wear low-heeled shoes, not because my height bothers me, but for comfort. I put on silver and turquoise earrings and a matching necklace and I was ready. I stood by the window, admiring the courtyard, while Clay dressed. Through the windows of the main wing, I could see a uniformed maid setting a polished mahogany table.

"Are you sure we're dressed okay?" I asked Clay as he tucked in his shirt. "That dining room calls out for black tie.''

"Wait until you see the rest of the house." He kissed

me on the cheek and said, "You look nice," and we went downstairs.

I felt better when I saw Eva Suarez wearing a dress very similar to the one she'd had on when I arrived, except the color this time was a ruby red that suited her skin and hair wonderfully. She took us into the great living room—the salon, she called it—with a baby grand piano at one end, a crystal chandelier, and a hearth large enough to stand under. She settled Clay in with Ghee in a seating area beneath the family oil portraits and offered to give me a tour of the house.

The rather bare entry hall and dull guest room had not prepared me for the rest. It was like an art museum or a baroque church, with overripe Italianate paintings covering the walls. The furniture, Eva told me, dated from the late eighteenth century. There were delicate tables dotted with family photographs and ornate chairs with silk brocade seats in jewel tones scattered about. I imagined a job-lot of antiques shipped from Europe and never uncrated until it arrived here.

Last, Eva conducted me to a small room off her sitting room. "This is my most dear possession," she said, her hand caressing the ceramic figure of Our Lady of Guadalupe. It sat on a white and gold altar that took up an entire wall and overflowed with rosaries, family photos, religious medals, candles, and paper flowers.

"She was one of three made for the Empress Carlota," Eva explained.

I gazed at the statue and thought of the tragic woman who had been empress of Mexico for four brief years. If she had prayed to the Virgin, the prayers did not seem to have helped the madwoman. Perhaps the madness had descended before she could pray. I compared the softly tinted face of this Virgin to the Saint Maker's carving. That face had character. This had a sort of flat serenity that one sees on such statues and nothing more. I glanced at Eva and saw the adoration on her face as she stared at the statue.

"It's exquisite," I said politely. The worn fabric of the prie-dieu before the altar testified to Eva's habit of kneeling in prayer to the Virgin. Was she a woman who lived too much on hope and not enough in reality? Or was reality too much for her to bear? She made the sign of the cross and genuflected before the statue just before we left to rejoin our husbands.

Ghee immediately gave me his arm, and with Eva on Clay's arm we made a procession of sorts into the dining room, where a yellow-headed parrot in a brass cage greeted us in raspy Spanish.

Four places had been laid at one end of the mahogany table that seated twelve in high-backed chairs as stiff and straight as sentinels. Platters of food filled a sideboard and we were waited on by the same uniformed servant I had seen setting the table. With hospitality as grand as the porcelain and crystal, Ghee offered the wine as often as the plates were refilled. Julia joined us for the enormous, slow meal, sipping a thin mix of wine and water, watching us and listening to the conversation, but remaining quiet unless spoken to by her father.

Eva remained almost as quiet as her daughter, while Ghee asked question after question about the trading post and my life growing up on the border. As I answered, he smiled, his eyes glowed, and he murmured words of encouragement. I realized that, relaxed by the wine, I had talked far too much and felt embarrassed. As if sensing my belated reticence, he shifted the subject of conversation to himself.

As a raconteur, he shone. He spoke of meetings at Los Pinos, the presidential palace in Mexico City, of meetings in Austin with governors and senators. With politics on the table, the talk soon turned to NAFTA.

"I understand," Clay said, "that Mexican workers feel they got snookered."

Ghee said, "Even the ruling party is having second thoughts. As for the rest of Mexico, in the South, they think about the free trade agreement not at all. Those *chilangos* in Mexico City think about it once a month. We *norteños* think about it every day. *Chilangos* talk endlessly about the past. We in northern Mexico have to work, work hard, and take bold, risky actions to succeed. We look to the future, a future increasingly intertwined with the United States. We prefer American goods, American business methods—"

"And American music and videos," Julia said.

Ghee said cheerfully, "She's going to be my American child." He put his hand on Julia's arm. "You must always remember, little one, America feeds the belly, but Mexico feeds the soul." His eyes shifted from his daughter to us, and he added, "All the world is my home, but like the Aztecs whose blood runs in my veins, my soul must return to Mictlan, the holy center of the north from which we were once driven out. For me, Mictlan is here in this desert."

Julia wrinkled her tiny upturned nose in disagreement, but did not contradict her father.

The talk went back to NAFTA and GATT and the feeling among workers on both sides of the border that the other side had won, the faults and virtues of the Salinas government, the effects of the falling peso, and the surging crime rate in Mexico City. By the time we finished the coffee, the purple dusk had descended and the lamps had been lighted. Eva sent Julia upstairs, and shortly afterward said good night herself. Ghee seemed as fresh as if the long day was only beginning rather than ending, and he invited us to his office for brandy.

"I have something that will be of particular interest to you, Texana," he said, opening the door and standing aside to allow me to enter first.

If rooms are revelatory of the personalities who live in them, this room clearly showed our host's "Mexicanness," what the poets and philosophers call *Mexicanidad.* In this case, Ghee's deep consciousness of his roots had resulted in one of the finest collections of authentic traditional arts and crafts I had ever seen outside a few museums in Mexico City. Rows of shelves displayed candelabra from Izucar de Matamoros, plastered with little clay birds, flowers, and human figures and used to pray for a sweetheart; papier-mâché Day of the Dead figures called *muertos;* magic paper figures from the mountains of Puebla used to make crops grow; paper watchdogs to guard against evil spirits; *rebozos* of raw silk from Juchita and bright embroidered shawls from Veracruz; small saints with ascetic clay heads and wire bodies draped ingeniously in paper.

While I surveyed the collection, Ghee poured brandy and offered Clay a cigar from a beautiful mahogany humidor incised with a coat of arms.

"These are from my tobacco farm in Honduras."

I turned and leaned over the humidor. "May I?" I asked, tentatively gesturing toward the box.

"Of course," Ghee said. With great aplomb he handed me the wide lighter from the desk. He waited until I had taken a few puffs before asking how I liked it.

"I usually don't enjoy the sweetish quality of a maduro, but this is splendid. A good, smooth taste." I let the fragrant smoke roll over my tongue and blew a few smoke rings. "Mild cocoa bean character with herbal notes."

Ghee beamed at me, one cigar-lover to another. "It has a long spicy finish," he said. He turned to Clay. "Did you teach her about cigars?"

"Until I met her, the only cigars I'd smoked were El Productos."

"I grew up on cigar smoke," I said. "My father loves a fine cigar."

"Which does he smoke?" Ghee asked.

"Hoyo de Monterrey Exquisito is his current favorite. He's tried Royal Jamaica Corona, Macanudo, Prince Philip...all the best," I said airily.

Ghee nodded in appreciation and for some minutes we smoked and paid silent homage to superb tobacco.

Afterward, I walked around the room examining the wonders of the shelves, pausing in front of a small, wall-mounted glass case with a brilliant, colored medallion inside. The eight-pointed, gold-rimmed, red cross had a rich blue center with the likeness of a man.

"That's the order of St. Gregory," my host said. "Presented to me by the local bishop to curry favor," he added with a chuckle.

I moved on, stopping this time in front of three hand-carved figures. I recognized Saint Michael the Archangel, sword in hand, looking like a warrior, and Saint Martin the Horseman, revered because he brings success in business, but I had to ask my host about the third statue.

"The Mayan Jaguar God," Ghee said, coming to stand beside me. "They have in common a fierce power, don't you think? The *santero* saw things always with an Indian eye. The racial memory of blood sacrifice is indelible. Think of it. We worshiped insatiable gods that drank so much of our blood. Then the Spanish friars told us of a god who offered up his own blood as the sacrifice. Is it any wonder we embraced the latter? These carvings capture the sense of both worlds, before and after the Conquest. Too bad the artist had to die. Such a gift of talent is all too scarce." Ghee puffed on his cigar. "Do you have any of the *santero's* works still for sale at the trading post?"

I shook my head. "Right after the first one sold, one rancher, a collector himself, bought four of the six I had. And I bought one for myself. An animal carving—a jaguar. It looks so real it almost breathes. It made me think the

Saint Maker must have seen the real animal, except that I guess there aren't any jaguar left in Mexico because of all the hunting.''

"I know where they're doing well," Ghee said, giving me a mischievous grin. "In the mountains northwest of here. Show up with a hunting rifle there, and if the marijuana growers don't shoot you, the soldiers will.''

I had known that the Sierra Madre was rich in fields of marijuana and, it was said, opium poppies. There were tales of long mule-trains moving the crop over the mountain passes. From time to time we heard of shoot-outs between army units and the growers, of *federales* manning roadblocks. It was rumored that the drug lords coerced the Indians into abandoning their corn and beans for poppies. Ironic to think the drug business provided more protection for a wild animal than the efforts of the handful of conservationists in Mexico.

"Come look at this, hon," Clay said.

"This" was a wonderful black and white photograph, a little fuzzy, of a bearded, compact man in a sombrero standing next to Pancho Villa.

"Ghee's grandfather," Clay explained.

Ghee said, "My father's earliest memory was of his father on horseback, gun in hand, riding hell-bent after a Texas Ranger running for the river.''

There were photos of Ghee with Mexican presidents De La Madrid, Lopez Portillo, Diaz Ortiz, Carlos Salinas de Gortari—a misunderstood man, Ghee said—and Ernesto Zedillo. Other pictures showed our host with George Bush in Maine, with Fidel Castro—both men wearing swimming trunks—on a beach in Cuba.

He directed us to leather chairs near his intricately carved desk. "From Juan Perón's palace," he said. Behind the desk was a large window overlooking the hangar and runway.

Ghee offered more brandy. I declined. He poured more for Clay and himself and we sat and watched out the window as the C-130 taxied for takeoff. When the blinking red lights of the plane had disappeared into the night, Ghee turned to us, and for the first time, his eyes looked tired.

"There are times when I wish we *norteños* could unsheathe a machete and slice northern Mexico off from those *chilangos*." He spat out the word as a curse though Mexico City residents call themselves by the term.

"My country is in disorder, and I'm getting old and fearful for the future of my children. We are a weak society dominated by a strong government. Until 1968 we were almost like Russia, with the government in control of everything. This weakened us. I want to build an independent civil society capable of organizing itself into a decisive, self-governing people." He finished his brandy and set the glass on the desk.

"And overpopulation that the government so foolishly encouraged," he continued, "has worsened the situation. The average peasant earns less in a day than an hour of your minimum wage. The poor see crime as the only way out of their poverty. I desire that Mexico become a country of laws. What we need is a *mano firme,* a strong hand to apply the law."

"Perhaps you should run for office," I said. He laughed and shook his head. "I like playing the game behind the scenes too well." He stood up. "I will say good night. Clay, we rise early for the cattle, but not tomorrow. Tomorrow you must relax and enjoy the company of your lovely wife."

We said good night to our host and made our way upstairs. Clay immediately got out of his clothes and hung them up. I kicked off my shoes and stretched out on the bed in my dress. It would have been grand to relax, and I was heavily aided by the wine and brandy. But I couldn't.

I kept worrying about how fast the news of the Saint Maker's death had spread, and Gringo in the lockup, so to speak, at the trading post. I raised my head from the downy pillow to ask Clay if he thought Ghee would mind if I called home.

He came out of the bath, toothbrush in hand. "Ghee would love it. His satellite hookup is new and he enjoys showing it off. His insistence that I call and invite you was just to get me to use the telephone, I think."

"Oh, that's flattering," I said, putting my feet into my shoes once more.

"There's a phone on a table at the end of this hall." A pause. "When you get back, if you're in the mood, I'll demonstrate how glad I am to see you."

"Possibly," I said.

Felicia answered on the second ring and I asked how things were going.

"Everything's okay, Texana, but that Sebastien man showed up four times today and wanted to take the dog away."

"I'm sorry he caused you trouble. Are you okay?"

"I'm fine. But that man is crazy. He said the dog was a killer and if I didn't let him cut the lock on the kennel and take the dog out to shoot him, he'd come back and shoot him right there in the cage. I told him if he came around here again or if anything happened to the dog, I'd call the sheriff."

"You handled it exactly right. I'm sorry about all this, Felicia. If I'd known there was going to be this much trouble about the dog, I'd have stayed home."

"No problem." Felicia gave a sly chuckle. "I took out all my frustration over my husband on that Sebastien. I think I scared him the last time. He won't be back."

"I'll start back first thing tomorrow morning."

"You stay until after lunch like you planned. I can handle things here. I like being in charge."

I laughed gratefully, told her I was glad she felt that way, and said goodbye.

"…one more thing," I heard her say as I lowered the receiver. I put it back against my ear in time to catch the rest of her statement. "Don't you worry about the dog. To be on the safe side, I brought him in with us." Before I could protest, she hung up. I tried to call her back, but she'd switched on the answering machine. The best I could do was leave a message telling her to put the dog back in the kennel.

I told Clay what had happened, and he agreed I should leave as early as possible. Neither of us could sleep right away, and we lay in bed, my head tucked into the hollow of Clay's shoulder, and talked for an hour.

"What do you think of Ghee?" Clay asked.

"Charming. A bit like an actor whose personality is imposed on the part, rather than vice-versa. Do you like him?"

"In spite of my suspicions, yes. He has real regard for his livestock. He's not brutal with the animals the way some owners are. I respect that."

"How did he know we had a pet bobcat? Did you tell him?"

"I don't remember, but I must have, mustn't I, since he knew."

And so it went, until I did relax, and we made love in the joyous, thorough way of two people completely at ease with each other.

ELEVEN

I SPENT a restless night, my nocturnal sighs and shiftings punctuated by Clay's efforts at reassurance: "Try and get some rest.... Don't worry—they'll be fine.... I gave Gringo all his shots and he never once so much as snapped at me."

Over Sunday breakfast Ghee announced to Clay that his people had put out the word about the reward for the dog and assured me that I could feel safer at home because this mad dog would soon be no more. I let that pass with a smile as I explained that a domestic emergency involving my stand-in at the trading post required my leaving as early in the day as possible. I apologized for disrupting the plans for lunch, and suggested I drive myself, adding that Julia could fly down that afternoon if she still wanted to see the bobcat. Ghee cheerfully informed me that he had already dispatched his most dependable ranch hand to drive my pickup home. His daughter, he added proudly, would have me across the border long before the pickup arrived. Lucky me. I called ahead and arranged for Ruben Reyes to meet us at the landing strip above El Polvo and drive us to the trading post. An hour later, I watched Ghee stow my suitcase on board the high-wing Cessna 210. I slipped into the rear seat, my anxiety over flying with a child-pilot only slightly reduced by my relief that we'd be home much faster.

In her Texas Rangers baseball cap and aviator glasses, Julia looked younger than ever, though Clay had informed me that she had recently celebrated her thirteenth birthday. I couldn't decide if that was any better than flying with a ten-year-old or not.

Julia ceremoniously kissed her father's hand in farewell and took her place in the pilot's seat. Mata crouched in the adjacent seat like some sleek animal. He wore chino pants and a white shirt. And his gun. During takeoff, I squeezed my eyes closed and prayed the Hail Mary with special emphasis on the *hour of our death* part.

When I felt the plane swing around to the northeast to meet and follow the river, I opened my eyes and looked down onto the Sierra Pilares, a picture in hues of brown.

Julia concentrated on the controls, Mata kept a watchful eye on her flying, and I kept quiet in order not to distract either of them. After a few moments, I actually began to relax a little.

We banked south and were cruising at about eight hundred feet. The Rio Grande trickled through a twenty-foot-wide riverbed, a desultory, muddy memory of itself that would not be refortified until it reached Ojinaga, where the Rio Conchos flowed into it. Desert scrub and the remains of abandoned adobes dotted the Mexican side. No signs of life except burros and goats. No roads or automobiles. A hundred years earlier, the scene would have been the identical.

I realized exactly where we were when I saw the first sign-point where I had turned off the day before to follow the dirt track into Mexico. Mata seemed to notice it, too, and turned to whisper into Julia's ear. She nodded and the plane dipped and turned to follow the road as it curved its way around the cliffs along the river. In a few minutes we were above a narrow canyon, and she jabbed a finger downward toward a settlement in the middle. "Providencia," she said.

I looked and spotted the village cemetery coming up right below us. A crowd had gathered inside around a freshly mounded grave that showed as a darker smudge of dirt against the parched earth.

"The *santero*'s funeral," Mata said, and then we passed over the village itself, the homes mostly thatch-roofed, mud-plastered *jacales*.

"I thought he was buried yesterday," I said.

"The priest had to attend a sickbed. The woman died last night, so he is here today before his Mass duty on the other side," Mata said.

"How do you know all this?" I asked.

Mata swiveled his head and let those feline eyes rest on my face. "In his territory, Señor Suarez hears the grass grow."

Julia said, "People tell Papa things to ingratiate themselves with him." Her words, sounding like a quote from Ghee, casually acknowledged the fact of the power and influence of her father's wealth.

We continued down the canyon to its end, rejoining the river just above El Polvo.

"Let's fly over the trading post," Julia said ebulliently, jockeying the plane into position.

The big tin roof came into view, with the flat long roof of Clay's office behind, and to my surprise, a familiar RV parked to one side. The Aplys had returned. Julia flew directly over the site, and I saw a figure step out of the RV and stare upward in response to the plane's steady drone.

A few moments later, Julia lined up with the landing strip above El Polvo. At one time it had belonged to a private ranch. The owner had generously allowed the local people to use it, and when he donated the ranch for a wildlife preserve, he had deeded the landing strip to the community. Julia descended into a very smooth touchdown, and I was home.

Ruben Reyes was waiting for us. As soon as his pickup stopped in front of the trading post, I told him to help himself to a free fill-up and with keys in hand and Julia and Mata close behind me, I hurried to unlock the front door.

The trading post is closed Sundays, but I had told Felicia that she could sleep over and stay as long as she liked in order that she have more private time with her daughter. I rushed inside calling Felicia's name.

In answer I heard Phobe's throaty greeting followed by a short bark. As I started down the central aisle, the bobcat ran full tilt from behind the counter with Gringo right behind her. The dog pulled up short when he saw me, then his ears flattened, he gave a throaty growl, and launched himself at me over the bobcat. A hand shoved me hard and I fell sideways.

"Don't!" Julia screeched, and I was deafened by the sharp sound of a shot fired too close.

Dog and bobcat bolted for cover. Felicia ran from the back and stood staring with wide, startled eyes, a frightened Kate peering out from behind her. I got to my feet, and gasped as pain rippled across my side. The shove had sent me across a saddle displayed on a wooden form, and the saddle horn had probably cracked a rib.

Mata stood clutching his weapon with Julia close beside him, her expression furious.

"What are you doing?" she demanded of Mata.

His face flushed as he choked on strangled anger and he slowly put the gun back into his shoulder holster.

When he answered his tone was unemotional. "I thought I was going to kill a dog about to attack Señora Jones."

"Another crazy man," Felicia said, throwing up her hands. "That dog wouldn't hurt anybody. He's been playing with my daughter and Phobe since breakfast. He slept in the bed with us last night."

Mata said defensively, "The dog jumped at Señora Jones."

I held my side and tried to stand straight. Felicia noticed and shouted, "You hit Texana!" Kate started to cry.

Julia said firmly, "I knocked his hand up. The bullet went through the roof."

"I'm all right," I assured them. "It's just a bruise. I got it when I fell. Will someone find Phobe and the dog and be sure they're okay?"

"I will," both Julia and Kate said at the same time.

I introduced them and suggested they go together. I was stalling for time, both to allow me to manage the pain from my ribs, and because I wanted to be careful how I handled Mata. If I could forestall further comments from Felicia, he might assume Gringo was merely a household pet. I'd stopped worrying whether Gringo was dangerous. Ghee's bodyguard seemed far more unpredictable and scary.

Kate gave Julia a shy smile and said, "I'll show you where they're probably hiding."

Julia gave Mata one last fierce look and followed Kate.

Felicia tried to help me by supporting my arm. I felt better standing and asked her if she'd supervise the children while I talked to Mata.

He stiffened defensively. Gently, gently, I thought. If I stabbed his ego, he might kill the dog to spite me.

"I appreciate that you were only trying to help me," I said. "I think I must have startled the dog. He was probably trying to protect—"

Behind us, the front door popped open and Pat and Boyce Aply appeared side by side.

"What's going on?" Pat said, her eyes flicking back and forth between Mata and me. "We thought we heard a shot."

"Just an accidental discharge," I said. "No damage done. Glad to see you back."

"We had to run into Presidio," Pat explained unnecessarily. "Boyce ran out of film for his camera." Boyce had already turned away. Pat gave me one more intent look and followed him, letting the screen door bang shut.

I turned my attention back to Mata, but he spoke before I could say a word.

"Who are those people?" he demanded.

"Tourists. A professor and his wife."

"If I am to protect El Señor's daughter, I must know about people who are to be around her."

"The Aplys are harmless. Professor Aply is a photographer. You can relax."

He flexed his large muscular shoulders and raised his eyes to mine. "El Señor does not pay me to relax."

"I think I'll see about getting everyone something cool to drink," I said. I'd have to catch Felicia in the kitchen and caution her not to say anymore about Gringo in front of Mata. I turned away from him and started down the aisle to the back.

"Señora Jones," Mata called after me, his voice soft and sure, "the dog looks like the one said to have killed the *jorobado,* does it not?"

He was young, arrogant, and astute.

I faced him and said quietly, "It is the dog we found in the chapel with the body. His owner turned him over to me later that day. As to whether the dog killed the Saint Maker, my husband will determine that when he gets home. He knows all about the kinds of wounds a dog attack would leave, and we have a photograph of the body for him to evaluate."

"You should let me take the animal outside and shoot him," Mata said. "El Señor would not wish for his daughter to be endangered by a mad dog. I gave my word of honor to protect her."

"My husband will decide if the dog is to be put down or not. Until then, the dog remains with me. I gave my word of honor to the owner that the animal would be protected until my husband returned."

Mata gave me a scornful look. "El Señor's daughter is more important than a dog."

"And my word of honor is as important to me as yours is to you. I wouldn't put Julia or anyone else in danger willingly. I'll lock the dog up, so Julia will be perfectly safe while she's here."

"Mata obsesses about my safety."

Julia had come up behind us and stood looking annoyed, holding a Coke in one hand.

"He's right to be cautious, Julia," I said.

"He doesn't have to be cautious here, for goodness sake," she said.

"I will get the bags from the porch," Mata said, and I gave him points for nicely avoiding an argument.

When he had stepped outside, I said mildly, "He's being conscientious. Doing his job."

She sighed. "I know. It's such a bore, always being followed and watched. My usual bodyguard is Felix. He's a lot older than Mata and not nearly so nervy. He's away, right now, because his wife is sick. I like him a lot, but I guess I should be glad Mata's around. I have a friend whose brother was kidnapped."

"What happened?"

"They grabbed him in front of his office—he's a stockbroker. His family paid the ransom. The next day they brought him back."

"He was lucky."

"For a while. He got grabbed again the very next month. His family had to pay a lot more, and I think the kidnappers hurt him. My friend's parents wouldn't talk about it and sent her away to school as soon as they could. They shouldn't have paid the first time. Papa says it never stops once you pay. He says if any of my brothers or I get kidnapped, we can consider ourselves dead. He says he'll track down the kidnappers and cut them and put salt in their wounds before he kills them. But he won't pay a penny."

The screen doors banged. "Where shall I put these?" Mata said. He carried my small suitcase, two duffel bags, and Julia's laptop.

"You can put them in back. I'll show you," I said, leading the way.

Julia followed after me, saying to Mata over her shoulder, "You better lose that gun, too, while you're here."

I would have given a lot to see Mata's face, but I didn't dare turn around and make him angrier than I thought he must be at the tone of casual command in Julia's voice. I only hoped he would follow her directive to put the gun away. I didn't much like the idea of him strutting around the trading post wearing a shoulder holster. He looked too much like a flashy drug dealer, right down to the gold Rolex on his wrist, and conceivably might draw the attention of the wrong people.

In the long, narrow room that serves as our living and dining area, Felicia sat on the couch with Kate curled under her arm. Phobe had folded herself up in Kate's lap and was yawning mightily as we came in. All I could see of Gringo were his hind legs. The rest of the dog was pushed in tight, hiding behind Kate.

Julia sat down beside Kate and reached to pat the dog's back, coaxing him to come out. I told Mata to put the bags down anywhere, and went to the galley kitchen to pour iced tea. I carried the tray of glasses to the table. Mata stood leaning against the door, his taut body denying his casual look. I offered Felicia and Mata glasses of tea and told the girls to help themselves to more Coke. The bodyguard drifted to a chair and finally relaxed enough to sit down.

After we had rested I did as I'd promised Mata and locked up Gringo in the storeroom, over Kate's and Julia's protest. The rest of the morning passed with the two girls roaming the front of the trading post, their talk voluble, their laughter free. Mata roamed outside, counting exits and entrances, I assumed. Felicia gave me a fuller account of Carl Sebastien's earlier visits, and I explained why I had to keep Gringo locked up. We had polenta pizza for lunch with a sauce that Felicia had learned to make at a restaurant where she had worked. Mata watched Felicia constantly, questioning her about where she lived and whether I employed her. Felicia, smart girl, gave away as little as possible about herself. I envisioned Mata collecting, using, and abandoning women in succession.

After lunch, I moved Phobe's box into the storeroom, and made a bed of feed sacks for Gringo. Tired from all the attention, Phobe joined her friend and curled up to sleep immediately. The girls wanted to stay with Gringo until he, too, fell asleep, and I agreed to let them, reminding them to shut the door carefully when they left.

I went back to the kitchen to find Felicia washing the dishes, with Mata standing close beside her, leaning near and speaking into her ear. She recoiled, saying something under her breath, and Mata jerked away.

Shortly after, Felicia went home to change clothes and make the long drive to Van Horn to be in time for the 5:00 a.m. start of her job. We had arranged that Kate would stay with me and I would drive her back to her grandmother's house that evening.

My pickup arrived at one, escorted by a second vehicle to take the driver back to Ghee's ranch. What a lot of trouble, I thought, to indulge his daughter's desire to see a pet bobcat. Mata asked if he might use my pickup, saying he needed to "see to the plane." I gave him the keys and he left. I fixed a big bowl of buttered popcorn and told the girls to pick out the videos they wanted to watch.

Mata returned, minus the gun, and sat on the front porch

in one of the tin folding chairs marked with the Corona Beer logo, drinking Coke and eating salted peanuts.

At seven, Julia and I drove Kate home. Back at the trading post, I showed Julia the spare bed in the loft. Her eyes drooped and she yawned, but she was far too dignified at thirteen to go to bed as early as nine. I wished her good night, and left her happily seated in the middle of the bed, legs crossed, working the laptop.

I had planned to unfold a cot for Mata to sleep on, but he beat me to it with his own bedroll on the floor right by the front doors, as if he expected danger to walk in that way. I told him he could switch off the porch light if it bothered him and wished him good night.

As always, with Clay gone I had a hard time dropping off. I lay on my back and listened to the sounds of the early night: the communal yipping of coyotes, the barks of nervous dogs answering back, the bray of an annoyed burro, and now and then the trill of a fox. Noise travels far in the empty air of the desert. Peace settled in about midnight, and I slept until the scratching and whining woke me around 2:00 a.m.

I padded in my bare feet to the storeroom, opened the door, and said, "All right, all right. Come on, you can sleep in my room." The bobcat gave me an irritable, *ferrrump,* and stalked by me. Gringo ducked his head hesitantly, and wagged his tail until the vibration reached his shoulders, then he ran after Phobe.

In five minutes I had them tucked in, Gringo put his back against Phobe's and stretched out full on his side. The bobcat slept with her paws bunched together, her head on my pillow. With one hand, I idly ruffled Phobe's tawny fur so that the pale cinnamon of the undercoat showed. I closed my eyes and waited for their breathing to slow in sleep before I completely relaxed. I half expected Mata to burst in demanding to know why the dog was out again. I

doubted that he'd like the only response I would give—
"So we can get some sleep."

At four, tired of listening to Phobe's snoring and
Gringo's dream noises, I eased out of bed and went to the
kitchen to put on water for coffee. While the kettle heated,
I wandered the room, then stopped in the doorway to the
front. The porch light glowed brightly, shining in through
the front windows and the glass of the top half of the doors.
Mata's bedroll was empty.

TWELVE

THE BELLOW and thud came from outside. I flipped on the back light with one hand and grabbed the wooden club I keep by the back door as I ran out.

Next to my pickup at the edge of the arch of yellow light, Boyce Aply, his face twisted in pain, lay curled on the ground, moaning, his arms holding his midsection. Over him stood Mata.

I barged between the two, gripping the club and wondering what to do next. A squeaking sound interrupted Boyce's moans as Pat, in robe and slippers, opened the RV door and charged out demanding to know why I was attacking her husband. She knelt beside Boyce and asked him where it hurt.

Mata, his face a bland mask, said, "I caught this man stealing from Señora Jones's truck and I struck him down."

With Pat's help, Boyce had rolled over and made it to his knees. He steadied himself with one hand against the pickup and pulled himself to his feet.

"Wasn't stealing," he wheezed.

"My husband has insomnia. He walks around outside to keep from disturbing me."

"The top of the toolbox is up," Mata said. "I caught him going through it."

"If you've damaged his kidneys, we'll sue," Pat said, supporting her husband on one side.

"Not me you won't," Mata said. "I'll be in Mexico." He pulled a pack of cigarettes and a lighter from his breast pocket and tapped out a smoke.

The wide toolbox was bolted to the pickup behind the

cab. Both sides were open. I checked inside. I didn't see anything missing, but I'd have to take everything out to be sure. Later. I turned back to the antagonists.

"I've got coffee on," I told them. "Let's go inside, I'll fix breakfast, and we'll sort this out."

I made the offer to be polite and diffuse the tension. To my surprise, Boyce nodded and nudged his wife toward the back door. Mata sucked deeply on his cigarette one last time before rubbing it out on the ground with the toe of his shoe.

Inside, Pat guided Boyce to a chair. As he sat down, he shook her helping arm off irritably.

"I was just curious what you carried for desert travel in the toolbox," he said, his voice back to its normal peevish tone. "I thought I might improve on my own kit."

Pat said, "My husband has an intellectual's curiosity about everything."

And that explanation was the only one forthcoming over the next forty-five minutes, while I cooked and served scrambled eggs wrapped in tortillas, coffee, and juice. Toward the end of the meal, after Boyce asked for a second helping, I mentioned the break-in on Friday and asked the Aplys if they had seen or heard anything. Pat said they had left for Presidio shortly after I had driven off with Carl Sebastien. I had no reason to doubt them and let the subject drop, but as soon as the pair left to go back to their RV, Mata demanded to know more.

I emphasized that kids had broken in before and probably had this time, that I had not bothered to notify the sheriff because I didn't see why he should have to make a long drive when nothing was missing or damaged beyond the splintered back door.

Mata asked, "And these Aplys were here when this happened?"

"You heard them say they left right after I did."

The suspicious look in Mata's eyes told me I had made a serious mistake in bringing the subject up in his presence. He probably imagined some plot on our parts to kidnap his boss's daughter. He disappeared while I washed dishes, and I assumed he was keeping a stealthy eye on the Aplys' RV. And me.

THIRTEEN

I DIDN'T SEE Mata again until Julia came down for breakfast at nine. By then I'd showered, dressed, done some house-keeping chores, and fed Gringo and Phobe, afterward put-ting the dog back into safekeeping in the storeroom. Phobe had refused to go, sailing past my feet and heading for her day place on the shelves from which she could observe the front doors.

Julia came down fully dressed and ready for the day. Shortly after she sat down at the table, Mata materialized in the doorway between the front and our quarters, while Julia munched cereal and read some of the tourist brochures on the area. The bodyguard accepted a fresh cup of coffee, stirring in two spoonfuls of sugar and drinking it standing up. I was relieved to see that after the night's events, he hadn't slipped the shoulder holster back on.

No one was in a talking mood except Julia, who had found a bat cave mentioned in one of the brochures and asked me twenty questions about that until the bell on the front door jangled, and I went to wait on a customer.

In a few minutes I helped three people, selling a case of motor oil, an air compressor, and two rolls of barbed wire to a rancher, the last of the bread and eight pairs of jeans to a truckload of men from the other side, and a car battery to a ranch couple who had walked a half-mile after their car died. Normally I'd have closed up long enough to drive them back to their vehicle, but I didn't want to leave the trading post with Mata there. I feared he might deliberately provoke the Aplys if they came in.

I had my back to the front door when the bell jangled

again, but Mata had come to lean against the wall behind the counter and the darkening of his eyes behind the drooping lids alerted me that he didn't approve of the new arrival.

I turned. Hector came down the aisle looking hesitant and uncomfortable. Behind him, just inside the door, stood a dark man with a distinctly Mayan face—strong, beaked nose, high flat cheekbones, and deep-set eyes that were ten years younger than his papery, wrinkled skin. He wore a white cotton shirt and pants and held a straw hat in his hands.

"Buenos días," Hector said, nodding his head.

I wished the mayor of Providencia good morning, glancing again at Mata's face. He seemed to be looking past Hector at the silent stranger. There was something in his expression, but whether it was mistrust or only the middle-class Mexican's contempt for the pure *Indio,* I could not fathom.

"Will you take my picture with Phobe?" Julia said, coming into the room behind us.

Mata lowered his eyes, took the camera Julia held out, and followed her into the back room. When I turned back to Hector, he stood alone, his companion gone.

I have never seen Hector when his natural social grace failed him, but now he appeared disconcerted, ill at ease, and embarrassed. I wondered if he had heard about the dog being here.

"May I help you, Hector?" I said.

He looked at me in solemn appraisal for a few moments. Then he shook his head.

"Do you need supplies?"

Again the shake of the head. Then he came forward slowly, as if reluctant. When he spoke, his kept his voice low, his eyes focused on the passage door behind me.

"I have news about the *santero*'s death, but perhaps this

is not the time. I will come back when you are not so busy."

Hector edged toward the door. I slipped from behind the counter and walked with him. I wanted to ask him to loan me the photograph Pat had taken of the Saint Maker's body.

"What news do you bring?" I asked as we stood on the porch. "Have you found the Saint Maker's bag and carving tools?"

"No, not that." He flapped a hand vaguely. "We have looked in every house in the village. I think the one who killed the *santero* must have taken the bag."

"What are you saying, Hector?"

"That, as you suspected, the *santero* was murdered. One of our men, old Lupe, in his youth worked as a stone mason. In spite of the pain he has now in his hands, he wanted to make something for the chapel. So he cut out of stone a doorstop in the shape of the old Christian symbol of a fish. It must have weighed ten pounds. Whenever there was work being done in the chapel, painting, or plastering, we used Lupe's doorstop to keep one side of the door open for light and air. When we searched, three of the men and I, for the *santero*'s bag, we realized the doorstop was missing. One of the dogs sniffed it out where it had been thrown among the rocks beyond the chapel. There was blood on the head of the fish. Whoever killed the *santero* must have held the doorstop by the tail of the fish and swung it at his face."

And hit him again and again, I realized, to do the damage to his face we had seen.

Hector said, "I think the dog must have been there with the *santero*. Perhaps it is the killer's dog and he left it."

I had to confess to Hector that I knew the dog and its owner, and that while I hadn't asked Pete where he'd been the morning of the murder, his wife had told me quite candidly about the dog coming home with blood on its face and body, not a thing she'd have mentioned if her husband had been involved.

"So," Hector said, "the dog does not lead us to the killer."

"Who would have killed the Saint Maker?" I asked. "And why? He seemed so harmless."

"The most harmless can give offense. Or offense may be taken when none was intended. I have seen one man knife another for refusing to have a drink."

From the porch, Julia called my name. Hector said goodbye, that we would talk again. He got into an ancient pickup, waved a hand, and was gone. There was no sign of the stranger that had come inside with him, and I wondered where the man had gone.

FOURTEEN

I INVITED Julia and her bodyguard to stay for lunch, but she explained that her father expected her back.

"Papa is very strict about times," she said. "He'd come after me if I was late getting home with the plane."

At eleven, I drove them to the landing strip.

"You're so lucky to live with a bobcat," Julia said. She gave me a dignified farewell handshake and asked if she might come back to explore the bat cave she had read about in the brochure. I promised to try and arrange something with the landowner, drove to the edge of the runway, and watched as they took off. I felt relieved to see the last of Mata.

His final comment to me, as he lifted Julia up to get in the plane, had been a reference to Boyce.

"I'd watch that professor if I were you. He's playing the fox."

He had spoken in Spanish, his use of the idiom leaving no doubt as to his meaning. The bodyguard thought Boyce sly and sneaky. In that, he credited the man with more deviousness than I did. Both the Aplys seemed to me to lack all subtlety.

Pat proved my point by coming into the trading post as soon as I unlocked the front door, demanding to know who Mata was, where he came from, and what he'd been doing there.

Her blunt force worked. In spite of my best intentions to avoid the subject, I found myself explaining to her all about Ghee, Clay's work at Rancho de Sierra Vista, and the reason for the visit by Ghee's daughter with her bodyguard.

"I can't think why any intelligent father lets a kid fly a plane," Pat said.

"Julia seemed to be very competent," I said, pushed by Pat's manner to defend something I thought unwise myself. "And Mr. Mata is a licensed pilot," I added in justification.

She prowled the aisles for a few more minutes, asking about Ghee's ranch: How big was it? Where was it? How far was it from the border? Finally she wound down and bought canned juice and cheese crackers.

When she paid, I took the opportunity to ask a few questions of my own: Were they still planning to stay until the end of the week as they had told me when they arrived? Had they located the film Boyce needed in Presidio—if not, could I order it for them? Would Boyce be going out to take photographs today, or was he still suffering from the effects of his confrontation with Mata?

They were staying indefinitely. Boyce had plenty of film. He felt dreadful but would bravely go out after lunch to take some pictures of the river, Pat informed me. As she left, she stopped in the doorway to make one last point, probably the reason for her visit, I decided.

"I think the least you could do to make up to Boyce for what happened is reduce our bill for the RV hookup." She left without waiting for my answer.

On the whole, I didn't think she had much of a point, but her suggestion had reminded me that I wanted to check the pickup's toolbox to be certain nothing was missing.

With Pat out of the way, I let Gringo out of the storeroom and let him join Phobe in our private quarters. Though Hector's admission that the wood-carver had been murdered made me feel less edgy about the dog's safety and that of my customers, I intended to be cautious until Clay could look at the photograph of the Saint Maker's wounds and see what he thought about how they'd been inflicted. I had been so surprised by Hector's changed attitude that I'd forgotten to ask him if I might borrow the photograph. I could have asked Pat for her copy, but I had felt reluctant to do so. I had the feeling she'd have pretended not to know what I was talking about.

And there was still the goat carcass waiting in my freezer to silently substantiate or refute Carl's accusation against Gringo. Until then, I wanted Gringo out of sight.

On a Monday that wouldn't be much of a problem. Except for gasoline sales, Mondays are always slow. Noon to four o'clock is a dead time because in the borderland we practice the long, late lunch hours of Mexico.

I nibbled on chips and iced tea and watched through the front window until a little after two when I saw the Aplys' truck pull out with Pat driving and Boyce slumping low in the seat beside her. They turned northwest toward El Polvo. I gave them a few minutes to get well away, then I went out to my pickup.

Twenty minutes later I'd removed every item from the toolbox, including my towing rope. I ticked the items off against my checklist of the contents—kept always on the corkboard beside the refrigerator. Not one small item was missing. So much for Mata's suspicions. And mine. Boyce was not a villain, merely a bumbling professor.

At four o'clock the Aplys returned, but Pat didn't make another appearance in the trading post and I had hopes of an Aply-free evening. At six, just as I was about to close, the brown United Parcel Service truck wheeled in so fast gravel peppered the porch. The driver jumped out, package in hand, and hurried in. As far as I know, Riley Bigham's route is the most remote in the state. Working out of Marfa, he covers a couple of hundred miles one way. And that in a region with a population of less than two people per square mile. The company must lose money on us.

Riley looked tired, dusty, and very hot in his starched khaki uniform. As he would after baking all day in the unair-conditioned truck in the 112-degree temperature. As he usually did, he stopped at the soft drink box. Instead of popping the tab, he lifted the can to the back of his neck, saying, "Ah, good and cold."

"Keep that one to cool your collar and have another to drink on the house," I told him.

"Thanks, Texana," he said, talking around the plug of tobacco in his mouth and walking to the counter, can in one hand, package in the other. "Just the one will do me. It's hot enough out there to melt the can. Could I ask a favor?"

I like Riley. He's a good, kind man who takes an interest in the folks on his route, not out of nosiness, but because his customers expect him to know and relate what's happening. Living in isolation as we do, we look forward to hearing news of one another.

Riley's knowledge of our habits is not only useful as a news source. More than once he has saved a life. When a rancher who always left the gate open for UPS failed to do so, Riley had climbed the fence, walked two miles to the ranch house, found the man collapsed with a heart attack, and telephoned for the sheriff. A helicopter had air-lifted the rancher out to the hospital. The burly driver's other exploits included making a hospital run for an expectant mother in unexpected, too-early labor, and rescuing a ranch hand from a flash flood in an arroyo.

"Someone not home?" I said, guessing he'd tried to deliver the package he carried to an empty house. The trading post is the designated drop for UPS, and I often accept delivery for locals who are away.

Riley nodded. "This package is for the schoolteacher. She gave me the okay to leave things with you if she wasn't home. She seems like a real nice lady."

I signed for the package. Riley pulled out his billfold to pay for his drink. Gringo and Phobe picked that moment to burst through the door behind me, chasing each other back and forth down the center aisle.

Riley eyed them for a minute, then said, "Better keep that dog out of sight. You know he looks like the one everybody's talking about, don't you?"

"Talking about?"

"Yeah, some white pit bull chewed up a man on the other side and a rich rancher is offering a big reward." He pocketed his change, picked up his soft drink, and banged out the door. I heard the engine start and the truck roared out to the road.

Damn that reward. Distance sure didn't slow down gossip any, I reflected. I put Irene's package beneath the counter and wondered how long it would be until the reward furor died down and Gringo would be safe. Hector's admission to me that the Saint Maker might have been murdered was a tribute to the man's honesty and conscience, but he would not broadcast the news for fear of drawing the attention of the authorities and all the attendant trouble that would bring the village.

Thank God the day was over, my guests gone, and the Aplys occupied elsewhere. I locked the front doors, pulled down the shades, and headed toward the back, leaving Gringo and Phobe in front. After dark, I'd take the dog out. First I intended to take a hot shower, then indulge myself by having a whiskey with my sandwich while I watched my favorite video: *Harvey,* with Jimmy Stewart as the charming soak Elwood P. Dowd.

After my shower, I slipped into a cotton tee and shorts, and was on my way to the kitchen when through the window I spotted Carl Sebastien standing inside the empty kennel out back.

I don't lose my temper often, but when I do, I make up for all the times I didn't. I barged out the back door, marched across the lot, kicked the kennel door shut with Carl inside the run, and closed the lock.

"Hey," he shouted, rushing at the bars. "Whadda you think you're doing? Lemme outta here!"

"Shut up, Carl, and listen to me. Or I'll leave you locked in there while I call the sheriff and slap a trespassing charge on you." I paused to let my words get past his ears.

He gave me a surprised look and dropped his hands from the bars.

"I wasn't doing nothing. Just looking around."

"A darn sight too many people have been just looking around my place lately. I'm fed up."

"That's no reason to take it out on me," he whined.

"There's every good reason. You're here," I sputtered.

Carl took a step back. "Take it easy, Texana. You're gonna bust something. You need a nerve pill."

His involuntary backing away from me eased my whole being and I felt the rush of power that bullies must enjoy. So that was the thrill of psychological and physical intimidation—and I was only enjoying it secondhand, since Carl's fear was of the sheriff, not me. Such pleasure could be a dangerous habit to form, I decided. I worked the lock and let the kennel door swing open. Carl hesitated so long, I motioned to him to come out.

He moved without enthusiasm, his eyes not meeting mine, his arms locked defensively across his chest.

"Felicia told me you'd caused some trouble while I was gone," I said, keeping my tone mild.

He shook his head. "No trouble. I heard that dog killed a man on the other side, so I came to warn you. I told you that animal was dangerous. I thought she ought to have let me shoot it. Not very smart, keeping a killer dog with a little kid around. Trying to help is all I was doing."

"Do you know Hector Cruz?" I asked him.

He shook his head. I explained who Hector was.

"He came to see me today to tell me that the dog didn't kill the man."

"Does that mean there's no reward, like I heard about?"

So that was it. Greed had brought Carl snooping around, looking for a chance to kill Gringo.

"It means," I almost shouted, "there's a murderer around here somewhere. That's a lot more to be worried about than a dog."

Carl's face shut down into mulishness. "I still think that dog killed my goats," he said.

"Well, no one's offering a reward for that," I said, losing my patience.

Carl looked disappointed enough to cry and I decided to take advantage of that.

"I'll tell you what, Carl. I'm going to compensate you ten dollars apiece for those goats. You wait here. I'll go get the money." A bribe, pure and simple, to get him to stay away.

I trudged back into the trading post. While I was getting the money from where I hide the cash receipts, Gringo came sniffing around and stopped to lick my hand.

"You're not worth it," I told him, kissing him on top of his hard head. If I didn't watch it, I'd be calling him my baby, just like Pete did.

Carl hadn't moved an inch from where I told him to wait. I counted out five tens into his grubby hand.

He looked at me. "There was six," he said. "I bought six goats off old man Haskell."

"Mr. Haskell *gave* you six goats. I happen to know that one fell out of the trailer while you were hauling them and broke its neck."

"Man, everybody knows everything about everybody else out here," he said, giving me a grin like a possum caught foraging in the garbage can.

"Do me a favor, Carl. Put the word out that the reward

is off, and if anything happens to the dog, I'll file animal cruelty charges against anyone in sight."

"Sure thing." He frowned. "Did you say somebody had been sneaking around here? 'Sides me, that is."

"There was the jimmied door, then someone went through my toolbox on the pickup." I didn't mention Boyce. No need to sow suspicion. "By the time you came along, I was out of patience."

"Sounds to me like somebody's looking to find something worth the trouble," he said.

He moved off a few yards, turned back, and said, "You sure the reward's off? You wouldn't be planning to collect it yourself?"

Without waiting for an answer, he loped away.

After the face-off with Carl even Elwood P. Dowd couldn't rid me of the jitters. Instead, I played tag with Phobe and Gringo, fed them, and took the dog out before settling the pair in the storeroom for the night. And it was still only a little after nine.

I usually enjoy being alone, and seldom have to search for ways to occupy my time, but tonight I craved company. I went out and sat on the porch, watching the sun slip behind the mountains of Mexico, and hoping that the schoolteacher would stop to pick up her package and visit for a while. When she didn't, I decided to deliver it.

Before I left, I gave an extra tug on the storeroom door to be sure it was shut securely. I wouldn't put it past Carl to come creeping back, and I didn't want the dog visible to anyone looking in a window from outside. I had dismissed his suggestion that someone was searching for something around my place as nonsense, especially since he'd accused me of trying to ace him out of the reward so I could keep it for myself. Carl suspected everyone of the same avaricious motivation under which he operated. Which either made him a cynic or a shrewd judge of human nature.

I walked to my pickup with Irene's bulky package under my arm as the light faded from purple to black. I had not put on the back floodlight. I enjoy the anonymity of darkness. But I used my flashlight on low beam to watch for snakes that might be taking advantage of the brief temperate period between the intense heat of day and the cold of the desert night to hunt. We were seeing more than the normal number of snakes because the drought was killing off the prey and the reptiles were coming in after food and water. Almost every morning I could see the signs where they had crawled across the cool sand around the hose, and one morning I had watched, fascinated, as a kingsnake had held his mouth open beneath the hose connection to catch the drip.

As I neared the pickup I switched the flashlight off and reached for the door handle. A slight shifting of the shadows beyond the edge of the lot caught my eye and I froze.

"Who's there?" I called, my hand moving toward the gun at my waist.

"No one, señora," came a meek voice. "It is I."

A lighter shape than the desert background glided forward. As my eyes adjusted to the faint light from the quarter moon I recognized the Maya who had come with Hector. Though he stood with his eyes downcast, I had the feeling he was watching me as closely as I watched him.

A night breeze came whispering across the lot and stirred the leaves of a mesquite nearby. Seeming to come from everywhere and nowhere, a shuddering cry rose on the air and echoed down the river as it had the night I first locked Gringo in the kennels.

"Mountain lion," I said.

A pause. Then the Maya said, "No, señora. That is no mountain lion.

"Then what is it?"

"I think it is a woman weeping."

FIFTEEN

HIS NAME, he told me, was Antun Tanhol.

"You come from southern Mexico," I said. Not a lucky guess. The name, in the Indian language of Nahuatl, told me as much about him as his Mayan face. Though Mexico is basically an Indian land, the Aztecs have long since adopted and adapted and changed into a composite of Spanish and Indian cultures that is Mexican. Not so the Maya. The most fierce and persistent warriors against the Conquest had held on to their ancient view of the cosmos, held on to their language, and held on to their identity.

He said nothing, letting his silence give confirmation.

I tried again. "You're a long way from home."

And what was he doing here?

He acknowledged my comment with a nod. "Farther than ever I have been," he said, then lapsed back into silence.

"You came in the trading post with Hector this afternoon. Did you wish to see me about something in particular?"

"I'm ashamed I ran out. Too many strangers. The farther I am from home, the more I fall back on my people's teaching that to go among strangers is to lose a piece of one's soul."

"I moved away from here, once, to live among strangers," I told him, thinking of my first, miserable marriage, "and I felt a little like I was losing a part of my soul."

"What did you do?"

"I came home."

He nodded slowly. "I, too, wish to return home. But you

are going somewhere and I keep you too long.'' With a long sigh, he merged with the darkness like a vanishing ghost. I stood there feeling stupid because I still didn't know why he had been waiting for me. Then a suspicion, planted by Carl, made me wonder: Had the Maya been waiting for me? Or had he been snooping around, looking for something?

I got in the pickup and circled the lot with the lights on high beam trying to spot the man, but the desert stood empty.

My trading post is two miles as the river—and thus the road—runs from El Polvo. The church sits on a rise at the southeastern tip of the community, and the schoolhouse and teacherage stand slightly back and three hundred feet on the other side of the adobe-walled cemetery. Overlooking the cemetery is a small adobe, formerly the home of Doña Aurora, godmother of the community and a clairvoyant, who had died peacefully in her sleep the previous winter. Above the empty house a high ridge runs for several hundred yards.

Someone had left a flickering candle on top of one of the *sillar* block tombs. I slowed and looked to see whether someone was holding a private vigil, then realized that the weak halo of light shown atop Rhea Fair's grave. Since the death of the *curandera,* her simple tomb had become a shrine of devotion. In life, she had healed many people. In death, believers said she healed still, and they came to pray for her assistance and leave gifts called *milagros.* These small tin arms, legs, eyes, and other body parts represented miracles of healing left as testimony to others. Others left paper flowers, crutches, photos, letters. The poorest of the poor left river stones as tokens.

Beyond the cemetery a bright light shone through the two front windows of the teacherage, but no one answered my knock. I turned to go, assuming that Irene was away for the night. A feeling of unease, perhaps prompted by the odd things that seemed to be happening at the trading post, made me check behind the house for the teacher's car. The green Volvo stood parked near the back door. I lifted my eyes toward heaven in a silent prayer that nothing had happened to Irene and saw against the brighter dark of the starry streaked sky the denser black silhouette of a woman whose head and upper torso were wrapped in a shawl.

La Llorona. Or someone dressed up as the weeping woman to frighten children.

Anger propelled me up the steep path to the top of the ridge. Panting for breath, I had nearly reached the figure when it spun around and cried, "Oh!"

"Irene?"

I saw her put her hand to her heart. "Texana? You scared me to death," she said.

I heard the shiver in her voice. The first hour of darkness had chilled the air. Without clouds or humidity to push down the heat, the desert cools rapidly after nightfall.

"It's cold up here. Let's go inside," I said.

I followed Irene down the path. "You're as surefooted as a goat," I told her. "You must come up here often."

"I like the view of the river and town. I walk up here most nights to get my exercise in."

"It's a wonder you haven't been snake-bitten."

"I wear boots, and the denim skirt is thick."

When we reached the back door I explained that I had a package for her in the pickup and went to get it.

The teacherage is tiny, only three rooms.

Irene had taken the shawl off and stood waiting for me in the front room. She had been hired in June to replace Ned Little, who had married and moved downriver to Lajitas where his wife ran a river rafting business. Irene had moved from Dallas. She was a large woman with a gentle, soothing face and masses of gray hair. Now she put on another lamp, and I saw that her face was haggard, her eyes red and puffy.

I tossed the package onto the rattan daybed and reached out to lightly touch her arm. "Are you all right?" I asked.

Tears brimmed in her eyes and a sniff turned into a hiccupping sob. "Oh dear, I have such troubles I don't know what to do."

SIXTEEN

"HE WANTS me to smuggle him in a gun," Irene said.

"That wouldn't be wise," I told her.

"He says the others have guns. There have been shoot-outs in the prison yard."

"I don't doubt it. Money is the official language of prisons in Mexico. If you've got the money, you can get anything you want, even guns."

"Kyle is only eighteen," Irene said, as if that explained everything.

And maybe it did. I'd have hated to be held accountable for some of the stunts I tried when I was that young. But my empathy wouldn't help Irene accomplish what she wanted to do: get her son out of jail.

"He says his lawyer tells him that twenty-five thousand dollars will *expedite* his case through the courts. He's been in that horrible place for seven months and he has no idea how long it will be until his trial. He says he didn't even buy the drugs the man offered him."

"The lawyer is probably being realistic." I didn't have the heart to tell her that in Mexico anyone with a bachelor's degree could practice law.

Her face seemed to cave in even more at my words and her hands balled into fists in her lap.

She had to clear her throat before she could speak. "Kyle wants me to borrow against my teacher retirement. I don't know what to do. He sent an airmail letter begging me to bring him cash. He said to come in person, that he would never get the money if I mailed it." She looked at me questioningly.

"He was right. About the only mail that gets attention on the other side is airmail. Anything else disappears down the Sepomex black hole. And mail from the States, I imagine that's mostly opened on the chance there might be cash, checks, or money orders inside."

She leaned against the back of her chair as if that was the only thing holding her up.

"Kyle said there were people in the cells who would kill anyone for twenty-five cents. He said that's the daily rate for a bed for the Mexican prisoners. It's more for the gringos. He said he had to have five hundred dollars to get a safe place to sleep. I didn't believe it until I went to the prison the first time and saw what it's like."

"Is that why you took this job? To be where you could visit Kyle?"

She nodded. "As soon as the spring school term ended I packed to come here. I saw the ad in the paper for a teaching position here the same day and called to apply. The school board member hired me over the phone based on my sending proof of my teaching credentials. He explained about the house being included and I asked if I could come early. He said yes. I resigned from my job, rented out my house, and drove out here the next month."

She paused to take a deep breath. "I took Kyle the money the first day I got here. He looked so bad. Dirty. Thin. And barefoot. He said someone had stolen his shoes. He'd been sick from the food. Beans and rice. He said that's all they served every day, beans and rice. He buys his meals from the prison vendors now, and I take him food when I visit." She shuddered. "I hate going there."

"Would it help if you had someone to go with you?"

"Oh, Texana, would you?"

"When is your next visit?"

"I was waiting on that package you brought. It's clothes I ordered for Kyle."

"Give me tomorrow to make some arrangements."

"Thank you. You must have thought I was crazy, pacing back and forth on the ridge. But every night I would sit here until I felt like my head would burst from worrying about Kyle for hour after hour. When I couldn't stand it any longer I'd go up there, to the ridge. With the stars, and the clean air, and the sounds of the trees by the river. Then I'd remember Kyle all locked up and I'd start to bawl like a baby.

I didn't tell her I'd heard her. I did admit why I'd chased up to the ridge after her.

"When I saw you up there tonight, I thought you were the Weeping Woman. Someone dressed up like *La Llorona* and playing some kind of game scaring people."

Irene hadn't heard of the legend, and I regretted bringing it up since it was hardly the most pleasant tale of motherhood. I told her an amended version of a woman wronged and searching for her lover.

Her need to talk and my desire for company made the time speed by. When I finally did leave, I was surprised to see that the clock in the pickup showed 11:45. We had talked for nearly two hours. Phobe and Gringo would be tearing at the storeroom door to be let out.

I parked in back, unlocked the door, and put on the lights.

Stub tail thumping the floor, Gringo sat right in front of me, panting and eager to be petted.

"What on earth! How did you get out?"

I went around him and headed straight for the storeroom. The door stood open.

With Gringo at my heels, whimpering as he picked up on my fear, I searched every corner and shelf in the place, calling Phobe's name, dreading I'd find her injured or dead. I didn't find her. On the second wave of my search I discovered that the screen on one of the kitchen windows had been cut through right up against the wood frame on three

sides and now curled outward. At that moment I didn't care
about who had cut the screen or why. Phobe had gone.

I went outside and stared into the darkness of the desert.
Phobe had been a pet all her life. I didn't like to think what
might happen to her out there.

SEVENTEEN

AT 5:45 A.M., drinking strong black coffee and slotting the cash into the register, I noticed the jaguar carving had vanished.

Phobe had not come for her breakfast. The night before, I had walked into the desert with the flashlight, calling her name over and over. The bobcat had been intrigued by the desert she watched through the windows and played at the edges of when Clay and I took her out with us. When I had gone to bed about two, I risked letting in all the bugs in the universe by leaving the screen pushed out. If Phobe had gotten out that way, she'd try to come back in at the same place. Only a very real fear of snakes kept me from leaving the back door cracked open for her. Stretched out on my back in bed, Gringo at my feet, the ceiling fan whirling overhead, I had dozed lightly, jerking awake at the slightest sound, thinking it might be Phobe climbing in the window. Every hour or so, I had gone to the back door and called her name. If the noise and flashlight had disturbed the Aplys in their RV, they had never once looked out to see what was going on. The incident with Mata must have really put the fear into them.

Toward dawn the morning star had burned like a yellow lamp in the east and I had watched the pale flush of first light spread and brighten. The old school wall clock had chimed the new hour, and I had put the coffee on.

Now, staring at the empty space atop the cash register where the carving had stood, I puzzled over why someone had cut the screen, unlocked the storeroom, and stolen a wooden statue. Nothing else of value—not even one of the artifacts in the display case, for example—was missing. The drawer of the register had been half open as I always left it. The most easily negotiable of items on the other side, cigarettes and liquor, were untouched.

The place had been broken into and searched twice in four days. Carl, it seemed, had been right. Someone was looking for something valuable enough to risk breaking in twice. But what? And who? I was sorry I'd promised to go to Chihuahua with Irene. Every time I went away, someone got in. Maybe that might be used to my advantage.

The bell on the door jangled as the first customer of the day arrived.

The morning passed with me pumping gas and making a few sales to locals. I told everyone that came in to keep an eye out for Phobe. At eleven, Pat Aply showed up and bought a magazine, remaining silent except to say that "poor Boyce" still suffered soreness from tangling with Mata. She swore that Mata had used his feet as well as his fists on Boyce. I had no reason to doubt her. A clean fighter wouldn't be worth much, I suspected, as a bodyguard.

I told Pat the bobcat had gotten out, without explaining how, and asked if she might have seen or heard anything between dark and midnight. She said that both she and Boyce had taken sleeping pills "to relax and get some rest."

I told her that I would be gone either the next day or the following day and the trading post closed, in case she needed to buy anything to tide her over. She said she'd tell Boyce in case he needed to put gas in the truck.

At noon I locked up and drove in to the post office to collect the mail and put up a hand-printed notice offering a reward for Phobe. I asked Lucy Ramos if one of her grandsons might want to work for me on Wednesday or Thursday. She promised to let me know.

I spent the afternoon sitting on a stool behind the counter, thumbing through some old magazines and trying not to worry about Phobe. The only customers I had came from the other side, three tired, hungry-looking *leneros* who traded me four burro loads of stumps and driftwood they had collected from along the arroyos for beans, coffee, sugar, rice, and lard. The desert is the only place where you dig for wood, and the *leneros* made a thin living using their shovels, axes, and machetes to unearth roots of dead trees to use as firewood.

At six I locked up, had a skimpy meal at the table by the window, and watched the first short shadows stretch across the desert. I tried a Thin Man video, but my lack of sleep the night before caught up with me and I dozed through most of the old black and white movie. At nine Lucy called to say her grandson Jorge would mind the trading post for me. I called Irene and she agreed we'd leave the next morning for Chihuahua.

Again, I left the screen open in the hope that Phobe would find her way back home.

EIGHTEEN

THE NEXT MORNING I rose again before dawn and looked for Phobe. No answering *mer-rrr-ump,* which passed for a meow with the bobcat. No round eyes reflecting the beam of my flashlight.

Over breakfast I could not keep from thinking about what Clay had said when Phobe first came to live with us.

"Bobcats are more affectionate than domestic cats. They crave affection and attention."

Wherever she was, she would want company. She would try to come home.

A half-hour later, I went out to Clay's office, returned, and pushed the cut screen back into place before feeding Gringo, who had no appetite and missed his friend. He'd roamed the trading post nearly all night, sniffing and looking into corners for his playmate.

Rubbing Gringo with my foot, I sat at the table and finalized my plans for the day. Clay had said he might be home by noon, so I wrote a note telling him where I'd gone and that Phobe was missing.

A little after seven Lucy's grandson arrived. Jorge looked a little skeptical after I explained what I wanted him to do, but agreed to spend the day in Clay's trailer keeping watch over the trading post for anyone trying to get inside.

"If someone does get in, take no chances," I told him. "Don't do anything except get a description and a license number if you see a vehicle."

For playing detective, I would pay him for a full day's work, and as soon as Clay arrived, Jorge could go home.

Irene arrived, parking beside the trading post to take ad-

vantage of half a day's shade for her car. We were going
in my pickup. As we left, the Aplys emerged from their
RV and got into their truck. They pulled out right behind
me and followed all the way on the fifty-mile, winding
drive down to the dusty streets of Presidio, the only official
cross-border link in the 450 miles between El Paso and Del
Rio. I lost the Aplys when we turned to cross the bridge
into Ojinaga. Odd, I thought. There was more for tourists
to do on the Mexico side. Presidio did have several good
places to eat. Maybe they were going to Las Pampas for
breakfast. Just across the bridge on the right, I stopped to
show my driver's license, registration, and title for a car
permit, also paying four dollars for the minimum daily auto
insurance, necessary for traveling further than twenty miles
into Mexico.

A bit more than an hour into the trip the highway crosses
a mountain pass, enters a narrow valley, and ascends an
even higher mountain. At the top is a parking lot, and a
path leading to the overlook of one of the most spectacular
river canyons in the world, the Peguis, with the Rio Conchos flowing deep down the middle. I asked Irene if she'd
ever stopped to see it. She looked blankly at me and shook
her head. She had started the trip in a nervously talkative
mood that drained away the closer we got to the destination.
Now she was quiet.

I didn't mind. Mexican Federal Highway 16 is often busy
with the bulked-up Mexican trucks whose drivers are *muy
macho*. This means they take their half of the road out of
the middle, yield to no one, and look upon slowing down
as a character flaw. Watching for traffic, and dodging pot-
holes and the rocks used by the truckers to stop tires while
they change flats kept me busy. Small talk, I didn't need.

Chihuahua City sits on a high plain near the junction of
the Sacramento and Chuviscar rivers. The population numbers around a million. For those foreigners who know only

the big border towns of Mexico, Chihuahua is a nice surprise. Its citizens are courteous, friendly, and there are few beggars. Downtown the city has wide boulevards and stately Profiriato buildings. The *penitenciaria* is only two blocks from the railway station where visitors take the train to see the famous Copper Canyon. It houses the unlucky—those who got caught, including plenty of Americans. One lasting contribution to Mexico by the three-year rule of Maximilian, other than good French bread and a number of French-fathered Mexican families, was the guilty-until-proven-innocent precept of the Napoleonic code. There is no distinction in Mexico between jail for those convicted and those awaiting trial. They are housed together.

We parked on the side street and I fell a few paces behind Irene as she hurried toward the front of the prison carrying the package of clothes for her son, her purse swinging from a shoulder strap.

I saw the old Volkswagen taxi pull in beside her. A man leaped out of the passenger seat with knife in hand, grabbed the purse and sliced the strap in one smooth motion, shoved Irene hard, and slid back into the cab. As the vehicle made a tire-squealing takeoff, a bus coming the other way made a bumpy U-turn over the curb and took off after the cab. A young woman across the street came running to help Irene. Together we got Irene up. The fall had knocked the breath from her.

As we stood there, rubbing her back and holding her hand, a *preventivo,* a regular beat policeman, approached. In the seconds before he reached us, the young woman whispered, "Don't give your real names and addresses to him. Don't let him take you to report this to *policia* headquarters."

Warning delivered, she hurried away in the opposite direction from the closing cop.

The policeman had reached us, asked if we needed assistance, and before I could stop Irene, she told him she'd been robbed. He invited us to accompany him to press formal charges with his superiors.

This time Irene hesitated and looked at me for a decision. I thanked the officer profusely, asked him to make a report for us, tipped him generously for his time, and got us out of there quick. We nearly reached the gates when the bus pulled up and the driver called to us, holding his arm out the window with the purse in his hand, explaining that the cab passenger had flung the bag out the window as the vehicle escaped down an alley too narrow for the bus. He waved off my suggestion of a reward, and drove off, his passengers waving to us.

Irene checked the bag and went white.

"All my cash for Kyle," she said, her voice strained. "Oh, and the guard at the gate…he expects…"

I edged up my shirt, extracted some cash and pressed it into her hand.

We walked to the front gate of the prison where a small group of people, mostly women, chattered and gestured, clutching packages and baskets of food and waiting for the one guard on duty to pass them in through the swinging door.

The tight-bellied guard looked like a desperado in street clothes, cradled an Uzi, and when it came our turn gave Irene's package a cursory examination, accepting the two dollars she offered with a broad smile that showed the metal caps where his teeth had probably been knocked out.

Immediately inside we passed by a courtyard that divided the prison offices from the general prisoners' area. A black car with the front end crushed nearly to the windshield almost blocked the street-side entrance.

The prisoners' yard had the appearance of a village, with small houses or apartments layered against the walls, some with balconies and TV antennas. The space overflowed with

men and a large number of women and children, all with
faces that reflected bewilderment, belligerence, or boredom.
Loudspeakers blared, announcing visitors and calling prisoners. Radios played from every direction.

I followed Irene past a taco stand, a makeshift video ar-
cade with a madonna framed by flashing lights, and a general store with a display of electric fans out front. Tattooed
men crouched in the spare shade of corners looking scruffy
and predatory, and a couple of young men wearing
women's clothes and garish makeup sashayed by, arm in
arm.

A young man with brown hair touching his shoulders and
wearing a red T-shirt and baggy jeans advanced across the
yard, his face a mask of indifference.

"Kyle," Irene said, relief evident in her voice. I'm sure
the only time she didn't worry for his physical safety was
in such moments as he stood in front of her.

Irene introduced me, and Kyle said, "Come on to my
house."

"We call the prison El Pueblo," Kyle told me as we
walked to his ground-floor dwelling. "I'm not on the high-
rent side, you understand. Those guys have servants and
bodyguards hired from the prisoners in the tanks. That's
where they stuff everybody who can't pay. It's bad in the
tanks. You don't want to be there. Here's my place. Come
on in."

Kyle's house sported three rooms, a tiny kitchen, a bath,
a living room with a sofa bed, a small black and white TV,
and a cherubic young man with blond hair and red cheeks
sitting on the sofa reading *Alarma!*, Mexico's blood-
drenched tabloid. He put the newspaper aside and stood up
to be introduced as Josh.

"Josh was in the tanks," Kyle explained. "He's an
American, too, so I offered him a place to stay till he can
get on his own. We gringos gotta stick together."

I saw the worried look on Irene's face as she plainly bit back the question she wanted to ask. To his credit, Kyle saw it, too.

"It's okay, Mom. Josh isn't in for drugs or anything. He's a Mennonite."

"Think Amish," I said, seeing Irene's blank look.

"Except we use trucks and tractors instead of horses and buggies," Josh said. "The conservatives in the group got huffy that we were getting too modern and left for Guatemala. Why don't you sit here, Mrs. Pick, Mrs. Jones."

He moved aside to let Irene and me have the sofa, while he perched on a milk crate that served as a coffee table. Kyle went to the closet-size kitchen and came back with a tray of food. Separate bowls held shredded chicken, beans, rice, tortillas, and a sauce made from red chilies.

"Dig in," he said, handing round plates and sitting down cross-legged on the floor. He and Josh both piled a little of everything onto their tortillas. I took chicken and rice with sauce. Irene hesitated.

Kyle said, "It won't make you sick. We have someone who buys the food and comes in to cook. We make sure it's done right."

Irene smiled weakly and took a bite.

"Are you from one of the *campos* near Cuauhtemoc?" I asked Josh.

He nodded.

"What are *campos*?" Irene asked.

"Settlements," Josh said. "We live in groups of about twenty families in settlements strung out along Highway Twenty-four. We farm and dairy. Some of the men do woodwork and the women do embroidery for the tourist trade."

"The Mennonites are famous for white cheddar cheese," I said. "When I can get it, I stock it at the trading post. It sells out in a day or two."

Josh smiled, looking more and more like a bas-relief angel from a cathedral ceiling. Given the ascetic lifestyle practiced by his sect, I couldn't imagine what Josh had been arrested for. He told us.

"I had a car accident."

"And they locked you up for that?" Irene said.

"I met a friend to celebrate a business deal. We celebrated a little too much. I was arrested for drunk driving and destruction of private property. Seems like I hit some parked cars."

"No insurance?" I said.

"I wasn't driving my car. I'm not used to drinking and I don't really remember what happened. The cop said I stole a car. Unfortunately, the car I was driving belonged to the warden."

"Not the black car in the courtyard?"

"Yeah," Josh said. "Can you believe the warden had it towed back here where he lives? The fat fool goes out every morning and stands there staring at that car. It's just a beat-up old Dodge, but he says it's a collector's item."

"Do you have family to help you, Josh?" Irene asked.

"My family and I are sort of on the outs right now. I'm a little tired of communal living. I want to see a little bit of life. I expect they'll come around after they think I've had enough time to learn my lesson."

We finished the meal and made small talk. Irene told them about a mad dog suspected of killing a wood-carver in a church. Fortunately, she didn't seem to know I'd been there when the body was found so I didn't have to tell the tale again. For a time Josh kept the conversation going with *campo* stories, but the talk soon grew a little thin.

Kyle suggested we walk around in the yard. I stayed back with Josh to give Irene some time alone with her son. I knew she had to tell him that the cash he expected had been stolen.

I questioned Josh about prison life. He admitted that the place scared him, but said that with the right connections and money a man could live in reasonable comfort and safety.

"Lots of the prisoners have their families here with them," he explained. "The wives can come and go to shop and do laundry. The women prisoners will cook and clean if you pay. You can have anything delivered from town if you can afford it."

I looked around at the wary-eyed inmates and listened to Josh describe what he called "the neighborhoods" of the prison. Apparently there were blocks preferred by drug addicts, gamblers, gays, single men, and families. Even poor, middle-class, and rich neighborhoods.

Ahead Irene spoke earnestly to her son, gesturing with her hands for emphasis. Kyle looked upset. I turned to say something to Josh and caught him staring at something with an odd expression between dismay and amusement.

I followed his glance and saw a plump young woman emerge from one wing of the building, smile, wave, and hurry toward Kyle and Irene. Kyle's back tensed, he gave a shake of his head, and the girl changed course to avoid mother and son, pausing to look stealthily back at them, a melancholy expression on her face. Irene never saw her.

Josh, seeing that I had noticed the little drama, felt the need to explain. "She cleans and does laundry for us."

Irene and Kyle talked for a few more minutes, then came over to where we stood. It was time to go. Irene looked teary, but she held herself together and managed a smile.

"I'll say goodbye here, Mom," Kyle said, turning to me and thanking me for coming, as if the visit had been merely a social call. He lightly touched his mother's arm then turned away and walked away toward his house. Irene watched him for a moment, a tear sliding down her cheek, then hurried toward the gate. I managed a glance backward and saw Kyle embracing the young woman, smoothing her hair with his hand.

Irene, I reasoned, might have more to worry about then getting a son out of jail. It looked to me as if there was a grandchild on the way.

NINETEEN

THE PICKUP parked in front of the trading post belonged to the Presidio County Sheriff's office. I didn't recognize the car.

"I hope nothing has happened," Irene said.

"The sheriff is an old friend of mine," I told her, but my stomach constricted in fear. Had something happened to Jorge?

I let Irene out by her car, and as I drove around to the back I noticed the Aply's RV still in place and no sign of activity from the odd couple. Whether that signaled good or bad, I didn't know. I parked next to Clay's pickup. Knowing he was home made me less anxious.

The back door was open and I could hear voices.

Clay sat hunched at our dining table with three other men, the sheriff and two strangers in lackluster suits.

My friend Andalon, the sheriff, sat leaning back in the chair, arms folded across his chest, watching the others, and looking almost apologetic. My husband wore his thin-lipped, stubborn expression. That and the jutting chin told me he was angry.

One of the suits, a thin man with the lined face of a life-long cigarette smoker, leaned across the table, talking and making emphatic gestures right under Clay's nose. The other stranger had the air of a cautious backroom clerk. He noticed my arrival before the others, tapped his hand on the shoulder of the man aiming words at Clay, and jerked his head in my direction.

"Good afternoon," I said, announcing myself. The conversational man snapped his mouth shut and stood.

"This is my wife," Clay said. "These men are from the El Paso office of the Drug Enforcement Agency."

The smoker extended his hand and managed a smile with no pleasure in it.

"I'm Agent Kemp, Mrs. Jones, and this is Agent Hale. We've been trying to convince your husband to help us out."

I must have looked bewildered.

"And my answer is no," Clay asserted. Had they known his tone as well as I did, they'd have quit right there.

Kemp said to me, "Maybe you can change his mind."

"I rarely try," I said. Clay is a better judge of character than I. If he didn't approve of them, it wasn't likely I would. I glanced at him.

"Go ahead," he told Kemp.

The agent said, "It's a simple thing. We've been working with your local people on surveillance of the increase in drug activities in this area since Operation Hard Line has slowed the traffic at the border crossings."

I knew what he referred to. The newspapers had been full of complaints on the letters-to-the-editor page since the U.S. Customs Service had added agents and made more frequent stops and thorough inspections of cars and trucks crossing all along the border. A thorough inspection meant trailers had to be unloaded, X-rayed, and the contents opened if the drug-sniffing dogs so much as whined. Everyone complained about cross-border drug trafficking, but no one wanted to be personally inconvenienced.

Kemp was saying, "We'd like you to answer a few questions about someone we have reason to believe is a major player, one of the five *patrones* controlling the border drug trade from Tijuana to Matamoros."

"Who?" I asked.

"Gordon Mateo Suarez," Hale said.

Kemp said, "We think he's heavily involved in the trans-shipping of Colombian cocaine into the States."

"And producing, processing, and smuggling brown heroin and marijuana," Hale added.

Clay said, "I've told them—"

Kemp held up his hand. "Let your wife decide for herself, if you don't mind."

"Don't tell me what to do in my own house, if you don't mind," Clay said in an ominously quiet tone.

I looked at Andalon and said, "I take it you're the local Mr. Hale referred to?"

He nodded and looked rueful. Andalon is full-faced, stocky, and sports a *bandido* mustache. He dresses western and projects a folksy manner that masks a quick intelligence. Outsiders sometimes underestimate him. He's no rube. I've known him all my life. We went to school together, dated briefly, and remained good friends. I had chaired his campaign the first time he ran for sheriff. Presidio County covers 3,855 square miles, and Andalon patrols it with the help of only three deputies and one constable. I knew he depended on the goodwill of all the agencies working the region—Border Patrol, Customs, and the DEA—for timely help and information. Along the border cooperation is vital.

And I appreciated Clay's feelings. I wanted to smooth things over for all our sakes.

"What exactly, Agent Kemp, are you asking us to do?"

"Provide us with a little information, that's all. Trust me when I tell you we have enough to widen the investigation on this side and bring in the Mexican authorities," he said, affecting an earnest manner.

"But I had the impression from Señor Suarez that he worked with our government," I said. "With the CIA."

"Well, that goes a long way toward proving criminal intent," Kemp said in a tone that sounded only half-joking.

His partner chimed in. "Here's what we see so far. You have access to this man. What we'd like to do is debrief you about your visit to the Suarez ranch. And we'd like you to follow up your acquaintance with the family. Be discreet, but be alert. Notice everything. Give us names. Who comes, who goes. No one is too minor or too important to ignore."

"I'm sure my husband told you why we were at the ranch. That he was consulted as a vet. We aren't exactly on the same social footing with the Suarez family. I doubt we'll hear from them again."

Kemp said, "We frankly hoped—"

"That I'd spy on a man who employed my professional services," Clay said, getting to his feet. "You people tolerate thousands of smaller drug dealers, then build up the agency's reputation by exposing one or two big ones. Do you think I don't know the kind of retaliation to expect from playing games with the Pacific Cartel? Your own boss had a brother gunned down in El Paso—"

"That was a carjacking."

"—as a warning. We're on the line in more ways than one here. The border is not holding against the drug lords. They're taking it over. I'm not going to place my wife in jeopardy or risk my business or my life for something that won't change anything. Arrest one drug lord and another moves in. You want to stop the drug trafficking? Try jailing all the junkies who snort their noses away. You walk in here and ask me to be patriotic, and when that doesn't work you try and pressure us to help. You forget one thing. I'm not a fool. When it's all done, you walk away. We have to live here."

Kemp said, "You can trust us to—"

"You don't stand for anything I trust," Clay said.

Kemp's face went red.

Andalon eased his chair back, saying mildly, "It's not

going to happen, gentlemen. Give it up. Time for us to let these folks get to their supper."

Kemp looked at me as if he might try again to persuade me to help, but evidently saw something in my face that caused him to change his mind about making the effort.

"You think about what I've said," he told us with a hint of menace in his voice. "If you decide to cooperate, the sheriff knows how to reach us."

Lucky you, I mouthed to Andalon as the agents turned their backs and marched toward the front.

Clay and I followed them to the door as much to be sure they were gone as to be polite.

Andalon said he'd be in touch.

"That was distasteful," I said, watching them drive off.

"It sure enough left a bad taste in my mouth all right," Clay said. "Let's lock the doors and open the bottle. I've got dinner ready. Cold sliced brisket and potato salad."

As we walked back to the kitchen, Clay put his arm around my shoulders and said, "I read your note about Phobe. Don't you worry. She'll be back."

I didn't believe it, but it made me feel better to hear Clay say it.

"Do you think they'll catch Ghee?" I asked him as we set the table.

"No. Drug money is what's keeping the Mexican economy going." He sliced the meat and forked it onto a platter, adding, "One thing bothers me, and it has nothing to do with the drug question."

"What?"

"As much as I enjoyed the man's company, Ghee doesn't strike me as a social egalitarian, so why bother to turn on the charm with us?"

"I imagine he operates on automatic. That charm gets things done for him. If he'd been a horse's rear end you wouldn't have gone to Ojinaga to see his cattle off to their new homes.''

"I guess," Clay said, wiping the carving knife and dropping it in its slot. "Let's eat."

As we sat down, I squeezed in two questions. Had Jorge been here when Clay returned and what had he said? Was Gringo okay?

"I put the dog in the bedroom when Andalon showed up, and Jorge said to tell you it was a washout. He didn't see anyone and nothing happened. So what's that all about?"

Before I could answer, he jumped up, saying, "Hold your story until I let the dog out. He's pining for company."

Gringo followed Clay back into the kitchen and sat at our feet while we ate.

I told Clay about the jimmied door, the cut screen, the missing statue, Mata and the Aplys, Hector and the mysterious Maya. That took us through the end of the meal and beyond.

Afterward we washed up, fed Gringo, then took our after-dinner whiskeys to the front porch where we sat and watched the sun dip below the mountains of Mexico.

In the first still minutes of the dark, before the sounds of the desert night began, I asked Clay what he thought was behind the two break-ins.

"Two things strike me," he said. "If Mata had his bedroll by the front doors, how'd he happen to hear this Professor Aply messing around your pickup when it was parked in back?"

"Maybe he was already outside."

"Maybe he was. But why?"

"He's a smoker. Maybe he was being thoughtful and not lighting up inside."

"He didn't strike me as the thoughtful type."

"And the second thing?"

"Hector. He wanted to avoid drawing the attention of the Mexican authorities to the Saint Maker's death, and he was happy to blame it on the dog. So why'd he make a special trip over here to tell you they'd found the murder weapon? The whole village would keep quiet about that to protect themselves. So why did Hector come here to announce to you it was murder?"

I couldn't begin to think of an answer.

TWENTY

IT WAS ONE of those frustrating mornings when everything goes wrong. The coffee maker burned out, I broke a glass and cut my hand, and the first customer of the day tripped over a bootjack in the shoe section and sprained his wrist.

At nine Andalon called and in his understated way cautioned me.

"These federal types," he said, meaning Kemp and Hale, "can get a little paranoid. When you don't jump at a chance to help them, they tend to think you have something to hide."

"Help or hinder, is that it?"

"More or less. They're doing serious business. Necessary business. A few more years and Mexico, instead of just moving drugs for Colombia, will be the primary traffickers for heroin, cocaine, and methamphetamines into this country. Right now, most of it's coming through Juarez to El Paso and from there to all points north. Around here, the Mexicans are walking it over on their backs a few pounds at a time."

"Are you saying you think we should have gone along with them on this?"

"I'm saying don't get in the way. For the next few weeks don't do anything that might look suspicious to these guys."

"Like visit the other side."

"You went to Chihuahua yesterday."

"They had me followed?"

He chuckled, "Clay mentioned it before he knew who the others were. They found it very interesting."

"I find that very intimidating," I said. "Do they know I went to the prison?"

"Well, I didn't. I don't know what they'd make of that," he said, sounding puzzled himself.

"A mission of mercy," I said, to explain in case the agents really did take an interest. Andalon doesn't gossip, but if it would help me, he'd pass the information along.

"I drove the new schoolteacher to visit her eighteen-year-old son. He got picked up on a drug charge."

"That's bad. Now if he'd killed somebody, he'd be out sooner. I hope his mother is a realist."

"Her experience of Mexico is *Ballet Folklorico,* but she's learning fast. I think she's over the stage where she thinks things on the other side should work like back home. Anyway, she feels better because he's got a Mennonite for a roommate."

"A Mennonite? They're rarely lawbreakers," Andalon said. "What's his name?"

I detected the slight inflection in his voice that signaled real interest behind the simple question.

"Josh Van Gurton."

For a moment, silence. Then, "Joshua Van Gurton, age twenty-five, blond, blue-eyed, medium build and height."

"He has a record?"

"He's wanted over here on drug charges. He got caught for marijuana possession. First offense. Agreed to return for trial. You know the Mennonites have an agreement with Mexico that allows them to come and go as they like. Van Gurton was released on bail when the Mennonite elders agreed to be responsible for seeing that he returned for trial."

"He didn't show."

"The elders did. Told the judge they washed their hands of him. Seems he stole a pickup and some money when he left the *campo.* Stupid of him. A first offense for a small amount, he'd have been probated out. What's he done in Chihuahua?''

"He said he got drunk, stole a car and crashed it. I saw it. I swear to you it's a duplicate, minus the bulletholes, of Pancho Villa's car. I think the warden had delusions of—"

Andalon laughed so loud I had to hold the phone away from my ear. "I guess," he gasped between laughs, "I can close his file. Stealing a warden's car, a man who emulates the great *bandido*. By the time Van Gurton gets out he'll be too decrepit to make trouble over here."

Fine for him to laugh, I thought, but what did I tell Irene about her son's roomie? Nothing. What good would it do?

Andalon rang off with a final caution. "I'm not kidding about watching out for anything the federal guys might mistake for wrongdoing. If a vendor hawking fake Rolexes or some wet-haired sharpie wearing Armani comes into your place, chase him out. Those agents will jump on anything, however small, that smacks of smuggling. The border is leaking drugs like an earth dam in a forty-year flood."

I said goodbye, thought of Mata, and hoped the DEA agents didn't know about me flying back in Ghee's plane.

At ten o'clock I heard an enthusiastic but tuneless humming.

The voice trickled out and Clay came in saying, "That dog never killed those goats, or at least not the one that Carl character stuffed in the freezer."

"What did?"

"Mountain lion, though from the looks of it I wouldn't be surprised if the animal wasn't dying on its feet already. You said he claimed all five goats were killed at the same time. That may be why. They were too sick to run far or fast. I'm going to go to the post office before lunch and put up a notice warning everybody to keep their kids and dogs in."

"Speaking of dogs," I said, "Now that we know Gringo

is innocent of manslaughter and goatslaughter, I think I'll take him home. He's used to lots of doggy company. He's lonesome here."

"Good idea." Clay poured himself some iced tea, and asked, "Are you leaving now?"

"After lunch. If I go now, Zeferina will ask me to share their meal. With all the grandchildren living with them, they don't need another mouth to feed.

For the rest of the morning nothing much happened. No sinister strangers showed up, and my fear that the DEA might be playing a game within a game receded.

The Aplys came in at eleven, bought Cokes, and sat at the table near the coffee maker to read the *Big Bend Sentinel* and the Presidio *International*.

For the first time, Boyce rather than Pat made conversation, asking me if I ever considered selling any of the artifacts I displayed.

"I know of someone who'd be very interested in the whole collection," he said.

After I told him that I turned down someone wanting to buy them once or twice a year, he persisted, saying he knew a man who'd pay cash. I supposed he thought because barter made up much of my business at the store, especially with *fronterizos* from the other side, that I was dodging taxes and would leap at a cash offer.

He looked so drawn and ill I felt guilty about the incident with Mata, and considered whether I should salve my conscience by foregoing the ten dollars a day charge for the RV hookup as Pat had suggested. I decided to let that ride until later and settled for making polite conversation with the pair.

"Did you enjoy your trip to Presidio?"

Pat gave me a fish-eyed look. "It was okay. Did you and your friend go someplace special in Ojinaga?"

"We went to Chihuahua. My friend has a relative staying

there,'' I answered, shading the truth enough to protect Irene's privacy, knowing that half of El Polvo probably knew already that the new teacher had a son in jail, and the other half knew the charges. Any stranger among us is an immediate source of intense interest and scrutiny, and gossip takes the place of radio and TV in the borderland as a source of entertainment. Word passes back and forth across the river every time a *fronterizo* crosses over.

"Are you going to be here all day? Seems like any time we need something, you're closed," she said.

In my irritation at her implied criticism, I forgot about my plan to take Gringo home and stated emphatically that I would be open all day.

As the Aplys walked out, a pickup with more rust than paint on the finish and four mangy dogs barking in the back rolled to a stop, nudging the porch with its dented bumper. A stringy man wearing a red gimme-cap, faded black pants, and a grimy undershirt opened the door, almost falling out of the driver's seat, and honked the horn.

I rushed out, smelled the beer on his breath from ten paces, and asked what he wanted.

"Dogs," he said, stepping out onto the ground as if unsure of the solidity of the ground.

He smiled proudly and gestured toward three poor mutts whining and panting in the pickup, their heads drooping, their tongues lolling with thirst.

"Let's get them in the shade and to a water bowl," I told him.

The animals were tied together with a dirty rope, and the man led them around back to the kennels where I filled the trough with water.

"These are your dogs?" I asked him, as the animals lapped. I held my finger over the nozzle and sprayed a fine mist over the dehydrated pups.

Slowly, with much mumbling and repeating, the man explained that they were strays he had rounded up after hearing that the señora at the trading post was paying cash for white dogs.

"I can get as many as you want," he told me solemnly. "No *problema*."

I told him to wait, went inside and got three packages of tortillas and a half-pound bag of jerky, a five-pound bag of beans, and a six-pack of soft drinks.

I explained that he was mistaken, there was no reward for white dogs, and he could have the groceries if he promised not to bring me any more dogs. He didn't understand, and asked me three times if I was certain of my information. Finally, philosophically, he announced a poor man must take what he's offered, accepted the groceries, and aimed himself in an irregular line toward the front and his pickup.

"Wait," I cried. "You forgot the dogs."

He removed his cap and made a sweeping bow. "They are yours, señora. I make you a gift. Don't thank me. It's nothing."

Hopeless to argue. I untied the rope around the dogs' necks and put down plenty of food while trying not to look at the animals too closely. Unless someone claimed them, and that was unlikely given the excess of dogs around here, Clay would have to euthanize them.

I had put the CLOSED FOR LUNCH sign on the door when Clay came in carrying a foil-wrapped package. Lucy had sent homemade tamales. Our postmistress had been born in El Polvo, but her parents were *norteños* from Chihuahua. Northeners scorn the fat white tamales of central Mexico, the kind made commercially in this country, as all dough. Once you've eaten the small tamales of northern Mexico, you'll never enjoy the others again. I followed the aroma to the kitchen.

Clay scooped spoonfuls of instant tea into a pitcher, and

I unwrapped the package of tamales and inhaled the fragrance of pork flavored with *chilies anchos* and cumin.

After lunch Clay checked over the new arrivals in the kennel, then left to play catch-up with his local calls, including a stop at Carl Sebastien's place to be sure the man understood that his goats were dying of neglect when the mountain lion came along. I smiled when I thought of the thorough chewing-out Carl would get. Clay has no respect for people who mistreat their animals.

I loaded up Gringo and went to see Pete.

When I reached the footbridge, Gringo gave three staccato barks and leaped onto the swaying boards, his right leg folding as he nearly skidded off midway, but he righted himself and ran on. As soon as his paws touched the ground on the other side, he broke into a flat-out run, barking as he went, and vanished from my sight.

I caught up in time to see the children, including a pale Alejandro, swarming around the dog.

Pete emerged from one of the goat sheds, shouted "Gringo!" and opened his arms. The dog bounded toward his master, made a flying leap into Pete's arms, and licked his face all over.

When man and dog had calmed down enough to separate, I told Pete that Hector and the others at the village knew the dog hadn't killed the Saint Maker.

"Superstitious *imbeciles*," Pete spat. "Some of them you'll never convince my Gringo isn't a *nagual*."

Gringo whined at Pete's angry tone, and his master knelt and patted his head. "I'll watch out for you, my baby. Anybody comes round here to kill you, I'll string up their hides like a goat skin."

I have never known Pete to speak harshly to a child or an animal, but he issues loose threats with the bravado of a tavern drunk. I have always wondered whether Pete made such boasts in company where he might be taken seriously.

He rose and called to Gringo to follow him, and I walked with the pair to the dog compound where Gringo's friends bounced and barked a welcome. Pete put him inside, shut the gate, and stood there watching his dogs and smiling.

"How is Alejandro?" I asked. "No ill effects from the snakebite, I hope."

"He still has some swelling and pain, but he's showing off his scar to the little ones and the snake gets bigger every time he tells the story."

"It was plenty big enough."

Pete agreed, then changed the subject abruptly enough for me to know something was up.

"Say, what's going on with these people living in the big trailer at your place?"

"You tell me. What do you know?"

"They friends of yours?"

"No."

"Word is, they're nosing around this side."

"Why?"

Pete shrugged. "That's what everybody wonders. Maybe looking for drugs. A hand shipment that's past due. That's what people figure."

"Thanks for the warning, Pete."

"I overheard them talking about you. Seems like they thought I couldn't speak English after they said good morning to me and I didn't answer until they said *buenos días*."

"What did they say?"

"The man said, 'Of course the Jones woman has probably already sold them,' The woman said, 'How could she? We've been here the whole time.'"

I thought about the words. "I have no idea what they were talking about."

"They didn't sound friendly. They give you any trouble, you send word. Me and my boys, we can handle them good."

I visited briefly with the rest of the family, and left, more troubled than before that the DEA agents might have real reason to be suspicious of Clay and me. My bright idea to add the RV park didn't seem to be working out. The Aplys could be innocent, taking pictures, ignorant of the risks they ran, both from encountering drug smugglers and being taken for them. Or they could be guilty. But of what?

The rest of the day passed quickly and without a hint of trouble, though I felt now that it was lurking, waiting to happen. Clay came in late, tired, and sleepy. I kept Pete's warning to myself. Time enough to share the worry tomorrow.

Around midnight, on the edge of sleep, I listened to Clay's steady breathing.

The barking sounded loud enough to be in the room, but it came from outside.

"What the hell?" Clay mumbled, stumbling out of bed and reaching for his pants. I grabbed my robe and the flashlight, slipped my feet in my shoes.

Clay yanked open the drawer of the bedside table and got the pistol. I followed him to the back door and flipped on the floodlight.

Clay was already out, headed for the kennels, the source of the furious barking. The mutts were jumping at the bars on the closest side to the trailer and making a full-fledged doggy commotion.

Clay swept the surrounding dark with the flashlight, watching for whatever varmint had triggered the dogs.

The Aplys' RV door squeaked and they appeared, huddled together, and stood watching us.

"Did you bring your gun?" Clay asked me. I shook my head.

"Then wait here. In case it's the mountain lion."

He moved to the end of the trailer and around to the far side. In a few minutes I saw the beam of the flashlight hit the slope behind the trailer. The desert scrub cast giant shifting shadows as the light moved up the hill, sweeping in a wide arch. In a few moments, it came back, the beam aimed straight ahead and bouncing as Clay walked over the rocky scree.

Pat and Boyce had moved up beside me by the time Clay reached me, and the dogs had calmed down.

"What happened?" Boyce asked.

Clay said, "Some varmint disturbed the dogs in the kennel, that's all. Probably a coyote. I think I saw some tracks leading up the hill. Sorry you were disturbed."

The Aplys turned away and disappeared around the corner. Clay stood there watching until he heard the door of the RV close.

"What's going on?" I asked.

"Let's get inside. You know how voices carry out here."

In the kitchen he snapped off the outside light and we stood there in the dark.

"What?" I hissed. "Did you see mountain lion tracks and not want to scare the Aplys, because if you did—"

"I saw tracks, all right. Footprints of someone in sneakers. A set right under the window of the trailer."

"Did the tracks go up the slope?"

"No. I went that way to double-check that there weren't two sets of prints. The sneaker marks came from around front."

"We should have checked out front, then. We'd better look now," I said, half turning. Clay stopped me with a hand on my arm.

"The tracks pick up with the person walking from the front corner of the trailer where the gravel ends and stopping under the window. When the dogs started up, the person twisted around and ran back in the same direction."

"And?"

"And Boyce and his wife were fully dressed. And he had on sneakers."

TWENTY-ONE

CLAY DID NOT take to my idea that we stay up and search the trading post together for whatever someone seemed to be looking for.

Not even after I told him about the remark by the Aplys that Pete had overheard.

"It makes no sense," I said, as we got back into bed. "We have nothing of enough value here to warrant this kind of attention."

"Someone thinks we do," Clay answered.

"I could tell the Aplys to leave."

He turned out the light, and I heard him say through a yawn, "We don't know that Boyce wasn't just being nosy peeking in the window of the trailer."

"Oh, right. The way he was just peeking in the pickup's toolbox. One time, I'll swallow the insomniac defense, but not twice. Next thing, he'll be claiming he was chipping golf balls in the dark." I could have saved the sarcasm. Clay had turned over and gone to sleep.

He rose early, cooked our breakfast, gulped his food and coffee, and left for a conference at Sul Ross University in Alpine. Planned months ago, the meeting would bring together experts in range management, animal science, and wildlife habitat with local ranchers, area vets, and county commissioners from the entire Trans-Pecos region. As official veterinarian for Presidio County, Clay would be one of the pack, as he had put it, to discuss the severe effects of the drought that forecasters predicted would be prolonged.

He'd prepared a report on the wildlife die-off because of

starvation. There had been other casualties as the 18.7 million acres of the region wilted and withered, and the always precarious ecological balance between humans and wildlife shifted under the stress of nature's extremes. Sitting on my stool behind the counter I read in the *Avalanche* that a two-year-old male black bear had been sighted foraging for food in the garbage cans at Kokernot Park in Alpine. The police, the Brewster County Sheriff's office, and the state Parks and Wildlife personnel searching for the animal had found it dead. Shot.

And the human toll had been terrible. In three months' time, five illegals had been found dead of dehydration and exposure, empty water bottles by their sides. Our sixty-mile stretch of border is the most isolated part of the Rio Grande. Illegals can cross and hide from the Border Patrol spotter planes easily. After that, it stops being easy. The long, mountainous route they must travel is over some of the roughest, emptiest terrain in the country. Their journeys are born of desperation, and too many end in tragedy.

"You look like you could use some cheering up," a voice said.

I dropped the paper and looked up to see Irene Pick. Smiling, she put a gift-wrapped package down on the counter and nudged it toward me.

"My bow-tying isn't the best," she said. "Go on, unwrap it. It's for you."

I took off the pale blue paper and lifted the lid of the deep, narrow box. Nestled in tissue paper was a statue of the Virgin of Guadalupe. About ten inches tall, carved in dark wood, it was a replica of the one in the chapel at Ruined Walls.

I lifted it out and set it on the counter to admire the fine craftsmanship.

"The Saint Maker carved this," I said.

"Yes. I heard at the post office that someone had taken

your statue of the jaguar. I thought you might like this almost as well.''

''How generous of you. But you should keep it yourself, Irene. I think his works are valuable.''

She shook her head. ''I want you to have it. I can't ever repay you for going with me to the prison. I'd have gotten into terrible trouble over my purse being snatched if I'd been alone. I want you to have this.'' She touched a finger to the smooth wood, adding, ''To be honest, this has bad memories for me anyway.'' A pause. ''I'll show you.''

She picked up the statue, turned it over. ''See, there's a tight plug of wood here. You can see the chip where I forced it open with a knife. Before that you could hardly see it because of the grain of the wood.''

On the border, there's only one reason anything—big or small—has a hollow compartment.

''The Saint Maker was a smuggler,'' I said.

Irene nodded.

''Yes. He knew about my son. I guess everybody around here does. Anyway, he seemed to know I needed money. I married young and I stayed home and raised my kids. I was doing the perfect-wife-and-mother comedy routine. I had no work experience, so when my husband cleaned out the bank account and ran off with his dental hygienist I had to go back to school. I spent the little money I had on college tuition to get certification. When Kyle needed quick cash, I was pretty desperate. The Saint Maker said to hand the statue over to a man waiting along the highway to Marfa, and he would hand me five hundred dollars. I was to keep half.''

''And did you?''

''No. The Saint Maker brought this statue to me a few days before he died. I'd had time to think about how stupid I'd been to agree and what a risk I would be running. And I was so scared it might be drugs I was passing, I pried it open. Feathers, that's all that was in it. Can you imagine? I took them out and spread them on the table. There were ten of them, from an eagle or a hawk, I think. Before I could decide what to do, a gust of wind blew them out the window. By the time I'd gone around by the door, they'd blow off into the scrub and I could only find one. I don't know what I'd have told the Saint Maker. I was supposed to meet the old man and give him his share of the money the day he died."

The bell jangled and a customer came in to pay for gas.

"You keep the statue, Texana," Irene said, "I don't want to be reminded of what I nearly did." She left while I waited on the customer.

Afterward I sat holding the Virgin, admiring the fine workmanship the Saint Maker had put into something to be used to fool Customs agents. Maybe the wood-carver had reasoned that the finer the workmanship, the less likely to draw suspicion. Was the old man's smuggling the reason someone had taken my jaguar statue? It seemed likely. Before he approached Irene, had he been using someone else as a go-between? Had that someone thought my statue had been hollow, too?

It didn't shock me that the Saint Maker had been a smuggler, an honorable profession along the river, and one practiced for centuries. Horses and cattle journeyed both ways long before the free trade agreements. A Texan from Alpine pioneered the smuggling of *candelilla* wax before World War II. And radios, televisions, washing machines, and hundreds of other American-made appliances had been transported illegally into Mexico for generations. The men and women who traded Indian artifacts to me for food and clothes were de facto smugglers. Drugs and human traffic moved across the border pervasively. If someone somewhere wanted something unobtainable, a smuggler would emerge to supply the desired object. The Saint Maker had been doing what comes naturally. Fulfilling the law of supply and demand.

And what of Irene? What would she have told the old man if she had met him that day. She had lost the commodity—the feathers. She didn't have the money to make good on his share of the cash. She had needed more money than she had to keep Kyle out of the tanks. I stopped my speculation right there. I liked Irene too much to envision her swinging the stone doorstop at the Saint Maker's face.

I needed information. I called Andalon.

One nice thing about my friend the sheriff—he doesn't expect me to waste his time on small talk.

"What can you tell me about the smuggling of endangered species out of Mexico?" I asked him.

"Thinking of branching out?"

"Don't be facetious."

"It's a busy border. Wildlife smuggling is at an all-time high. Everything is coming across. Mounted animals, skins, bones, feathers, live animals, plants, snakes."

"How's all this transported—and don't say 'any way they can,'" I told him.

"Just like narcotics. For instance, there's a big market in yellow-crowned parrots. The Indians in Chiapas and Central America trap them and sell them to a middleman who brings them north by bus. They're passed on to smugglers who raft them across the Rio Grande or pack them into hidden compartments and drive them into the States at the border crossings."

"How come you know so much about the trade in parrots?"

"Remember Luis Trooper?"

"The kid from our class who became such a high-powered defense attorney?"

"Son-of-a-gun put himself through law school smuggling parakeets and parrots. You can buy the birds for fifteen or twenty bucks from street vendors in Mexico. Grandmas in Winnebagos get caught by Customs every day of the year with a pretty parrot in a cage.''

"How serious is the penalty?"

"For one bird, not very. A fine and probation. On the high end, fines can reach one hundred thousand dollars and a year's jail time. That's for big-ticket items, like eagle feathers that can retail for eight or nine hundred dollars each, or exotic skins. One lizard skin can bring a thousand bucks. All for some *tonto* to have made into boots.''

"Thanks for the information," I told him.

"Care to tell me why you're asking?"

"I'm not sure myself, yet," I said.

"Tread softly, Texana. Couple of months ago, I was playing backup for some guys from Fish and Wildlife and an agent from Customs on a stakeout to catch the pick up man for a drop by plane of exotic animals skins worth about eighty thousand dollars. The drop never happened. When the agents gave up waiting and closed in to check the drop site they found the body of the informant who had tipped Customs. He'd been beaten to death."

I thought about what Andalon had told me for a long time. Including just how much Irene could have realized from those feathers. A lot more than the two hundred fifty dollars the Saint Maker had promised her.

After I served my last customer—Kate, buying her candle—I closed the doors and ate a peanut butter sandwich, wishing we weren't so far from a source for fresh milk. Even chilled, the powdered stuff just doesn't taste the same.

By then I had made up my mind what I was going to do next. I showered and put on fresh clothes, wrote a note for Clay in case he got back earlier than expected, and went to the pickup, where I sat for a minute with my hands on the steering wheel. When I finally started the motor and drove away, I deliberately went around the opposite side of the trading post from the RV hookups, hoping the Aplys wouldn't notice me leaving.

TWENTY-TWO

ALL OUR INDIVIDUAL and collective prayers have failed,'' Hector said. "The rains have not come, so the corn and beans have not grown. Now the water well has dried up and our goats are starving. So we hold a rain ceremony. This is the third and last day. We would be honored if you would join us.''

The sun-scarred adobes of Providencia are built in the old and classic U-shape of a Mexican village with a plaza of rough, uneven ground in the middle. Everyone had gathered at the open end. The women clutched candles, the children held hands with each other or clung to their mothers' skirts. The men led the twenty-five-minute procession up the steep, rocky trail to the altar.

The site overlooked the whole length of the canyon. I stood at the edge of the group of women and children and watched as four men took their places at each corner of the rickety, low table on which rested bowls of bread, a cup of water, and a tin can serving as a brazier. Behind this makeshift altar, a tall cross of sotol stalks tied together had been erected.

A bent old man approached carrying a white pouch. Crouching before the altar, he sprinkled a minute amount of powdery substance into the tin can, and in a few moments the light smoke of *pom,* dried tree sap, scented the air with its sweet smell. I thought of the description recorded in Bernal Diaz's diary of the Indian shaman passing a brazier of *pom* incense over Cortez's clothing, and I marveled at the capacity of the people to pray to the god of the

Conquest without destroying their pre-Conquest vision of how the cosmos works.

With his voice pitched in a high octave, the old man began a prayer. "Here we come to light candles for you, to bring you food, to burn incense for you. We have planted our seed in the ground and it does not grow because there is no rain. Father, do not abandon us. Bring rain in plenty. Not too much, not too little, but enough so the earth will be content."

For nearly twenty minutes he chanted softly, circling the cross, while the men at the four corners of the altar clapped small wooden blades together.

"It is to make the sound of the lightning," whispered the woman next to me. Around us all the men imitated the *ruum, ruum* sound of thunder.

The old man added more incense to the small burner. The white smoke rose and hung above our heads. Dipping his fingertips into the bowl of water, he sprinkled the table, raised his face to heaven and cried out, "Restore the earth and nourish it. In the name of God the Father, God the Son, and God the Holy Ghost. Amen."

My eyes strayed, and I saw the darkly etched shadow of a hawk climbing the mountain wall enveloped by a larger darker shadow. I looked up. A cloud passed above the mountaintop, and everyone heard the distant rumble of thunder.

"San Juan weeps," whispered the woman. "God has heard our prayers."

In the dusk the people made the procession back down the trail. At its base, I stopped, turned, and looked back at the gold-lined cloud. From out of the heart of the great stone mountain, a dark shape gathered and grew into a dense black cloud that rose to meet the gold and broke into a lacy network of wings that soared upward, thinning as it spread against the blue remnants of sky.

"The old ways say the spirits who bring rain dwell in the same cave with the bats," Hector said.

He had come to stand beside me. The villagers flowed around us, going back to the plaza and paying no attention to the regular feeding flight of the bats.

"May the rain bless your land soon," I told the mayor.

I respected Hector. A natural leader and organizer, he had long been at odds with the other villagers over the advantages and disadvantages of different crops. Hector's opponents stubbornly held to the custom of growing *maiz* and *frijol,* corn and beans, because the staples required no fertilizer and if the crops couldn't be sold, they could be stored and eaten.

Hector, a man of vision, argued that while the crops might keep the people from starving, they also prevented them from going to the bank with any profits. And the goats, Hector preached, were a recipe for poverty, slowly eating the land into barrenness.

Hector wanted the villagers to work together to grow the *flor de zempoaxochitl*—the marigold. Long cultivated for Day of the Dead ceremonies, the flowers are used as a chicken feed additive to make yolks golden. But the mayor had based all his hopes for a marketable crop on the fine well the village possessed. That hope had vanished with the drought.

"We have fasted for the three days of the rain ceremony," he said. "Now we feast. Please join us. We have killed three goats and many chickens."

I followed him inside the dilapidated building that served as a community center. Bowls of beans, finely chopped chilies and the young pads of prickly pear cactus, rice, fresh tortillas, hot sweet bread, shredded chicken and goat meat almost hid the long wooden table. I ate as much as if I, too, had fasted for three days.

Afterward, the younger women carried the children off

to bed while the older ones removed dishes and bowls, swept the floor, and wiped the table. The men went outside to smoke and gossip, all but Hector, who pulled up a chair opposite me, saying how glad he was that I had been present to share in the prayers and food.

I acknowledged his good wishes and addressed his unspoken question: Why was I there? I had thought hard about the best way to approach Hector and had decided on an appeal for his advice and help. I made it now.

"I'm in trouble, Hector, and I don't know why."

An elegant dip of his head, a kindly expression in his eyes indicated that he was at my disposal.

"Twice since the Saint Maker died someone has broken into the trading post. The first time, I couldn't find anything missing. The next time, whoever got in took the statue I bought from the Saint Maker..."

Hector eyes darted around the room, though no one was near us to overhear. I waited until his eyes came back to my face, and then finished my sentence.

"...but that can't have been why the first break-in happened because the statue was in plain sight then. Also, someone went through the toolbox in my pickup and tried to get in my husband's office. Hector, whatever the Saint Maker was doing, I wasn't a part of it. But someone seems to think I was.

His eyes had gone expressionless. Either he didn't believe me or he felt so determined about keeping the village clear of any hint of trouble that he wasn't going to help.

I tried again.

"Hector, did you come to the trading post that day to warn me, because you thought I was helping him?"

"The one who kills once does not mind doing it again."

"I can't avoid danger if I don't know what it is or where it's coming from. Can you tell me anything that might help me understand what's going on?"

He thought it over.

"You have always been good to the people of Providencia," he said. "I believe what you say. I will tell you what I know."

He glanced around.

The four women had finished their chores, and were putting out the lamps, except for one just inside the door, and preparing to leave. Hector waited until they had gone before speaking.

"The *santero* sold clandestine goods."

Subtle Hector. He would not call the Saint Maker a smuggler since to him such movements of goods from seller to buyer was a matter of commerce, and no business of governments.

He continued, "Small things. Bird feathers. Insects. Once someone asked him to transport butterflies. He would not. The Maya believe butterflies are the souls of the dead, you see. But other things, yes. He acted as a go-between for the source and the buyer. He could move anywhere along the river with his wood-carving as a reason. And the carvings sold well, too. Not only to churches and the devout, but vendors bought his works to sell to the tourists. The *santero* journeyed so far from home to help the people. For the Indian, loyalty to the community is unquestioned. The money he got went to buy guns to send South to the Zapatistas."

Even our Texas newspapers, which write far more about Europe and Asia than of our nearest neighbor, Mexico, had headlined the Maya takeover of San Cristobal de las Casas in Chiapas, Mexico's southernmost state. The romantic figure of the young Ladino who commanded the fighters had intrigued the world's media. They had named themselves the Zapatista Army of National Liberation and demanded Indian autonomy. Maya rebels, the shaken government had dubbed them, responding with force and firepower. The newspapers had reported that one hundred forty-five people had died. Inspired by the Maya, other Indian groups had joined in. A year later the influence of the spirit of rebellion had sent ranchers and farmers in northern Mexico marching on the government in Mexico to protest high interest rates, and more recently to make open complaints about the failure of the NAFTA agreement to help the Mexican economy bounce back. As for Chiapas, the so-called peace negotiations continue to this day, as well as the military presence. I know only one salient fact about Chiapas other than that the state lies next door to Guatemala: Its poverty is crushing.

"Guns are expensive," I said.

"Any guns would be more than the handful the Zapatistas started with. They buy what they can, as they can, one gun at a time, if necessary."

"I thought the Zapatistas had pretty much abandoned the fighting and become a peaceful political movement."

"There are always those who hold to the hard line. Maybe the *santero* worked for a guerrilla group. I don't know who they are or what their program is."

It sounded to me as if Hector knew more than he cared to admit, but I wouldn't gain any more information by saying so. My next question stretched my luck—I was probably pushing too far for answers—but I figured I could learn something of the truth, if only from Hector's reaction.

"Could the Saint Maker have been bringing in drugs?"

He answered without hesitation. "If I had thought that, I wouldn't have allowed him to stay in Providencia. I don't know what he transported that is so valuable there are those who still search for it; if that is why they search your business, and I think it must be so, for myself, I owe you an apology. I did think you might be helping the *santero* because it would be so easy for you. Everyone knows you will take some things in trade. Pots, arrowheads, figurines.

These old things are not important to us, you understand, and our people like it that you are not fussy about accepting them. If you chose to pass them on..."

"I don't resell them," I said.

He shrugged, indicating the matter was of no importance.

"You still haven't found the Saint Maker's bag with his tools?" I asked.

He shook his head. "You are thinking that whatever is being searched for is in the bag?"

"Yes."

"That's possible, but I don't know where else to look."

"Thank you, Hector, for talking with me." I rose stiffly, and Hector got up with me. He lifted the oil lamp off its hook and, lighting the way, escorted me to pickup.

I opened the door and when the dome light came on, Hector extinguished the lamp, no doubt to save the oil. Normally the village would rise and go to sleep with the sun. Lamp oil would be saved for special occasions or serious necessity. I paused and told him I had met his friend Antun Tanhol.

Hector had never heard of him.

"Stupid of me," I told him. "He came into the trading post behind you and I assumed he was with you."

I slammed the door. The dome light went out. In the silent dark I heard Hector's footsteps moving away. I turned the key in the ignition.

All the way home, my eyes focused on the faint track on the desert floor, I asked myself what Antun Tanhol was doing here.

TWENTY-THREE

I HAD NEGLECTED to leave the porch light on at the trading post, so I didn't see Antun Tanhol sitting on the front steps until the headlights illuminated his stolid figure. It took me a few seconds more to register that Phobe nestled in his lap.

I braked and jumped out of the pickup, motor running and lights on, without the slightest thought that I might be doing a very foolish thing.

The bobcat climbed into my arms.

"Where have you been? I've been so worried about you," I said, cradling her in one arm and scratching her behind her ears with my other hand. She allowed me to hug her, chewing on my fingers while resting one big paw against the side of my face. Only when Phobe squirmed to be put down, did I remember her companion.

Sitting so still he seemed half flesh, half stone, Antun Tanhol watched me with an enigmatic smile. Looking into his eyes, I had to fight the instinct to trust him. I had to remind myself that I knew nothing about him.

Phobe rubbed against him, making her throaty meowlike sound and rolling over so he could rub her stomach.

"She likes you," I said.

He stroked her. "She is a good companion. I call her Shunka."

"I call her Phobe," I told him. We both smiled, each recognizing the other as an animal lover.

"I see how well cared for she is," he said. "One who takes good care of one animal has respect for all life. I think this little cat is your soul companion."

I thought of those moments of face-to-face confrontation in which I glimpsed the pulsating intelligence behind Phobe's large, golden eyes. And the feel of the warm, muscled form of the wild animal beneath the tame as she sat pressing trustingly against me, a flow of life distinct, unique, and equal to my own. Soul companion, I decided, was a perfect term for the bonding between animal and those humans lucky enough to share such wonders.

A squeaking noise, metal on metal. Immediately and sharply aware, Antun Tanhol's eyes shifted toward the sound. For snoops, the Aplys were careless in not oiling that door. I went to the pickup, cut the motor and lights, and locked it. As I pocketed the keys, I touched the pistol at my waist, a gesture of comfort and caution, reminding me that I could protect myself and also that I should proceed carefully. Moving up the steps past the Maya, I whispered, "Come inside."

Phobe didn't have to be invited. She ran past my feet, and in the dark I could hear her going toward the kitchen. Rather than take the Maya into our private quarters, I put on a small light near the coffee machine and turned around. He waited just inside the doors.

"Come in and sit down," I told him. "Would you like something to eat?"

"Some water only."

"Are you sure you don't want some food?" I knew he must have been living off the land. I appreciated the ability of the Mexican to live and work and never seem to tire on less calories a day than most Americans consume at one meal, but this man had to be hungry.

"I am used to eating nothing," he said.

I took that to mean he was running on empty. In the kitchen, I fed Phobe then returned with a pitcher of water and a glass for Antun and went to find something for him to eat. We live out of the freezer and I didn't have much in the refrigerator. I had to settle for microwaving the last of some stew, and serving it with tortillas, some cheese slices, and an apple.

He accepted it gravely, taking one small bite and chewing slowly and thoroughly before going on to the next. When he had finished, I cleared the plates away and sat down opposite him at the table. He looked at me as if prepared to wait forever without once feeling the need for patience.

"Smoke if you like," I told him.

From around his neck, he took a small pouch on a leather string, opened it, removed some cigarette papers and some black, rough-cut tobacco, and rolled a smoke. The smell was pungent.

"I am an *Indio*," he told me. "I work as a guide for tourists at an archaeological preserve. I show the ruins of the temples of the Maya. My home is a hut at the edge of the preserve's land. When I am a boy, all the land is jungle. The people gather medicine plants from the jungle floor. From my mother, I know one that cures headaches." He laughed. "Never do I suffer a headache. And I remember the butterflies. So many colors. So many kinds. One of the scientists who comes there tells the names of over a hundred different ones. Inside the preserve is the last of the jungle. All around the trees are gone. Cut down. The loggers move into the preserve. I walk in the jungle because I love it. They give no thought to the jungle except to take the lumber. I plant trees to replace the ones they cut. Someday, they cut down my trees, also."

He smiled cheerfully, as if in appreciation of the incongruity of his efforts versus his apocalyptic attitude. He added, "But a man must try, must he not?"

I agreed that he must.

"What I tell you now, I say in trust. You understand my meaning?"

"It stays between us."

He nodded solemnly. "I am fifty-eight years old and my life is governed by a dream. Not a dream of something I wish to have or want someday to do, but by a dream I have as a boy."

He inhaled deeply on his cigarette and, exhaling, sent a coil of dense smoke that held its shape above our heads like a genie released from a bottle.

"My people, the Zinacantecos, believe that each man has an animal spirit companion that shares with him an inner soul. At the moment a Zinacanteco is born, the animal is born. Throughout life, what happens to one happens to the other, so that if one is injured or killed the other suffers the same injury. These souls—jaguars, coyotes, ocelots, and all the small animals—live inside the Great Mountain above our village. Our ancestors care for these animal spirits. Sometimes, one is let out to wander in the real forest."

Another puff of the cigarette and the smoke genie grew larger.

"As a small boy, I dream that I wake during the night to find *el tigre* sitting on my chest."

El tigre. The jaguar.

"I feel its breath warm against my face. I hear the thud of its great heart beating against my chest. I smell the sunlight trapped in its fur. With its great eyes it looks into mine, and I know I am seeing my animal spirit. And then, it vanishes and... Someone watches us through the glass, there, at the front door."

I jumped up and spun around. One of the metal folding chairs on the front porch made a clatter as it was overturned. By the time I reached the doors and went out, the watcher had vanished like the Maya's animal spirit. I lowered the blinds and went back to my visitor, sitting calmly under his cloud of blue smoke.

"You were saying..."

"The hut I live in is open-sided, with a tin roof. I sleep

in a string hammock under the stars. One night, three years ago, now, *el tigre* visits. Not a dream animal this time, but a real one. From the jungle he creeps upon me and watches me. We stare eye to eye. He sniffs the air, tasting my scent, then turns and creeps back into his jungle. This is an omen, I tell myself. To warn me that my animal spirit is loose in the jungle and I must be on my guard. I think perhaps that my animal spirit has taken the real form of *el tigre,* and I must protect him from all who would hunt him." A pause. "I am here because I fail. Because I have fail, I suffer a soul-loss."

As the old man spoke these words, I saw a stricken look such as I have never seen in the eyes of any man.

"I don't understand."

"I live in the jungle," he said, "but all around the land is gone to cattle. My neighbors are *ganaderos* who hunt *el tigre* because sometimes he kills a cow or calf on one of their ranches. Also poor *Indios* hunt. The price of a spotted skin in the fur market brings enough to buy a dozen or more range cows. The worst are the hunters who kill for sport. The foreign hunters come, led by *Indio* or mestizo guides. They kill with bow and arrows, crossbows, guns, dogs. Even spears. In my lifetime there will be no more *el tigre.* I am here because I follow a man, a gringo, who comes here with the skins of six. Almost the last from the preserve. I ride many miles on the buses with him. Never does he see me. To him I am one more dirty old *Indio.* This man passes the skins to the crooked one. Alas, the crooked one is an *Indio* like me. Not so easy to follow him without his knowing. He goes on foot, and I must track him across the desert. I keep an hour behind or he will know that I am there. I track him to a village where he is known and is living. From the hills above I wait and watch for three days while the crooked one works and eats and sleeps, but goes nowhere. I grow tired. Careless. On the fourth day,

I wake and take my place in the rock. I see no sign of the crooked one. Halfway through the morning, the villagers leave. When the people return, they go indoors, shut the doors, and stay. A truck drives up with a cloth-covered body in back and three men carry it into one of the buildings. That night, from the dark, I listen. All the talk is of the dead man and the *nagual* that has killed him. I understand the crooked one is dead. I wait until he is buried in the *campo santo* of the village. I show myself and ask for food and work. They have no work for me, but they feed me. As I eat, I listen. I learn of this place where the crooked one had sold his carvings, and I think this may be where he has passed the skins on. So I come here to watch."

"And what did you see?"

"I see a fat woman and a skinny little man cut the screen of a window at the back. She waits outside watching while he climbs in. When he leaves he is carrying something small in one hand. What, I cannot see. He and the fat woman go into the trailer and close the door. I wait. In a while, I see the little bobcat stick her head out. She looks, then she leaps and runs, playing. I follow her. At first, she likes her freedom, but then she is afraid. I talk to her and she runs to me and we travel together. I think you have her to sell, so I will keep her. But she is friendly like a puppy. And unafraid. Her coat and eyes shine. I change my mind that you are a person who would trade in animals, live or dead. I believe you are a person I can trust. I bring her back."

His cigarette finished, he mashed it out with the tips of his fingers and put it into the trash.

"I'm very glad you did. I hope this means you'll believe me when I say I don't know anything about the skins of the jaguars. I only learned today that the Saint Maker, the crooked one as you call him, smuggled contraband. And you're right. I wouldn't trade in animals. Do you happen to know what the Saint Maker carried the skins in?"

He stood up. "Like this," he said, arranging his hands to show the size. "A satchel with a strap over the shoulder."

"Yes, I've seen it. He had his carving tools in it. He had it with him when he came here and left some of his carvings for me to sell. It disappeared the day he died. I think it's what the man and woman you saw coming in through the window were trying to find."

"They buy the furs?" he said.

"I don't know. They may just be go-betweens for someone else. I understand that's how these things work sometimes. Why don't you go to the authorities? The Customs Service would help you. They'd be glad to—" I remembered the informant Andalon had told me about. Beaten to death. I couldn't ask this man to place himself in danger he might not understand.

He was shaking his head. "Already I am farther than I understand. This desert is another country. I find the skins, take them home, burn them, and bury the ashes beneath the trees where *el tigre* raises his head to the sun. It may be one of the skins is my spirit companion. If so, then I go home to lie down on my reed mat and die there at the foot of the tree with the bones of my spirit companion."

He spoke with such simplicity and sincerity, I had tears in my eyes.

"We must find the skins for you," I told him.

TWENTY-FOUR

ANTUN DEPARTED a formal handshake. I offered him a cot, but he refused, saying he would rest better on the porch where he could see the stars. I gave him a pillow, but he placed it on one of the folding chairs and settled his head on his arm to sleep.

I longed to talk over with Clay what I had learned about the Saint Maker, but that would have to wait until tomorrow, since he had planned to stay overnight in Alpine. Too keyed up to sleep, I searched the trading post again, this time knowing what I looked for. Antun had explained the space the skins would take up. A jaguar is large, leopard-size. Six skins, tightly rolled, could be squeezed into a duffel bag.

Four hours later, I'd removed a lot of cobwebs from corners and underneath shelves, but I hadn't found the skins. I stretched across the bed in my clothes and dozed fitfully, waking every hour on the hour and staring at the clock face glowing in the dark. At 4:30 a.m. I got up.

The coffeemaker, burned out and not yet replaced, I brewed my two cups the old-fashioned way. I heaped two teaspoons of ground coffee into the pot and poured in boiling water. Before I could pour my first cup, Phobe joined me, demanding to be fed. Worn out by her adventures, she had slept through the night. I cut a chunk off her food log, chopped it up and put it in her pan, and filled her bowl with fresh water.

I poured my coffee and carried the cup with me to the back door, opened it, and stepped outside into the sweet, cool air. To the east, the morning star burned in the sky.

Lucero—the lamp—the Mexican ranch hands call it. The pale flush of dawn had spread itself across the Sierras. From a distance came a sharp bark, a howl, yapping, culminating in many vibratos. Clay tells me the vocalization of the coyotes is social behavior. I say they sing the sun up.

Over the voice of the coyotes I heard a motor start. I trotted around the corner of the building in time to see the Aplys' blue pickup turn onto the road in the direction of Presidio. They might be going anywhere, of course. To one of the ranches Boyce claimed to be scouting out for photographic tour locations. To Ruidosa, where they could turn off on FM 2810 for a forty-eight-mile drive through Pinto Canyon to Marfa. Or across to the other side, where Pete had said they had been seen frequently.

I set the cup on the ground and walked to the door of the RV. They'd been poking around my place. Time for me to investigate theirs. I tried the door. Open. Two steps up and I was inside.

The interior was an orderly arrangement of space designed to utilize every inch for storage. The overlay of the Aplys' daily living was disorder. Table and countertops were a mess, littered with paper plates, candy wrappers, soft drink cans, and coffee cups. I moved front to back, starting with the built-in couch that wrapped one end of the space. I lifted cushions and examined the storage beneath. Boyce kept his cameras and extra film there, plus a file box with notes in a tight-fisted hand on places he had photographed. That much was true, then. He had been taking pictures. I moved to the kitchen and looked in every tightly packed shelf. I even checked the microwave oven. I glanced at the shower and toilet facilities, too tiny to hide much of anything. The closet opposite held only clothes. Next came the bedroom, with the built-in bed tucked close enough beneath the overhead storage bin to give me claustrophobia just thinking about sleeping in it. The only thing that made breathing possible in the close space was the window above the bed. I winced at the bright morning light hitting the closed curtains.

I took a second look. The image burned on my retina had not been the accident of shadow and sun and curtain folds. On the rim of the window, behind the curtains and silhouetted against the light, was the jaguar carving. I reached across the bed, pushed the curtains aside, and picked it up.

I heard a sound. It had been going on for some time, a dulled ringing resonating against the silence. Like two stones being clicked together. The kind of warning sound I'd read the Indians used. Warning! Antun.

Too late I heard a vehicle pull in next to the RV. I headed toward the door, clutching the statue. As I reached for the handle, it swung in, forcing me back.

Pat entered first, her bulk filling the doorway.

"What are you doing in here?" she said, goggling at me. "Boyce, get in here quick."

Her husband stuck his head in, looking more than half afraid.

When in doubt, attack.

"Yes, Boyce," I said, "come in and explain how you happen to have this." I held up the statue.

"I found it lying out in the edge of the desert late yesterday," Pat said. "I was going to return it when you opened up this morning."

I looked at Boyce, who had come all the way in and stood eyeing us both with equal nervousness.

I told him, "Someone saw you cutting the screen, climbing in, and getting out."

"I didn't take anything except the statue," Boyce said.

I looked at Pat, expecting rebuttal. Instead, she sat heavily down on the couch. Her face reddened and tears streaked down her cheeks. She made no effort to wipe them. Her hands lay limp in her lap.

I looked at Boyce to see if he intended to comfort his wife, but his squeezed-up face and trembling hands made it obvious that he was in as much distress as she. I'd get no help from that direction. I went to Pat and sat down beside her.

"I thought I was the one in trouble, but it looks like you two need help more than I do."

Sympathy made Pat cry harder and loosened her tongue, but not to coherence. I thought she said, "If they don't kill us then the others will arrest us and send us to jail."

I didn't want to ask for an explanation of that until I was back in my own territory.

"Have either of you had anything to eat this morning?" I asked, looking to Boyce for an answer. He managed to shake his head.

"Come on. Let's go inside and get some food and coffee into you. Then we'll talk things over and work out a solution."

I helped Pat down the RV's steps and took her arm to support her. I could feel her nervous trembling. As I glanced back to make sure Boyce was coming, too, I saw at the edge of the desert, outlined by the sun, Antun Tanhol standing as still and silent as the rock around him. Knowing he was watching and waiting, I felt safer.

TWENTY-FIVE

THE HOT COFFEE went a long way toward restoring the Aplys' emotional equilibrium, and the English muffins and bacon did the rest. Their eyes still reflected fear, but it was contained enough for me to get the story out of them.

As usual, Pat did the talking, beginning with self-justification.

"It was to get us over the hump, so to speak, of our financial losses. We invested badly—"

"You invested badly," Boyce snapped. "She got a cash settlement from the hospital for her back injury after some lunatic patient shoved her down the stairs."

"It was a gang member who came in with a gunshot wound," Pat said. "He was running from the police."

Boyce said, "We were in great shape until she goes and invests with some broker in high risk stocks—"

"You liked the idea as much as I did," Pat said.

"I didn't—"

"Could we get back to the main event?" I said.

"What was I saying? Oh, yes. We had to do something to make up the money we lost. Boyce has an associate who does research in southern Mexico and Central America. He put us on to something—"

"Smuggling animal skins," I said. Why didn't they look surprised that I knew?

Pat said, "There were a few lizard skins, too. And snakes. But mostly it was jaguar and ocelot. They bring the most money. And it was so easy. We were already coming down here for the photography tours. They knew us at the border crossings and the checkpoints."

I could see her confidence coming back as she talked, her own story convincing her, if not me, of the harmlessness of their activities.

"We were just the go-betweens—isn't that so, Boyce? We picked up and delivered. It's the Mexicans who are killing and selling them. And they'd do it anyway, so why shouldn't we take advantage of an opportunity?"

"But they're endangered," I said. "Protected."

"Not down there they're not," Pat said vehemently.

"Didn't you worry about what might happen if you got caught?" Even as I asked I remembered what Andalon had told me about the rarity of stiff penalties.

Pat ignored my question and went on with her tale. "We always met at some isolated place on the other side. Boyce would get a marked map in the mail showing where to meet. We had a shop teacher friend fix a trunk with a false bottom. The courier would hand the skins over to us and we'd pack them in the hidden compartment in the trunk and pile all Boyce's cameras and tripod and film on top. We'd drive them across, and deliver the skins to a contact on this side."

"And that would be?" I asked.

"The primary buyer or someone the buyer sent. One man used his secretary to collect the skins from us. I know that because she told us. She was mad at having to make the trip."

"Just a little side journey, and we got paid in cash," Boyce said wistfully. "The free trade policy between the U.S. and Mexico made it so easy. With all the traffic hitting the border crossings, customs hardly had time to check any vehicle. When they did, it was for drugs."

Pat said, "The sniffer dogs don't care diddly about anything but drugs. Anyway, the skins are treated with some chemical to keep them from smelling."

"How many times did you make these little side trips?"
I asked.

"Same as my tours," Boyce explained. "Four a year
over the past two years. Two in summer and one each at
Christmas and spring break."

"Was the courier, as you called him, always the same
person?"

Pat looked at Boyce, who shook his head.

"But this time it was the Saint Maker," I said.

"Yes," they said in unison.

"Do you know where the skins are?"

"God no!" Boyce almost shouted. "What do you think
we've been hanging around here for?"

Pat said, "He thought they were in the old man's bag
and hauled it all the way back—"

"Shut up!" Boyce's small face flushed and he balled his
hands into fists in his lap.

Unfazed, Pat said, "We thought you had them. That's
what we told the DEA agents."

For once, Pat had said something for which I had no
comeback.

Boyce's words rushed into my stunned silence.

"I didn't kill him," he said to me, then twisted his head
to face his wife. "You made it sound like I killed him."

"I can't think why she'd think that," Pat said. "Look at
you."

Boyce squeezed his eyes shut, leaned his head back, and
pleaded. "Christ, give me patience."

Pat gave him a contemptuous glance and said, "Boyce
was set to meet the old man at the church at nine that
morning to get the skins. When he got there, the doors were
open. He went in and found him dead."

Boyce said, "Just barely. He was pouring blood, the dog
started howling its head off—"

I said, "You're the one who went off and left the dog locked in?"

I concentrated on the dog to keep from thinking about the scene Boyce had described.

"I didn't mean to. I like dogs. *She* won't let me have one. The mutt followed me—"

Pat said, "Because you fed him."

Boyce pretended she hadn't spoken. "I tried to get him to come to me, but he went crazy and I was afraid he'd bite me. The smell of the blood scared him—"

"Like it scared you," Pat said.

"You weren't there," Boyce told her, thrusting his chin out.

"I had the presence of mind to get the picture of the body so we could prove to the buyer the old man had been killed."

"You knew he was dead when we got there?" I said to Pat.

"Boyce dragged the old man's bag of junk all the way back here without even looking to see if the furs were in it. It was all I could do to get him to stop yammering about the blood and the dog so I could find out what happened. After I got him calmed down enough to tell me, I checked the bag myself. Like I said, junk. No skins. I told Boyce to go take pictures somewhere he'd be seen so he'd have an alibi for the morning. The way people around here pay no attention to time, I figured if they saw him any hour that morning it would be okay. Nobody would know exactly what time they saw him. Then I came over to see what you were up to."

"What do you mean?"

Pat said, "I thought maybe you sneaked out early and crossed over and bashed in the hunchback's face to get the skins for yourself. Don't look so surprised. Boyce saw you were a smuggler right at the start. All those arrowheads—"

"Points," Boyce said. "They're called points."

"Whatever. Points, then. You have a whole display case full of points and things. Boyce says if those are the ones you keep, you must be getting big money for the ones you sell to collectors—"

This time I interrupted Pat. "I don't sell any artifacts."

She ignored me. I began to sympathize with how Boyce must feel.

"No telling what you could get for the skins with the connections you have."

"So you deliberately worked it to get me to ask you to go across the river to the chapel," I said.

Pat smiled. "It's amazing how in life, if you're pushy, it's the polite people who give in first. I knew about the dedication service from talking to that woman at the post office. I wanted to see for myself what had happened. When you said you were closing, I figured it had something to do with the chapel. You having so many friends on the other side."

"How does the DEA come into this?" I asked weakly.

"You really don't have the skins?" Boyce said.

"I really don't."

Boyce swallowed and looked sick.

"The buyer already paid," he said, almost moaning. "Ten thousand dollars apiece to have them brought up here. We were to get a thousand for each skin we delivered. He'll never believe we don't have them. He'll think we stole them and tell the people in Mexico and they'll kill us for stealing from them."

I tried again. "What about the DEA?"

Boyce said, "We got *caught.* It was *her* fault. She bought prescription painkillers for her back and we got stopped by the Highway Patrol for speeding. The damn boxes of pills were piled in plain sight right there on the seat."

Pat said resentfully, "We weren't breaking any federal

law bringing them back. How was I to know Texas had its own stupid laws about quantities?''

Boyce said, ''I told you not to buy the damn things. You had a prescription at home.''

''They're a lot cheaper in Mexico. If you can buy two or three years' supply, I don't see why you can't bring it back.'' Pat crossed her arms and sulked.

''Please explain what you're talking about,'' I said.

Boyce, enjoying his wife's discomfiture, resumed the story.

''The highway patrolman arrested us for having, according to him, illegal amounts of a prescription painkiller. Amounts sufficient for sale and distribution, is how he put it. At headquarters, they confiscated the pills and searched the RV to make sure we didn't have any more. They found the skins. They called in an agent from the Fish and Wildlife Service. Next thing we know, we're talking to some big shot DEA agent who claims that contraband skins are being traded for drugs, and he's looking for a trail to connect back to the source, and if we cooperate he'll work something out on the charges and fines for the pills and the skins.''

Boyce's voice turned whiney again. ''If I had been charged, and the case went to court and I was found guilty, the pills alone could have gotten me nine years. The university would have fired me. I'd have lost my pension. All the money we accumulated from the other trips in fines. They said the fines could go as high as a hundred thousand. They intended pressing for a severe penalty—''

''Bluff. All bluff,'' Pat snapped.

''That's not what you said then.'' Boyce threw his hands in the air and mimicked his wife in falsetto: ''Oh, what will the neighbors say!''

''So you agreed to cooperate,'' I said.

Boyce nodded. ''We notified them when this trip came

up. They told us to collect the skins and bring them for marking before we delivered to the buyer.''

"What did you tell them about the Saint Maker's death?''

"God! Nothing. I was afraid they'd think I killed him. I thought when I grabbed his bag I had the furs. That's all I could think of. No furs. Go directly to jail.''

"But you had a set date to collect the furs. You had to tell the DEA agents something.''

"I told them there'd been some kind of cock-up and the courier had been here early. I told them I thought you had the furs.''

"Why?''

"Like my wife told you. All those artifacts out there in that case. It seemed obvious that you trade with smugglers.''

Pat said, "He had to tell them something.''

"*When* did he tell them this?''

They looked at each other, then Pat answered. "Our arrangement was for a five-day zone for collecting the furs from the courier. That allowed for delays. You know how things are over there. The bus driver's not going to worry about a schedule if he wants to stop and visit friends or have a meal. And that doesn't even allow for the things that can happen to the couriers that walk—''

"Just tell her,'' Boyce whined.

"This morning. We met them in Presidio,'' Pat said.

"When you told them you thought I had the skins, what did they say?''

Pat frowned slightly, and said, "You know, they looked kind of odd for a minute. Then they told us to come back here and stay put. That they'd be in touch.''

I touched my hand to my head in anticipation of the headache I would have. No wonder the agents had looked odd. The day before yesterday, they'd been trying to recruit me and Clay. Had they been successful, no doubt they'd have asked us to keep an eye on the Aplys. Then along come the Aplys to denounce me as a smuggler.

"Just to set the record straight, you were the ones who broke in the back door, right?"

"Yes," Boyce said. "I was sure you had the skins. When we didn't find them, we took off. But we had to come back. I've got to get those skins."

"And Mata did catch you going through the toolbox trying to find the skins?"

"Yes."

I looked at the pathetic pair. "Where did you hide the Saint Maker's bag?"

"Come on," Pat said. "I'll show you."

I supposed there was little point in seeing the bag, but I wanted to test the truth of at least some part of their story. I followed the pair out the door.

"We'll have to drive," Pat said. "I buried it under some rocks down by the river."

We took my pickup. Pat directed me to a spot not far from the crossing point. I parked and we walked single-file down the bank to a spot beneath some wilting salt cedars. Pat pointed and said, "Right there."

I had to stand in the water to reach the rocks and lift them out of the way one at a time. I moved five large stones before I was able to tug out the sodden leather bag. I carried it dripping to the bank and spread it out. The water had soaked the fawn-colored leather black. The handmade bag resembled a large knapsack or an outsized shoulder bag. Pat had wrapped the stout strap tightly around the bag before submerging it and weighting it down. I had to use my pocketknife to cut it free. The top of the bag had no closure except an extra length of leather in one side. I turned it back, pulled the sides apart, and took out the sodden contents.

A plastic box with an old straight-edge razor and a dissolved lump that might have been a bar of soap. A handmade leather pouch with pockets and straps that held the Saint Maker's few precious woodworking tools. A pair of thick, white, cotton pants. Nothing else.

I looked over my shoulder at Pat, standing on the bank, looking tired and old. I realized that I had gotten used to her boisterous pushiness and I almost missed it. As his wife shrank in personality, Boyce seemed to compensate by asserting himself. A balanced marriage, I guess.

I stood up, holding the bag at arm's length to keep it from dripping all over me.

"I was hoping to learn something from this. But it tells me nothing."

"Whoever killed him got the skins," Boyce said. "Son of a gun has probably already sold them to some taxidermist for cash. I think the DEA was right. Drugs are involved. The killer could have gotten maybe sixty thousand dollars for those skins. Some rich guy's got one displayed in his house right now, I'll bet, looking so real it might walk."

"I can't think why anyone would want to look at a stuffed animal on their mantel," Pat said.

For once, I agreed with her.

"Why did you take the jaguar carving?" I asked Boyce as I drove them back to their RV.

"As proof the old man had been at your place, in case I needed it."

"Why didn't you give it to the DEA agent?"

"I intended to. I was nervous. I forgot to take it with me."

I stopped at the trailer, and they climbed out and stood looking at me like two kids being put off the school bus for misbehavior.

"I assume you're going to be here until the DEA tells you otherwise," I said. "I want to be sure we understand each other. I don't have the furs. I don't know where they are. I am not dealing in smuggled anything. Not drugs. Not skins. Not artifacts. If I find so much as a crack in a window of my place or a door open that shouldn't be, I'll call the sheriff and have you arrested for the two previous break-ins. The charge may not be as serious as the wildlife smuggling, but I will make sure it is just as embarrassing. After your names appear in the police report of the *Big Bend Sentinel,* I will send a copy to the president of the university and the Austin newspaper. Understood?''

Boyce drew himself up to his full five-foot, six-inch height and said, ''Ms. Jones, I owe you an apology. I'm very sorry for involving you in this mess.''

He took his wife's arm, and they turned away. I watched him help her up the steps and into the RV before driving around back to park. I sat in the pickup, my hands resting on the wheel, too dispirited to move. I heard the telephone ringing inside the trading post, and thinking it might be Clay I rushed in to answer it.

Instead of Clay, Julia's piping voice sounded in my ear.

''Oh, Texana, I have my father's permission to come and see the bat cave. He says if you truly don't mind taking me. I told him you wouldn't because you are so very kind.''

TWENTY-SIX

IF HECTOR was surprised to see me again so soon, he didn't show it.

I had brought along two fifty-gallon drums of water for the village. I had loaded the drums empty by rolling them up a ramp of two-by-fours, upended them, and filled them from the hose.

The villagers lined up with buckets, bowls, and whatever other containers they had, handing them to the two men standing in the pickup who used gourd dippers to fill them. In no time, the drums had been emptied.

"We are very grateful," Hector told me.

"What have you been doing for water?" I asked.

"Let me show you."

He crossed the plaza to a pickup and we drove five hundred yards beyond the buildings to the rocky soil of an arroyo that, if it ever rained, would be a flood of rolling, muddy water. In the center of the gully three men with buckets and a dipper crouched around a hole. Behind them a wide, waist-high pile of chunks of clay soil and rock testified to their efforts.

Hector jumped out of the pickup, leaving the door open, and motioned for me to follow.

As we approached, the men grinned up at me with dirt-lined, tired faces and smiled proudly, moving aside so I could have room to stand close.

"Look," Hector said, pointing into the hole.

The sides had been shored up with boards hammered into the stiff clay soil. Water had pooled in the bottom of the deep, hand-dug hole, and a thin plastic hose ran from the seep to a bucket. The men were siphoning out the precious liquid.

"We fill half a bucket in about thirty minutes," one of the men told me.

"You see," Hector said, "we survive."

"With this kind of spirit, if it ever rains, you'll thrive," I told him.

"When it rains," he corrected me.

We walked back to the cluster of adobes, golden-walled under the amber sun, and sat on the porch of the community center.

Hector asked after Clay. I inquired about his children. We talked about his plans for the crops *when* it rained and the well had been restored.

"This land sustains little. Certainly not so many of us as are here now. The village keeps alive only because our young men go to the United States to work and send money back. If I were younger, I would go, too, and find land where I could grow sage and chilies. And onions. I have seen the onions growing in Presidio. Fertile land and plenty of water, that is what I dream of. Nature makes all the demands. We can only respond."

"As with your rain ceremony," I said.

He smiled. "Such things give the people hope. We can say we have done everything possible."

"That night, you mentioned that the rain spirits lived in the bat cave. Have you ever been inside the cave?"

"Yes."

"Is it safe to go in?"

"Do you want to see the cave?" he said, half rising. "Come, I'll show it to you now if you like."

"Not now," I said, and he sat down. I explained about Julia, and told him what I wanted, making it clear that I understood if he wished to say no.

"I like the idea," Hector said, smiling. "As you point

out, Señor Suarez is a man of much wealth and influence. It will do no harm to be gracious to his daughter.''

"Will you go with us into the cave then, to show us the way?''

"We will go together into the cave. Who knows," he said, "Maybe we'll meet a rain spirit. When will you come?''

"Day after tomorrow.''

I left with the whole village waving goodbye and thanking me again for the water. I promised to bring more.

As soon as I closed the door of the trading post, Clay's voice called from the bathroom, "Is that you?''

"Yes.''

"Where are the sinus pills?''

"How can your allergies be bothering you?'' I said, walking through to the bathroom. "There's nothing green enough to be pollinating.''

Phobe sat on top of the chest of drawers that I keep towels and medicines in. Clay rubbed her head with one hand and rummaged through the top drawer with the other.

"I ate dust all the way home,'' he said. "The wind has picked up like a front is coming through.''

I pulled the drawer farther out, looked in, found the Benadryl, and handed it to him.

"Why were you driving with the windows open?''

He tried to extricate a pill, fussed as usual as the pack refused to cooperate, and handed it to me to open for him.

"The air conditioner in my pickup has gone out. I think it needs coolant.'' He ran water into the bathroom glass and swallowed the tablet.

"I hate to hear that. Doesn't it mean you have to pay a lot of money to have the air conditioner reworked so you can use that new stuff that everybody's complaining doesn't cool?''

"It means I take a drive across the river and get the Freon put in."

He picked up Phobe, asked me when she got home, and carried her back to the bedroom, dumping her down on top of the bedspread and stretching out beside her. She settled down to chewing his fingers.

I explained about Antun Tanhol. When I got to the part about the jaguar skins, Clay's face darkened.

"I despise trophy hunters," he muttered under his breath.

After I told him about the part the Aplys had played in the smuggling, he lifted his feet off the bed and sat up.

"You should tell them to go," he said. "You wanted to the other night when we almost caught them at the trailer. You were right."

I revealed the part the DEA agents played in the Aply saga.

"I can't think of a way to get rid of them without increasing the DEA's interest in us. Can you?"

"Let me think about," he said.

"Right now, think about getting rid of that headache. You've got a call on the answering machine from Stan Able asking you to come out. A non-emergency, he said."

Clay groaned. "It would be emus. I'll be glad when the ratite fad dies out. I hate working on those birds."

I patted his arm. "I'll get the ice pack."

Clay napped for forty-five minutes, claimed his head felt better—though from looking at his eyes, I doubted it—and left for the Able place.

I stayed busy with video rentals, gasoline sales, and the usual number of locals coming in to shop, gossip, and spend a little time in the company of others. I made sure they each left with the news that the reward offer for a white dog was canceled and that the dog in question hadn't killed anyone.

Clay made it back home by six, his headache really gone

this time, and suggested we forget about the awful Aplys, the DEA, and the world at large by dining out at our favorite and only local restaurant.

La Casa Azul is twelve tables in the front room of the Reyes family home. The cooking is done in the family's kitchen. No alcoholic beverages served—too many customers have to drive too far to get here, and the Reyeses want them to get safely home again. In the hours between 6:00 and 10:00 p.m. on Fridays and Saturdays, when the restaurant is open, every table is filled and there is a waiting line.

We showered and changed, dressing up for the occasion in a skirt and blouse for me, slacks and a jacket for Clay.

"How'd the meeting go?" I asked Clay as we sipped iced tea and waited for our food.

"Good. Really interesting. A couple of the ranchers paid to bring in the cloud-seeding team that's been working in San Angelo, plus a couple of farmers from there. The team was hired to seed 6 million acres of cotton farms, and cattle and goat ranches. The weather has to be just right, what they called 'promising cloud tops,' which turned out to be an understated way of saying the pilot goes up into the lightning and the storm to eighteen to twenty thousand feet. He shoots silver iodide flares so the particles rain down through the cloud layers collecting water droplets as they fall."

"Hot plates," Ruben Reyes said, as he placed them before us, the white china hidden by steaming enchiladas in red sauce.

Clay said, "At least, that's how it's supposed to work. And the consensus is, it does. I liked the man in charge. He was honest about the critics who claim cloud seeding causes hailstorms. He contends objective data shows seeding diminishes hailstorms. Makes me wish we could try it. Things are getting bad. Some of the livestock sales are turning away ranchers' cattle because there aren't any buyers.

The cattle market is about as low as the value of the peso. We don't need rain, we need a hurricane.''

"You may get one," I said, telling him about the rain ceremony at Providencia.

"More power to them for trying," Clay said, digging into his food.

I waited until dessert to tell him about Julia.

"Do you approve of my plan?" I asked him after I had explained.

"I agree you can't have Ghee's daughter over here again. Not with the DEA spying on us. I don't say they'd assume the worst—"

"I do. What's more, I'm afraid they might walk in and try to question her."

"They wouldn't do that. They know better than to pull something that foolish."

"Are you sure?"

"I'm sure they don't want to offend Mexico just when they need the cooperation of the authorities in this drug business. Ghee is a powerful man. He'd make a powerful complaint." He eyed my dessert. "Are you going to finish that?"

"Too sweet for me," I said, pushing the dish his way. We were eating ice cream topped with caramel-flavored *cajeta de leche,* a paste made with thickened goat's milk and sugar. "But you don't think I should take Julia to visit the cave?"

Clay said, "I don't much like the idea. But then, I don't see how you can avoid it, either. If Ghee is what the DEA says he is, I don't want to draw his suspicion either."

"Or his enmity."

"You're satisfied the cave is safe?"

"Hector is, and I trust him."

TWENTY-SEVEN

NOTHING MUCH HAPPENED on Sunday. I went to Mass, prompting a remark from Clay that my unaccustomed piety wouldn't impress the watchers from the DEA. I laughed at the joke, but my purpose was serious. When the world closes in, nothing expands the horizon like reflections on eternity.

I came out of church to find a flat on the pickup. By the time I'd changed the tire it was eleven-thirty. When I got home, I found a note from Clay saying he'd been called out by a woman who thought her potbellied pig was dying.

I had a cold lunch, tried to settle down with a book, and ended up restlessly doing nothing much of anything, except waiting for Julia's telephone call.

She rang at two o'clock, breathlessly excited about the possibilities of the bat cave, and not at all disappointed that our exploration was not to be in the cave on this side of the river.

"It's here in Mexico?" she said. "Super! An undiscovered site!"

I didn't point out the obvious, that the villagers had discovered it. I was too relieved that she didn't object to the location. She said she would meet me there if I would give her directions and map coordinates. I did, and we set the time for three hours before sunset on Monday.

"Be sure it's all right with your father," I cautioned her with my last words before goodbye.

I spent the rest of the afternoon loading the truck with water barrels, a new spare tire, and a short list of other supplies such as goat feed and lamp oil. I owed Hector for letting me impose on the goodwill of the village.

Clay arrived home in time to fill the water barrels for me.

"How's the pig?" I asked.

"Okay now. It impacted on corn, so I had to clean out its stomach."

We spent a quiet evening. Clay had no more calls, and not a single person made an emergency stop for gas at the pumps. We relaxed over dinner, washed up the few dishes, and with Phobe flopped on her back between us watched Alfred Hitchcock's 1938 classic called *The Lady Vanishes.*

"Any word from the Aplys?" Clay asked me as the tape rewound.

"Not a sound or a sighting. I guess they've decided to keep a low profile."

"Everything set for tomorrow?"

"Yes. Julia loved the idea."

"Do you want me to come with you?"

"I don't think we should both cross to the other side. Not with the interest in our activities from so many directions."

"Just be careful. Take your gun."

"I intend to."

TWENTY-EIGHT

THE GRINDING ROAR of the motor and the *whomp, whomp* of the rotor blades sounded over the hills and bounced back from the mountain behind the village, bringing every man, woman, and child rushing out to shade their eyes with their hands and watch the landing.

Dust swirled around the barren plaza and the younger children covered their ears as the pilot set the chopper gently down on the clay flats a hundred feet beyond. The blades slowed, stilled, and Julia jumped down and came running to greet me, followed by the manly stride of Mata. She wore full hiking gear, while Mata sported serviceable jeans, boots, and a cowboy shirt with the sleeves rolled up to show his powerful biceps.

"I thought you'd fly the helicopter," I said to Julia, noting the pilot waiting behind in the chopper.

"No, Papa says I'm too young. He says helicopters are to pilots what motorcycles are to drivers."

I made the introductions to Hector and several of the other villagers. Julia behaved with perfect graciousness. Stern-faced throughout, Mata nodded briefly, shaking hands, saying nothing. I gave him full marks for his attendance on Julia, though. He kept his eyes on her. As he watched his charge, he had the expression of intense awareness and expectation of danger that one sees on the faces of Secret Service agents guarding the president.

The welcome and introductions over, Hector, in his worn leather shoes and work clothes, led the way up the path to the table of rock where the rain ceremony had been held.

"After this," Hector said, "it gets more steep."

And it did. We climbed, single file, sometimes using our hands. Hector hopped from boulder to boulder, never tiring, and pausing only to let the rest of us catch up to his pace. At our backs, the sun intensified as it dropped lower in the sky.

Just as I was almost out of breath and energy, Hector stopped. We had rounded a blind bend in the trail and reached a high point from which the view was as spectacular as it was scary, looking down hundreds of feet to the canyon floor. Behind us the wall of the mountain cracked in a long, jagged fault large enough at the base for several men to stand. This, Hector explained, was the cave entrance.

"I made this trip yesterday to be sure all was safe and as I remembered it," Hector said, turning to guide us in.

At the opening I handed Hector the flashlight I'd carried tucked into my belt. Julia took off her knapsack, opened it, and brought out three pencil flashlights, handing one to me and to Mata, and keeping the third for herself. Last she lifted out a larger, hand-held light.

"When we get inside we should be really quiet, so we don't scare the bats," she said authoritatively. "I want us to go in only as far as we have to to see them, then leave. I brought this red light for looking at the bats because it won't bother them a lot. Hector, you must shut off the big light as soon as possible."

Ghee's daughter, I reflected, had grow accustomed to command already.

Inside the entrance a boulder blocked the lower portion so that we had to squeeze past one at a time, except for Julia, who was small enough to slip through easily. Hector went first, I followed, then Julia, then Mata.

Hector kept the large beam of light aimed at the ground. The first twenty feet we traveled a dry, sloping passage that descended and widened into darkness over our heads. I could tell by the hollow sound of our footfalls that the darkness was vast. With every inch, the smell, a mix of ammonia and musk, increased.

Just when I thought my lungs would rebel, Hector stopped and barely breathed out the words, "We are here," and extinguished the flashlight.

Julia's red light came on and shot upward into the thick darkness, revealing more detail than I would have thought possible. The chamber was dome-shaped and festooned with multitudes of bats. As the light swept over them, thousands of glistening eyes in tiny faces turned down to stare back at us, and the upper air filled with the bickering sounds of millions of tinny bat voices.

I heard Julia give a delighted gasp, then saw her hand close over Hector's and the light dropped down to our feet.

"Could we get closer to them?" Julia's voice whispered, breaking her own admonition to us not to speak inside the cave. The adventurous child speaking over the budding naturalist.

Hector turned, cupped his hand over the light as a dimmer and started to guide us to the left. I saw Julia's pinpoint flashlight on his back, and followed that. I heard Mata move in behind me. Disturbed by our movement, the bats swirled, alighting on more distant walls. We walked along a rocky prominence that seemed to edge a pool. I stopped long enough to shine the light onto it and realized I was looking at a huge reserve of semi-liquid bat guano. There had to be fresh air coming in from somewhere or we'd be choking on the stench.

I looked up just in time to see Hector's light vanish as he stepped into one of the passages, a natural fissure in the rock. Julia's tiny beam of light went out, too, and I hurried to catch up, stumbling. A hand gripped my arm and kept me from falling. I recovered my balance, but instead of letting go, the grip crushed my arm until I could feel my pulse throbbing as the circulation closed off.

"If you have the skins," Mata's voice hissed in my right ear, "they are *not* to be passed on. Do you understand? There is to be no more smuggling of such goods. Remember the Saint Maker's fate."

He let go, a light shone on the ledge ahead, and Mata put his hand in the small of my back and prodded me forward. Fear kept me silent. That and my imagination. I saw myself drowning in bat guano. I guess that was the idea.

The passage curved sharply and immediately, explaining why first Hector's, then Julia's light had disappeared. After that, it erupted into a secondary chamber with a lowered ceiling and creviced walls. Hector stood waiting for us to catch up. Julia's pencil flashlight worked along a shadowed crack in the rock. To be safe from Mata, I decided to join her and stay close until we got out of the cave.

I started across. The floor felt slippery and I shone my light on it and saw a thin coating of mud and heard from somewhere the muffled sound of rushing water. My eyes had grown more accustomed to the dark and I could see better here than in the first vast cavern where the magnitude of the darkness swallowed the light. I had stepped within five feet of Julia when I realized the direction of the sound of flowing water. Down.

I heard her say, "I've got one. It's a free-tail bat." I dipped the light lower, saw Julia's boot-clad feet balanced on a heap of partially dried guano on a ledge at the edge of emptiness.

As I moved forward to pull her back, the pile of guano collapsed with a sucking sound and spilled over the edge. Julia gave a cry, her small body tipped, her flashlight went flying up into the air, then down, down, down.

I lunged, my hand contracting on the smooth fabric of her shirt. I held on, but her momentum carried me forward on the shifting mass and, as light as she was, I felt my hold slipping. From somewhere below came a deep *plop* as the gun I had carried in my pocket fell into the underground stream.

I stretched out my free hand, trying to find leverage, and grabbed air. We slipped forward. I tightened my grip until my knuckles ached.

Something yanked at my shirt and I sailed backward, taking Julia with me.

Mata's voice said softly, "I have hold of her. You can let go."

"I don't think I can."

Gently, his fingers pried my fingers one by one from their hold, then massaged my cramping hand.

A light shone in my eyes, and someone wiped my face with a handkerchief. It was Julia, recovered from near death with the physical resilience and the mental insouciance of the young and innocent, who cannot believe that bad things can happen to them.

"You saved my life," she said lightly, acknowledging the debt without any realization of the gravity of the deed.

"Mata saved us both," I said. "I can get up now."

"This is my fault," Hector said. "I would never have let the young lady go forward alone if I had known. I have been in this part of the cave before, but the chasm—it was not there." He shone the light, but I preferred not to look at how deep it went.

"Let's get out of here," I suggested, and with Mata holding Julia's hand and Hector walking with me, we made our way back to the main cavern. In a great swooshing sound, the bats took wing, swirling and chattering as they abandoned the chamber for the exit. Outside the sun would be setting.

I asked Mata for the flashlight. He handed it to me and I aimed at the passage from which we'd just emerged. I moved it slowly along the wall. A second passage lay to the left by only a couple of feet.

"I think, Hector, you mistook the passage. The two are so close, it would be easy. That chasm must have been there for eons."

"I think you are right," Hector said, his voice harsh with suppressed emotion. "I am so sorry this happened."

Julia said, "It's nothing. Don't worry."

We made a slower journey going out than we had going in. Outside the entrance we all sat down for a few minutes, and in the fast-fading light, Mata got a flask of water from Julia's knapsack where she had left it on the ground and passed it around. Tepid Perrier never tasted better. I smelled foul, I felt bruised to the bone, and I dreaded the downhill walk.

Mata put the empty water bottle away, hoisted the knapsack, and helped me to my feet. Julia looked back at the cave.

"I hope the bat is okay," she said.

"What bat?" Hector said.

"The one I was holding when the floor gave way."

"That's why they have wings, kid," Mata said.

Until then, I never suspected him of having a sense of humor.

The walk down took forever. Hector again led the way. I deliberately motioned Mata and Julia ahead of me. I didn't want the man behind me on that steep trail. One hand in my back could send me rolling hundreds of feet downward. I concentrated my eyes on the circle of ground in the flashlight beam and my mind on putting one foot in front of the other. All my energy had drained out the soles of my feet. Shock, the aftermath of fear.

Back in the village, I used a pint of their precious water to wash my face and hands. I needed a shower and a change of clothes, but that would have to wait until I got home.

The women had lighted the lamps and prepared a meal for us, and after I ate I felt better. The bottle of beer I drank to wash down the soft, bean and chicken tacos didn't hurt any, but it made me sleepy.

Julia spent the meal trying to make Hector feel better, and I think she succeeded. She suggested to him that he might consider collecting and selling the bat guano as fertilizer, explaining that she had read how it could be collected at times when the bats moved to other feeding grounds, thus protecting the source for the future. She promised to send him the information.

Everyone carried a lamp and went out to see the visitors off. I said goodbye to Julia on the porch of the community center. Hector escorted her to the helicopter. Mata flashed me a last look that I was too exhausted to fathom. In a few minutes, the noise overwhelmed the silence, and the helicopter lifted up and away, its lights mixing with the stars.

TWENTY-NINE

GETTING HOME had been arduous. I parked outside Clay's trailer and used his outdoor shower to clean myself up, then changed into a set of extra clothes he kept handy.

When I got inside, Clay took one look and said, "Are you okay?"

After I nodded, he added. "What can I do for you?"

"Coffee," I said, lying down on the couch.

Two cups of hot coffee laced with whiskey restored my physical stamina, while my mental state bounced among guilt at my own folly in taking Julia into that cave, fear at Mata's threat, and frustration at my inability to do anything about it other than shout to the world that I didn't have the jaguar skins.

I told Clay all about it over a glass of whiskey, my aching muscles finally relaxing into complete exhaustion. I vaguely remembered Clay guiding me to the bed and slipping my shoes off.

We talked things over at breakfast, which Clay brought me in bed. Toast, apricot preserves, and crisp bacon.

"It would simplify everything if we could find the skins," I said.

"Would it? I don't see how. You want to give them to your Maya friend. The Aplys are desperate to find them and if they get to them first, they'll take them. The DEA wants to catch us out in some wrongdoing. The skins would be it. And Mata? We don't know if he's working on his own or for Ghee."

"Why would Ghee want the smuggling of the skins stopped—oh, of course, what he said that day about—"

"—environmentalists. Might as well bring in the badges," Clay finished.

"He's afraid it will draw the attention of the environmentalists," I said.

"Unless Mata acted on his own. We need to know more about Mata."

"Does it make a difference?"

"I think so. By himself, he's dangerous. If he made the threat against you at Ghee's instigation, he's infinitely more dangerous."

I nodded. I had an idea how to find out more about Mata, but I had wasn't ready to discuss it yet.

Clay had some ranch visits to make, and left at eight o'clock.

I opened the trading post a little late.

The night's sleep had restored my physical stamina. My fear took care of itself, fading as the hours passed. You can't stay that shaken for long. The more distant the threat of physical harm, the less real it becomes. Sitting safe in my own business and home, it seemed very unreal. Not that I didn't realize the full implications of the threat. Mata couldn't have made it more clear that he had killed the Saint Maker. At least that was my reading, based on events. But if he had murdered the wood-carver, why didn't he have the skins? The only other alternative I could think of was that Mata wanted me to think he'd killed the wood-carver so I'd be too afraid to pass on the skins. I dismissed that. Mata didn't strike me as capable of that much subtlety.

My head ached with thinking about it. Until I knew enough to act, nothing would ease my frustration, much less get Clay and me out of deepening trouble on all sides. Squeezed between Mata and the DEA, I understood a little better how the Aplys must have felt.

Two seconds later, my empathy evaporated as I recalled the confrontation between Mata and Boyce over the search of my pickup. What if Mata had also been looking for the skins? I pictured Boyce lying on the ground where Mata had knocked him, and it dawned on me that the professor was behind Mata's assumption of my being in possession of the furs. It had come to mind so easily with the DEA because he'd already used it on Mata. Boyce didn't have the imagination to come up with a second story when the first had worked well enough.

I marched straight to the RV and pounded on the door with my fist.

"Who's that?" a little voice said from inside.

"Texana Jones. I've got some news for you about the skins."

Boyce opened the door and stood there wide-eyed and eager. "You have them? You know where they are?" Pat hovered behind him.

I put my foot on the step and kept going, saying, "It's better if we talk inside." I elbowed my way around Boyce and had Pat backing up to give me room. I sat down at the built-in table, gave them a hard look for a few seconds, then said, "Do you have anything to drink? And I don't mean your desert mix, Pat."

They gave each other a nervous glance. Boyce nodded to Pat. She opened the door of the shelf next to the microwave, took out a half-full bottle and three glasses, and put them on the table.

I told them to sit down, poured the Windsor scotch into two glasses, and pushed one glass at each of them.

"Aren't you having any?" Pat asked me.

"You're the ones who are going to need it. Drink up."

Pat lost all color. Boyce's chin quivered. Neither touched the liquor.

"I had an interesting chat with Mr. Mata yesterday."

Boyce downed one scotch and wrapped his hand around the second, his eyes looking everywhere but at me.

"I had to tell him *something*," he whined.

I have never wanted to strike another person in my life, but I swear if I had to live with that man, I'd be an abusive wife.

"What do you mean?" Pat said to me. "What's she talking about?" she asked Boyce.

"Boyce wasn't content just to name me to the DEA as a smuggler. He also told Mata that I had the skins."

She looked at her husband, saying earnestly, "You shouldn't have done that."

"No, he shouldn't have," I said. "He hasn't left me many options."

"What do you mean?" Boyce said.

"I mean I'll tell the DEA your fellow courier for the skins was found murdered eleven days ago, a fact you covered up. I'll tell them you were there, in the chapel. That you stole the dead man's bag and buried it under rocks in the river. It won't take them ten seconds to conclude that you killed him and took the skins. I doubt they'll have any trouble believing that smugglers, like thieves, sometimes fall out."

"But you can't do that," Boyce said, his voice rising. "It isn't true."

"That didn't stop you from telling lies about me."

Pat said, "We stayed here after the Saint Maker's murder. Why would we have done that if we'd had the skins?"

"You couldn't have left. The DEA wouldn't have let you. You had to remain here long enough to convince them that the courier wasn't coming, which you'd know if you killed him."

I didn't add that I only had their word that the DEA had demanded they stay. For all I knew, the pair had hung around hoping to find the skins and cash in.

Instead, I kept hitting while I had the momentum. "The villagers' desire to keep quiet about the Saint Maker's death and the natural reticence of *fronterizos* with outsiders made it unlikely the DEA would hear anything unless you told them, and you sure weren't going to do that. It suited your purpose perfectly to keep the murder quiet. You could wait it out and when the DEA got tired and gave up, you'd be free to go, having lived up to your part of the bargain with them. It was even better for you if you could give them some kind of answer. So after you saw the artifacts in the display case, you thought how convenient to direct their suspicion toward me as a smuggler. Then, if you had the skins, all you had to do was wait until the DEA and Customs got tired, leave, deliver the skins to the buyer, and pocket the cash. At least, that's what I'll tell them. A pretty plausible story, I think.''

Boyce said, ''You could have paid some friend of yours on the other side to kill the old man for you and take the skins. We were already cooperating with the DEA. Why should they believe you?''

''They already caught you smuggling. You agreed to betray the people you work with in order to save yourselves. Why should they trust you not to betray them, too? In order to have it both ways. Pretend to help them by blaming me, and keep the skins.''

Boyce looked so stubborn, I put my first high card on the table.

''The county sheriff is a personal friend. We grew up together. He'll vouch for me with the DEA. I think that puts the odds on my side.'' No need for them to know he already had, which might explain why the agents hadn't been back to question me after the Aplys had denounced me to them.

''What do you want us to do?'' Pat asked wearily.

''I want to know what else you haven't told me. I want to pick your brains about everything and every person associated with you in this smuggling business.''

Boyce said, "I don't think—"

"Tell her," Pat told him.

"Where do we start?" he asked.

"Who recruited you for the smuggling?"

"I don't know his name. I already told the DEA this. He was some kid, early to mid-twenties. He sounded American."

"He looked so innocent," Pat said. "Like one of those fat baby angels you see in old paintings in museums. What was it you called him, Boyce?"

"A blue-eyed cherub."

"With golden hair and rosy cheeks?" I asked.

"We aren't making this up," Pat said, assuming sarcasm where I had meant none.

"I didn't think you were," I assured her. "But if your blue-eyed boy had blond hair and a florid complexion, I think I've met him."

"He did," Boyce said.

I sat quiet, thinking about it.

Boyce said, "If you know him, if we could name him, it might satisfy the DEA. Get them off all our backs. An address would be even better. You know, where they could pick him up."

"Somebody's already done that," I said, and rising, I walked out of the RV and back to the trading post, leaving the pair to wonder and worry while I mulled over how to use this bit of information.

THIRTY

FOLLOWING a back-country road in Chihuahua is like following a game trail or a cow path. It will take you where you want to go with the least amount of effort.

I had left Clay minding the trading post in order to make the trip to Ejido de los Reyes.

This time the adobes were not deserted. As soon as the pickup came within sight, faces appeared at every window and someone stood in every door to see who was coming.

Before I had cut off the motor, Domingo and his wife and most of the rest of the people had come out to welcome me. Domingo invited me inside their cool adobe to sit down, offering me water after my long journey. After I gave them the gift I had brought, a garland of paper flowers for the grave of their granddaughter, they invited me to accompany them to place it on her grave. I offered to drive, and we went to the hillside cemetery and put the bright wreath on the wooden cross marking the small mound. Domingo's wife whispered that she would stay and say a prayer. I said I was in no hurry and would wait to drive her back, so Domingo and I crossed to the far side of the cemetery to talk.

Fifteen minutes later, after I had expressed a wish for his family's good health, inquired about the well-being of the *ejidatarios* in general, I broached the subject that was the purpose of my visit.

"Señor Domingo, your *ejido* sits on the boundary of Rancho de Sierra Vista. Are you familiar with a man named Mata who works for the owner?"

"This Mata," Domingo said, "he is a friend?"

"He is not a friend. I've had some trouble with him."

Domingo's expressionless eyes surveyed my face, then swept the panorama to the south, the high rims of the sierras backed by a blue sky faded by the sun. Clouds streaked the far horizon in runners of white, pink, and yellow.

"Serious trouble?" he said finally.

"He thinks I have something in my possession that I don't have. He threatened me. I need to know how seriously to take that threat, and to do that I need to know about him."

Domingo said, "I know this Mata. He is the intermediary for this *ejido*." Domingo's hand fluttered. "He is man little amiable."

Little amiable. In the fleeting and subtle use of understatement, Domingo had said much. The words removed the sting, but not the condemnation. In Spanish, the more diminutives attached to a word, the less its connection with truth. Domingo detested Mata.

I could understand why. With no collateral, *ejidatarios* had to borrow money at usurious rates from banks or moneylenders to buy livestock, and *maiz* and *frijol* seed crops. The term "intermediary" meant Mata was the moneylender who not only financed the purchase of stock, but bought the kid goats and crops and arranged the shipping—at a price set, not by the market or by the government subsidies, but by the intermediary's whim, thus giving the speculator a higher percentage of the profits, usually half to two-thirds. That and the high interest charged on the loan, kept the *ejidatarios* chronically in debt. The farther from a market the *ejido* was and the poorer the land the people worked, the more dependent on the moneylender they became. A despicable but very common practice. The *ejidatarios* knew the moneylender took advantage of them, but they were trapped between poverty and the corruption-riddled system that offered no alternative. What surprised me was that

Mata would expend his time on such small-time graft. Maybe it was the taste of power he liked. The control.

I was quiet so long, Domingo asked, "This information helps you?"

"The better one knows an enemy, the better one can defend against him."

Domingo's wife had finished her prayer and walked toward us.

"I'm grateful to you," I told him.

"It is nothing," he said, his eyes sliding toward his wife. I could see he wanted to drop the subject. Whatever else he knew of Mata, I would not be told. I couldn't blame him. I had imposed enough on the goodwill I'd earned by helping with the casket when the burro died on the road.

We made the drive back to the *ejido* in silence except for the few tears his wife wept quietly.

I said goodbye when I let them out. Domingo walked a few feet, turned, and came back to the truck and leaned in at the window.

"Be watchful of this Mata," he said. "He is known as *El Verdugo de Suarez.*"

Miles into the burning afternoon sun, my tired brain finally called up the meaning of the word *verdugo*. Not a word I heard much in daily conversation. Hangman. Mata was known as the hangman of Suarez. Or to translate the idiom into gangster lingo, a hit man.

Ghee's assassin.

THIRTY-ONE

As SOON as I got home, I did two things. First, I lit a candle to Saint Jude, the patron of lost causes, to aid me in finding the skins. Second, I packed away the artifacts that had given Boyce the idea I was a smuggler.

With Phobe helping me by shredding newspaper, I lifted each piece out of the display case, wrapped it in thick layers of newsprint, and placed it carefully in a box, cushioned by more newspaper. By the time I finished, I had filled six boxes.

I was carrying them one at a time to the closet when Clay came in from doctoring a puppy with a stomachache from having been fed hot dogs.

We discussed what I'd learned about Mata.

"If we sit quiet and do nothing, maybe they'll all go away," I said.

"Unlikely. Mata sounds like the type to act first and fast. It would be ironic, wouldn't it, if your Maya friend was wrong and what he saw being passed to the Saint Maker was, say, wood for his carvings."

"I know who may be able to tell us."

"Does this mean another trip? Because if it does, I think I should go with you this time."

"I won't be alone. Irene Pick will be going with me." I explained what the Aplys had told me about the person who had recruited them to smuggle the skins.

"Why should this kid tell you anything or admit to anything?"

"He's got nothing to lose."

"And nothing to gain. From what you saw, he's a young

man with an eye to the main chance. I think you'd better be prepared to meet his price."

"Can we afford it?"

"Depends on his price," Clay said, his brief grin melting into a grim expression. "I don't know about you, but Mata scares me. We may *have* to meet his price."

At the back someone honked three times. Looking for the vet.

Clay headed toward the door, saying over his shoulder, "Don't take that to mean you can't try and negotiate. While I'm out back, keep the front doors locked until you can see who it is." The screen door banged shut behind him.

I sat on my stool behind the counter, idly watching the doors and mulling over the alternatives, feeling impatient to do something and discouraged by my limited options.

The distinctive sound outside had me on my feet and moving. I reached under the counter, and only when my hand came up empty did I remember I'd lost my gun in the cave. I ran to the bedroom, took Clay's extra pistol from the drawer in the nightstand, and went to open the front door with the gun in my hand and clearly visible.

Mata's slick eyes lit on it instantly, and a grin flickered on his lips. He stepped from behind the Hummer—its motor had been the noise I recognized—and smiled, something I found more scary than his normally guarded expression. A pickup, motor running for the air-conditioning, waited behind the vehicle, its driver the lone occupant.

"You're wise to be cautious," Mata said, "but I am here to reward you. El Señor wishes you to have this"—he gestured toward the Hummer—"in gratitude for saving the life of his daughter." He opened the side door. "If you will get in."

"You'll excuse me if I keep on being cautious and stay where I am."

From inside the vehicle, a telephone rang.

"That will be the boss. He wants to thank you personally. Also he anticipated your reluctance. I will step over here." Mata walked away from the Hummer to the end of the porch. "You may keep the gun on me while you speak with him. If it makes you more comfortable," he added, managing to keep any intonation out of his voice that might indicate his certainty of my reluctance to shoot. In that he underestimated my fear for my life. He had told me to remember the Saint Maker's fate and I did. I had the gun cocked and locked, so I could fire fast and more than once if I had to.

The briefcase-size satellite telephone unit was on the front seat. I sat down, lifted the receiver, and said, "Hello."

"Texana," came Ghee's voice, urbane, authoritative, warm, and as clear as if he stood next to me. "I am indebted to you. You risked your own life to save my daughter. On your visit to my ranch you expressed a desire to have a Humvee. I am delighted to be able to fulfill that desire."

"That's too generous of you." I could hardly hear his voice over the sound of my heart thudding in fear as I told him, "I can't accept the Hummer."

"You are hesitant because of the other little business. That is done. Forgotten."

I choked. "I never had the, uh, items."

A pause. "I believe you."

I said, "There is something…"

"Name it."

"I think I should tell your representative here."

A pause. "A discreet woman is a prize. If it can be done, it will be done. I give you my word."

"I don't think it's anything you'll find difficult."

"Then consider it accomplished." He disconnected.

Astonished at my own audacity and presence of mind, I replaced the receiver, slid out of the vehicle, holstered my gun, and said to Mata, "In place of the Hummer I asked a favor. Señor Suarez said I should tell you what I want."

Mata's head dipped in a mock bow. "I'm listening," he said.

It didn't take long for me to explain and in five minutes, the Hummer vanished in a cloud of dust across the river, the pickup trailing in its wake. Even as I breathed again, I had to admit I did hate to let it go.

THIRTY-TWO

ALTHOUGH I FELT sure all Ghee had to do was pick up the phone to make things happen, the prison officials apparently moved more slowly and it was three days before Irene called, laughing and crying at the same time, to tell me she had received a call from the American consul that all charges against Kyle had been dropped and he was to be released.

"Think of it, Texana," she said breathlessly, "only yesterday I was so worried about his having enough money to buy his safety that I went to Presidio to arrange a loan to replace the money that awful purse-snatcher in the taxi took. Now I can go get my son and bring him home. He'd better never leave the country again if he knows what's good for him. I know I never want to see Mexico after tomorrow."

She accepted my offer to drive her without question. I could only hope that doing good under false pretenses counted for something.

We agreed to leave at seven the next morning.

When I told Clay the trip was set, he said he had no appointments scheduled and would do double duty, watching his office and the trading post.

Irene had been ready and waiting for me outside the teacherage for an hour, she told me, when I picked her up. She had packed her money for "tips"—as she preferred to call the *mordida*—more wisely this time, wearing a money belt under her loose shirt. More relaxed than I had ever seen her, she almost enjoyed the spectacular scenery of the river road.

The trip from Presidio to Chihuahua was uneventful, and this time I let her out right by the prison gates to wait for me while I parked. We moved through the same process as before, a cursory check by a guard and the tip.

The prison yard seemed a little less crowded than before, and the absence of people revealed the dismal atmosphere. This time I noticed the guards armed with rifles crouched along the high walls. They wore street clothes rather than uniforms, and appeared, except for the weapons, indistinguishable from the prisoners they watched. An unpleasant thought.

Kyle came running to greet us, looking euphoric and saying again and again, "I'm getting out!" Irene had to assure him four times that she had brought a copy of his birth certificate for the border crossing. His own papers and billfold, confiscated when he had been arrested, had not been returned.

We went back to his place, where he had already packed up the few clothes and other items in one small bag.

"I guess your friend Josh will stay here," I said, looking around at the cramped quarters.

Kyle's smile vanished and he looked somber.

"What's wrong?" Irene said anxiously.

Josh, Kyle told us, had been asked to the warden's quarters for a "consultation" about his plans to make reparations for the wrecked automobile. It was the third meeting that week, and Kyle had been asked by the warden to pay an additional sum or Josh would go back to the tanks.

"How much more?" Irene asked.

"They're just doing it to put pressure on Josh, Mom."

"And squeeze you for more money while they can."

"I've told them I don't have any more," Kyle insisted.

I said, "You're an American. You have more than most of them can imagine. To them, that means you're rich."

Irene said, "If Josh's family needs help, I have a little I could chip in." A nice person, Irene.

I said, "I may be able to help Josh. Why don't you two visit, and I'll wait outside for him."

I left mother and son talking excitedly, and went to stand with my back against the wall facing the prison area where the officials were housed. Fifteen minutes later, Josh came out, shoved along by a guard until he cleared the gate to the courtyard. Despite the high carbohydrate prison diet, he had lost weight and some of the bloom from his cheeks. He also looked shaken and scared, and I guessed he might have been pounded by the guards in places it wouldn't show.

He seemed to have to concentrate on walking straight, and would have passed me by if I hadn't spoken.

"You look like you need a friend."

"I could use a shot of whiskey, if I had any money to send out for a bottle," he said.

I reached into the inside pocket of the jacket I wore and pulled out the flask I had brought along so that, if the opportunity arose, I could look really friendly. I handed it to Josh, silently blessing the warden for his timing in exacting his pound of flesh from the Mennonite for having wrecked his prized automobile.

Josh tipped his head back and drank like a man thirsty for water before holding the flask out to return it.

"Keep it." I order the flasks from Mexico five dollars for a gross. I suspect if you keep one long enough the contents will eat through the thin layer of tin.

He sighed, said, "Thanks," and took another swallow before screwing the top back on and slipping the flask into his belt.

"What happens to you," I asked, "when Kyle leaves?"

"The warden will shove me back in the tanks." He eyed me speculatively, and I could see him make himself restore the look of benign innocence to a face beginning to show traces of the decadence of his true character.

He added, "Unless maybe, if you could help me out with a loan until my family—"

"Let's talk, Josh," I said. "Is there somewhere we can speak privately and maybe sit down? You need to get off your feet."

He glanced around. "There's only the food stalls. We could buy something to eat and sit at one of the tables. It's not private, but no one will bother us."

The tables turned out to be homemade affairs of wooden crates and five-gallon, heavy-duty plastic containers turned upside down for chairs.

"You'll have to pay," Josh said.

"Order what you want."

He got five tacos and beans. To make the proprietor happy, I asked for two tacos I had no intention of eating. I let Josh finish half of his food before I spoke.

"I know about the drug charges you face in Texas. And about the bail jumping, so I know you can't expect any more help from your family."

"I guess that means a loan is out."

"A loan may keep you out of the tanks temporarily. It won't answer your problem long-term."

"Something else will turn up," he said, trying for an air of bravado and only half succeeding. "There are ways of making money in this place."

I looked around and thought of the possible ways for a man to make money here. I wasn't a criminal, and even I couldn't think of much that was honest, except the food stalls. I couldn't see Josh doing that.

I asked, "What would it take to get the warden to forgive and forget about his wrecked automobile?"

"A bigger, better one."

"I can do that."

"You will?" Josh said, paying attention.

"I said I *can*. Semantics are important here, so listen carefully. I can replace the warden's car with something better. Whether or not I do so depends on you."

He looked hard at me, and then around at the prison yard. "I never thought much about dying till I landed in this place. Know what they call what they did to me in there this morning? *Calentadita*. A little warming up. If I go back to the tanks, I won't be thinking about dying, I'll be dead. What do you want?"

"I know about the smuggling, the jaguar skins, and a couple named Aply as couriers."

He picked up his last taco. "If you know all that, what do need me for?"

"I want you to tell me how the system works."

He ate the taco and gave himself time to think.

"Okay," he said finally. "A couple of years ago I went down to Chiapas with some of the Mennonites looking for better land. Some villagers approached me with an idea. They could regularly supply exotic animal pelts for smuggling into the States, but they needed someone to transport them to the border. I went them one better. I arranged for the Indians to act as guides for hunters from the States. I had some contacts who went back and forth from Chiapas—"

"A university researcher," I said, taking advantage of what the Aplys had told me.

Josh raised an eyebrow. "Someone has been talking to you. That lizard Aply, I bet." He shrugged. "What does it matter? The researcher put me in touch with a couple of travel agents in Dallas who fixed up the trips, just like these clients were taking a regular vacation to Las Casas. There's more money in it that way. The hunters pay up-front for the trip, the guns, the guides, the transport of the skins to the States. I found a couple of taxidermists willing to break the law and mount the trophies. For a sizable fee, of course. It's amazing what these trophy hunters will spend to get one more head for their wall. Getting the skins into the States was easy. Normally the locals brought them as far as San Miguel de Allende, where I took over. This trip I brought the skins all the way until I handed them to the old hunchback."

"Why did you change your routine?"

"A few times we flew skins over the border and dropped them, but there was a leak and we came close to getting caught. This was the largest number of pelts we moved at one time, so I did the job myself."

I suspected his real motivation had been greed.

"When I got arrested," he said, "I'd been celebrating my share of the profits. I didn't know about the old hunchback's death until you came to visit and Kyle's mother told us the story about the body found in the chapel. When I heard that, I knew it meant the last of our smuggling."

"Why do you say that? Surely you could have gotten another courier?"

"Because I've got a good idea who killed him."

I didn't breathe for fear of breaking his flow, wondering how far he'd confirm my own belief, consolidate my fears.

"We took a chance running a smuggling ring through somebody else's territory. Right after we nearly got caught, a man approached me. I agreed to pay him a sizable kickback for looking the other way and not informing on us to his boss or anyone else."

"Did this man have a name?"

He frowned, then his face cleared. "What the hell. I've got nothing else to lose. This would have been my last smuggling run with the skins. The hunting is played out down there. Guy's name is Mata, though why you care, I don't know."

"And his boss?" I wanted it confirmed in words.

He looked scared. Then I saw the last of his resolve wiped from his face by a wash of total weakness. I knew he'd give me whatever information I wanted.

He leaned in and said quietly, "Gordon Suarez."

"What do you know about him?"

"About his personal business, all I know is rumors, and those aren't verbalized, like my old English teacher might say. They're just passed along with knowing looks and raised eyebrows. What you don't say can't get you killed."

I let it go. I didn't need Josh to verbalize it for me, either. Charming Ghee *was* a drug lord. I went back to Mata.

"So this man Mata was—"

"—lining his own pockets at the expense of his boss," Josh finished.

"You did pass the skins to the Saint Maker. You're sure of that?"

"I took them out of the duffel bag I used to transport them, put them in his hands, and watched him stuff them into a leather bag he carried." Josh eyed me speculatively. "The skins are missing, aren't they?"

"Yes."

"You find them and get me out of here so I can make contact with the buyers, and we can collect sixty thousand for them."

"Do you have any idea where they are?"

"Mata. I bet Mata killed him for the skins. Not for his boss after all." He grinned, puffing up with optimism. "That means if you get me out, I'm back in business. Mata can't touch me because I can tell his boss about his little sideline."

"And what makes you think his boss will let you go on smuggling through his territory once he finds out that's what you've been doing?"

"How would he do that?"

"Don't you imagine he'd ask how you happened to know about Mata?"

His optimism deflated.

"What happened to the up-front money you got for the skins?"

"I had it on me when I got arrested. What do you think happened to it? The cops are buying shag rugs and color TVs with my cash."

"As I said, I can help you. If you help me. I want the names of the hunters, names of the travel agents, names of the taxidermists."

He took a last pull on the flask, draining it.

"I can supply more than names. I've got pictures of some of the hunters from the States, including a couple of big hats from Texas. I was saving them. Just in case. But I can't use them from in here.

"Got a pen and paper?"

THIRTY-THREE

RIDING ON AN emotional high, Irene and Kyle didn't object to a detour in Chihuahua to pick up something for Josh. Kyle kept the radio on the norteña music he'd developed a taste for during his jail time. Irene kept her eyes on her son.

The street had no name that I could find, not even high on a corner building as so many are painted, but Josh had written down the name of the cantina on the corner and once I spotted the sign of the Yellow Parrot, I knew where I was.

In spite of my carefully obeying every traffic sign, as I pulled away from the intersection Irene twisted around in her seat.

"I think that cop wants you to stop," she said.

"Ignore him," I told her. "I'm short on time and change."

"But he's running after us, blowing his whistle."

"He's just trying it on because he saw the Texas plates. He'll give up in a minute."

"Won't he call in our license and have us arrested?" Irene said, worried for her son.

"He doesn't have radio contact with anybody. These traffic cops work strictly on their own. We'll go back down another street to avoid him. It'll be fine."

Irene looked distractedly at the poor portly street cop, but when he huffed and puffed to a standstill at the next corner, she sighed with relief and faced forward once again.

I found the house Josh had described to me as the place where he rented a back cottage from the owner. The pot-holed street had parking under trees nearly leafless from the drought. I asked Kyle and Irene if they would mind staying with the pickup.

"Sure thing," Kyle said, buoyed with confidence now that he was headed home. Irene looked less happy and more nervous but nodded.

I got out and went to the wooden gate in the adobe wall surrounding the small, neat property. I found no bell at the unlocked gate and walked through. The inside courtyard had paving stones, a dry fountain, and a few well-tended plants in pots. I pulled the handbell by the front door and waited.

A tall, stoop-shouldered man with thin white hair opened the door and peered inquiringly at me over his reading glasses.

Josh had told me he rented the gardener's cottage from a retired American professor. "Dr. Faye?"

"I'm Joseph, please. I must say, you're very prompt. Come in."

"I think you must be expecting someone else."

"You're not from the museum?"

"No," I said, introducing myself.

He laughed at his mistake. "From time to time, the museum sends over a typist to do my papers. I never learned. My wife used to type all my papers for me. How may I help you?"

I explained that Josh had asked me to pay his next month's rent and collect something for him from the cottage.

"Certainly. Come in and let me get you a receipt."

I followed him into a large front room crammed with antiques and books. I paid the modest rent, and accepted the receipt he wrote out in beautiful script that dated the professor as much older than he looked. He told me to go around to the back and follow the path through the wall to the cottage, and he handed me the key, reminding me to return it before I left.

The cottage had three rooms. Neat, clean, furnished with leftovers from the main house, the only evidence visible of Josh's occupancy was the tape player and television. I found the envelope of photographs where Josh had said it would be, in a canister in the tiny kitchen. I examined them only long enough to make sure the prints and negatives were there, and were the kind of evidence Josh claimed before putting them in my pocket. I didn't want to stay too long and worry Irene. Dropping the key by the house on my way to the car, I was in and out in under five minutes.

"Find what you wanted?" Irene asked.

"Yes. We can go home now."

They were both so glad to be on the way that neither asked why, if I'd been picking up something for Josh, I didn't take whatever it was back to him.

Kyle talked all the way to Presidio about what he wanted to do and see and eat when he got home. I didn't think to ask him anything until ten miles up the river road.

"You want to know what Josh and me talked about?" he said.

"What Josh told you about himself, what he did in Mexico to earn a living, friends he might have mentioned, anything you can tell me." I thought it couldn't hurt to try and find out what Kyle might know that his friend hadn't told me. Especially since everyone from Hector to the Aplys had leaked only as much information as suited them.

"He didn't say much actually, except about the Mennonite *campo*. He really hated the life, you know. I mean, he had no freedom, no TV, no music, no dancing. The list of things those people couldn't do was way long."

I asked a few more questions, but concluded that Kyle had taken Josh at face value, never suspecting the flush of

villainy beneath the cherubic glow. We rode in silence for
several more miles before he spoke again.

"If he can get out of that place, Josh will do okay."

"Why do you say that?" Irene asked her son, saving me
the trouble.

"He told me he knew a man who worked for an *influyente*—see how I picked up the lingo? It means somebody
with lots of influence. Josh said in Mexico that means
money."

"Not just in Mexico," I said.

"Right. Anyway, he said this guy was ripping off his
boss. You know, cheating him on stuff the man was selling.
Josh figured if he turned him in to this *influyente,* he'd get
a job working for the rich guy as a reward."

"Did he mention a name?" I asked, already knowing the
answer but wanting confirmation.

Josh thought. "It sounded sort of like Motto."

"Mata?"

"That's it. You know him?"

"Vaguely." I said nothing more, and Josh lost interest,
his prison friendship devolving into a cleansed memory that
would become a tall tale—My Exciting Stay in a Mexican
Jail—to tell his friends, his fears and humiliations left behind like his pregnant young lover.

"What movies have come out while I've been away?"
he asked his mother, the somber facade of maturity he had
acquired in the prison yard dropping with the miles.

While Irene obliged her son, I thought about what Josh
might not have told me. How close was his relationship to
Mata—or had his bragging to Kyle been only the weak
man's litany of bluster, more to reassure himself than to
convince his audience? Most of all, I thought about Mata.

That day I had arrived home with Julia, Gringo had been
jumping, not at me, but at Mata coming in behind me. The
dog had sensed something he didn't like there. I'd have to

remember to tell Pete what a good judge of character his pet was. And Mata had tried to set me against the Aplys by his warning that Boyce was playing the fox. He'd probably similarly cautioned them about me. He had hoped by working against one another, we'd all be prevented from getting away with the skins. I didn't know what to do about Mata. And about what Mata might do next.

My anxiety made the uneventful drive to the border seem endless. While the sniffer dog went over the truck and I opened the toolbox and glove compartment for the Customs officials, Kyle jumped out to kiss the ground, putting a grin on the faces of agents and passersby alike. I dropped Irene and her son at the teacherage at a little after 6:00 p.m.

As I turned into the trading post's parking lot, Pat emerged from the RV and waved me down, her lips mouthing words before I could open the door to hear.

"What's wrong?" I said, getting out. The heat hit me like a bullet and I pulled Pat into the shade of the porch.

Pat grabbed my arms. Her words bunched together like cattle at a gate, all trying to get out at the same time. "They've been here asking questions, about you, about what we know about you, about what we know about the schoolteacher...about where you go on the other side...they think we're working together...they're going to arrest us all."

She could only mean the DEA. I almost smiled. For the second time that day, authority had exerted pressure where it did me the most good. Assuming guilt, the DEA had tried to promote rash and criminal action. The action I planned wasn't criminal. I could only hope it wasn't rash.

I disengaged my arms from Pat's grip. "The DEA can't arrest you. The charges against you are smuggling of a protected species into the U.S.—that's Customs and Fish and Wildlife business. And the state charge over the pills. Go back to the RV and wait for me. I promise, as soon as I shower and get some food in me, I'll come out and we'll talk this over. I got some information today that may help us all out of this mess.''

She didn't like it, she wasn't mollified, but she went.

THIRTY-FOUR

CLAY LURKED behind the front doors, blinds drawn, hiding
from Pat's frantic need to quell her fear of imminent arrest.

"I guess she told you we had visitors," he said.

I nodded.

"She's been at me ever since the DEA agents left to do
something," Clay said. "She talked so much Phobe hid in
the utility room and hasn't come out. I don't know what
she thinks I can do. Damnable woman."

"I know something we can do, and I'll need your help."

Over the throw-together meal we fixed, I outlined my
plan and had coffee while Clay considered it.

"I think it will work," he said with some satisfaction.
"And I'll sure take pleasure in seeing those hunters
caught."

I wiped my lips on the napkin and rose from the table.
"Here goes, then. Let's see if I can make the case with the
Aplys."

Clay laughed. "That's what I like about it. They don't
have much choice. We should go in the morning, so while
you talk to the terrible twosome, I'll make a few calls and
reschedule a couple of ranch visits."

I barely knocked and the RV door popped open.

Neither Pat nor Boyce said hello. We sat at the table in
a repetition of the tableau of the other occasion of my visit.

"Did you know," I said conversationally, "that the jaguar's spots are like fingerprints? Unique."

They looked at me with puzzled, disillusioned eyes.

"What's your point?" Boyce said.

"I have seen nice, clear, close-up photographs of two

hunters posing with stretched skins from three jaguars. Holiday pictures for the scrapbook. Both men are very public figures. Prominent. One is a businessman, the other a member of the state senate, and on his way to national office some say.''

The light of hope gleamed in Boyce's eyes. He said, ''Who has the pictures? Can we get them?''

I nodded. To tell them I had possession already would have cost me the controlling hand.

Pat said, ''I don't get it.''

Boyce said impatiently, ''We could take the photos to Customs and the other bunch and do a deal. The big names mean publicity if they can find the mounted skins in their houses. The photos mean they have a reason to search the men's homes to find the skins, and if what she says is true, a way to prove the skins in the photos match the skins in the pictures. They can legally hunt an endangered species in Mexico. They break a lot of laws when they bring the trophies into this country.''

''I don't think the U.S. Fish and Wildlife even need a search warrant,'' I said.

''That won't satisfy the DEA. What do we do about them?'' Pat demanded.

I said, ''You told me the agents thought the drugs and skins smuggling were mixed up together. With the high profiles of the people involved, my guess is that the agents will be more than happy to switch their attention to two men who should be dying to cooperate in return for a lesser plea or fine.'' I fervently hoped I was right.

''Who has these photos?'' Boyce asked again.

''Your first contact in the skins racket. He's in jail in Mexico and likely to stay there. In return for telling us where to find the photographs and negatives, he expects us to provide the means of getting him out.''

Pat said, ''How do we do that?''

''I'm glad you asked.''

THIRTY-FIVE

AT 7:00 A.M. the next morning, a parade of three vehicles left the trading post. At the head, the Aplys' small, blue pickup turned southeast on Ranch Road 170. The RV with Clay at the wheel followed. I came last in my truck.

The night before I had helped Pat clean and shine the inside of the RV. Clay had washed and polished the exterior while Boyce sulked, muttered, and complained.

An hour and forty-five minutes later, in front of the Presidio Information Center and Gift Shop, I handed the photographs and negatives over to Andalon as the Aplys watched, intent but unsmiling. Unwilling to trust the pair, I had called the sheriff the night before and asked him to arrange the meeting with the U.S. Fish and Wildlife agents, those with the real interest in the photographs. And it wouldn't hurt, I thought, for my friend to get some of the credit in his home county where it counted when election time rolled around.

"I can't imagine why you don't trust us with those photos," Pat had complained when I'd revealed that they were already in my possession. I had half smiled and presented her with the bill for the RV hook-up. I didn't expect to see the couple again.

While I met with Andalon, Clay went ahead into Ojinaga. I caught up with the slow-moving RV a few miles away, on the other side of the town, and we drove at a steady but sedate pace, only once having to pull off to make way for a rampaging eighteen-wheeler in the middle of the road. We reached Chihuahua in four and a half hours.

We parked near the train station, one tourist vehicle

among many others, and I walked the two blocks to the prison while Clay kept watch over the RV from a parking space down the block.

Because of his blond hair, Josh stood out as a solitary still figure leaning against the wall and surrounded by a moving, loud mass of dark-haired men pacing and talking. Josh looked shrunken, his shoulders hunched, his stomach hollow, his head bowed.

His head jerked up when he heard me say his name. The acute fear and desperation in his eyes shocked me, and without another word I held up the keys dangling from Pat's bright red key chain.

Quick as a pickpocket he grabbed them from my hand.

"What is it and where is it?" he asked.

I told him.

Suddenly he seemed happier.

"The owner donated it," I added. "It isn't stolen, but there's no paperwork in it. The owner didn't want his name and address on anything, but I understand that's no problem, that—"

"Right. Half the automobiles in Mexico came from Texas. Paperwork is no problem, getting it or getting rid of it."

"I'll buy, if you want a meal before you tackle the warden," I told him.

Already moving past me, he said, "I'm out of here." He trotted to the guard at the swinging gate to the offices. A moment's conversation and the guard stepped aside to let Josh into the courtyard beyond.

I picked my way around the food stalls to the entrance and walked quickly back to the pickup, joining Clay to wait and watch and see what happened.

"What if the warden takes the keys and leaves Josh locked up?" I said, worried after five minutes. I was under no further obligation to Josh, having delivered the replacement vehicle for the car as promised, but I felt responsible.

"He'll be reasonable. Look at it from the warden's perspective. He runs a prison without a budget, so the inmates must pay for their upkeep. He has to buy his own guns, uniforms. Everything he needs to run the prison. He gets nearly no salary except what he extracts in the *mordida*. To keep his job, he has to pay patronage to the guy above him. His power in the system is determined by the amount of money he can get. Within that tradition of graft, he'll behave honorably, which sounds like a funny way to describe it but—"

"Look."

A car with more dings and dents than paint pulled up to the RV and three people got out. A thickset, gray-haired man wearing a too-tight khaki uniform, a gun belt, and sunglasses surveyed the RV while Josh and a man with a rifle stood and watched. The warden walked all the way around the RV in one direction, then turned and made the circuit in the other direction. He stopped in front of Josh, said something, and held out his hand, palm up. Josh dropped the keys into it. Fat little sausage fingers folded over the keys and the warden smiled and clasped Josh in his arms in the *abrazo*, the formalized hug that is the greeting among males equal in honor. It is the symbol of respect, the cement of friendship, and the signal of acceptance. I could see the grin on Josh's face over the warden's shoulder as the fat fingers patted the Mennonite's back.

"We can go now," Clay said, starting the motor. "Let's go to La Fogata and have a steak to celebrate a mission successfully accomplished."

"Lovely idea. I hope the mission with the Aplys went okay. I'd hate to find the DEA agents camped on the porch at home."

"So what if they are. We haven't done a thing wrong."

I grinned at him. "Unless Boyce gets vicious and claims we stole his RV."

"It's the kind of thing he'd do, all right."

But Boyce had behaved, as Andalon reported to us when he telephoned the trading post at nine that night. The agents and Fish and Wildlife had been satisfied that the photos were worth investigation.

"The agents tried to keep the grins off their faces when they realized who it was in the pictures," Andalon said, "but they couldn't wait to get out of there and get going to set things in motion. You'll see some headlines over this, one way or another. If it turns out they can't prove anything, they'll still leak the names and maybe the pictures to the media. But from what the Wildlife Service agent said, it sounds like two good old boys are going to be very inconvenienced."

"What about the Aplys?"

"They're okay, but the agents really don't like them. I suspect the paperwork will go slow, and they'll get to plea out with a fine on the pills Mrs. Aply brought back."

"What about the charges on smuggling in the jaguar skins? Will they have to testify in court? Boyce was afraid for his job."

"They pay the minimum fine and walk. I doubt they'll be needed in court."

"And Clay and I? Are we still…?"

Andalon chuckled. "Kemp cussed a little, but that's mostly over hurt feelings from Clay's hard words. That said, I'd be careful who I socialized with in the future, if I were you."

"I'll stay away from politicians," I said.

"Easy, obvious shot." Andalon said.

"No, that would be lawyers," I retorted.

Clay and I talked over what Andalon had said as we sat in bed with Phobe, who was getting the attention she'd missed from being alone all day by playing pounce on our wiggling feet beneath the covers.

When the bobcat wore down and fell asleep with her head resting on Clay's arm, we turned out the light. In the still dark I remembered Antun, driven from my mind by the hectic events of the past few days. Was he still out there waiting and watching? I had not seen him again since taking comfort from his presence on the hill when I stole into the Aplys' RV. All the energy and effort I'd expended on fixing things for Irene, for the Aplys, for Josh, for me and Clay, and I still hadn't been able to help the person I most wanted to.

Clay had fallen asleep instantly. I could hear his steady, deep breathing. I got out of bed and went to the front to the display of votive candles, selected a plain vanilla one, and lit it in front of the Saint Maker's statue of the Virgin of Guadalupe. Maybe Saint Jude needed some help, I thought, as I said a prayer that the jaguar skins might yet be found.

THIRTY-SIX

THE CANDLE had melted down and gone out in the night. I used a knife to lift the cold, pooled lump of wax out of the glass and threw it in the trash.

No miracle of the jaguar skins had occurred, and when I opened the trading post and stood on the porch I had no glimpse of the Maya. Perhaps he'd given up and gone home.

Relieved at being back to my normal routine, I spent the morning sweeping the worn wooden floor and dusting the shelves, between serving customers stocking up for the weekend and buying gas for the long Saturday drive to Presidio or Alpine or Marfa to eat or see a movie.

My only customer for the afternoon was Kate, to buy her candle. She spent less time in making her selection, and I thought soon she would stop praying for a miracle and accept that her father might never come home.

At 5:45 p.m., Father Jack came in with a message from Hector inviting us to attend Providencia's fiesta Saturday night in honor of its patron saint.

"Are you going?" I asked him.

"For the first part of the evening." He sighed mightily. "I'm doing an exorcism in the morning to rid the chapel of the spirit of the *nagual*. It's the only thing I can think of to do that might convince the villagers to use the chapel. I wish I'd never met that wood-carver and paid him to come here to make that statue."

"It's a beautiful carving, though."

"Is it? The more I see of it, the less divine and more dark it seems. The old friars were right, I think, about the cult of the Virgin of Guadalupe being a return to the worship of the goddess Tonantzin. At the time of the Conquest she'd fallen out of favor, replaced by the cult of two male gods in the Aztec pantheon, Quetzalcoatl and Huitzilopochtli. I guess the Indians figured if the Spaniards could defeat those two, then Tonantzin deserved their prayers, and they needed her help.''

''See you at the fiesta,'' he said as he left.

THIRTY-SEVEN

FIESTAS IN MEXICO usually begin at dusk in order to end with fireworks.

An hour before dark on Thursday Clay and I started for Providencia with a box of firecrackers and four bottles of tequila clinking together on the back seat.

We could smell the cooking for a half-mile before we arrived. The women had set their fires outside and stirred black pots over glowing embers. Soup steamed, fat sizzled and popped as strips of cabrito fried, and *barbacoa* cooked down to a density that allowed it to be spread on flour tortillas and eaten with the fingers.

The villagers wore their Sunday best. Little boys in stiff new jeans bought a little too big to last longer and little girls in pink or white polyester dresses cut and sewed by mothers ran barefoot in the thick dust of the plaza, working off excitement that had begun as early as the preparations for the celebration. By the time dinner was over, they would be drooping with fatigue and sent to bed.

"Welcome to our fiesta," Hector greeted us, and Clay handed over our contribution to the celebration.

"*¡Cohetes!*" shouted one little boy who spotted the firecrackers, bringing the others running. Hector lifted them above the children's reaching fingers and passed them over to another adult to divide and distribute.

We walked with Hector to the community center where a skinny old man played the guitar on the porch and a handful of older children danced and swayed to the music.

We sat at the edge of the porch, and Clay and Hector immediately began a conversation on the health and keeping of goats, vanishing in no time in the direction of the pens. Vets, like doctors, are always on call.

I watched the children, talked to the women, and carried food inside to the table. As the sun set I raised my eyes and watched the massed shadow of the bats sail into the darkening sky. Not a single villager paid attention to the daily spectacle. The women lighted the lanterns, the men broke out the beer and tequila, and everyone moved toward the community center. Hector and Clay came in arm and arm, prompting me to conclude that someone had been at the tequila early.

Father Jack arrived with bottles of water and boxes of groceries. I helped him unload and asked how the exorcism had gone.

"Fine so far. Hector persuaded most of the men and a couple of the women to attend. I sort of made it up as I went, to cover this specific event and their sensibilities. Whether the people will use the chapel or not remains to be seen. That reminds me…" He felt in his pockets. "Well, Sister Mary Joseph! I left the key in the chapel door. Ah, well, no harm for one night. I'll tell Hector to collect it for me in the morning."

We got everything inside in time to sit down for the meal. Father Jack gave a blessing. Hector rejoined with a toast that called for a grand celebration, "so that tomorrow we dine on *desayumo de campeones*. The breakfast of champions. He referred to menudo, the hangover cure.

I tempered my drinking to a sip of beer now and then to wash down the food, and quietly reminded my husband sitting beside me that we wanted to leave before the drinking got serious.

For remote places like Providencia, fiestas are nights to forget one's poverty and worries. The universal Saturday night, no matter the real day of the week. Later the noise of gunfire would compete with the bursts of firecrackers. A good time for gringos to be at home.

In no time, the party moved back outside. A flickering of candles carried by three women proceeded the entrance of the statue of the patron saint. Held on the shoulders of two men, the wooden statue had been painted like a garish doll's face, the skin shiny pink, the eyes brown circles, the mouth a red pout, and the costume a floral-patterned cape crowned with paper flowers. The villagers shouted and clapped and set off firecrackers that echoed in the hills.

Father Jack tried to talk over the noise. "These poor folks had such bad luck with their old patron saint they buried the statue upside down in the sand and asked me to suggest a new one. That's Saint…"

I missed the rest. "Saint who?" I asked. But the priest didn't hear me and moved away, drawn by a child who wanted his help with more firecrackers.

The men had lowered the statue from their shoulders onto a wooden platform in the center of the plaza. Everything that had gone before had been a prelude. Now the fiesta took off. The night overflowed with the rumblings of friendship and beer. The guitar began again, and with the old man's belly full of drink the chords almost ran away with themselves as his fingers plunked the strings. Men and women danced, while tired children drooped on the porch or in the arms of the old women in their shawls. Hector and Clay sat under the lantern of the porch, a wobbling table between them, swatting bugs, sipping tequila, and playing chess with plastic pieces.

Weaving my way among the dancers and children I moved closer to the patron saint. I stood on tiptoe and looked close. Beneath the paint was a familiar face. What was it Father Jack had said? The old man had carved Tonantzin. The face on this statue was the same face on the small statue that Irene had given me. Both identical to the face on the Virgin of Guadalupe in the chapel. No wonder the old man had completed the carving so quickly. The more refined ones, like the jaguar and the other animal figures I had sold, he'd probably brought with him on his journey up from the south. Once here, the large saint, carved to a well-known pattern, had taken little time to execute.

I walked away to a clear spot near the end of the porch from which I could watch the festivities until the fireworks began. We could not with good manners leave before the most important event of the night, for which the village had no doubt spent too much money.

My eyes returned to the statue, and as clearly as if someone had spoken the answer in my ears, I knew where the skins might be. I glanced at Clay and Hector, scowling intently over the chessboard. I slipped the pickup keys from my pocket and went around the edge of the plaza to the far side. I could drive to the chapel and back in fifteen minutes without disturbing anyone. And Father Jack had left the key in the door.

Backlit by a full moon, dark clouds spread across the high desert sky and once I was well away from the noise of the fiesta, I heard thunder and saw a lightning flash.

I kept my headlights on low beam most of the way because the moon made following the shadows cast by the raised, rough edges of the track easy. I went alone and secretively because if I was right in my guesswork about where the skins had been hidden, I wanted no opposition from anyone in what I intended to do. Father Jack might counsel that I turn the skins over to the authorities. Hector and the villagers would say: The animals are dead, the skins are valuable, and we are poor, so let us sell them. I had an intense aversion to anyone profiting from the destruction of what Antun Tanhol had said might be the last of the jaguars. If I found the skins, I would give them to the Maya. *If* he appeared. If not, I would burn the skins and bury the ashes here in the desert, hoping that Antun would sense somehow that I had tried to fulfill his wish.

The white chapel glowed in the moonlight like a ghost building. I parked right by the doors, saw the key still where Father Jack had left it, cut the lights and the motor, and stepped into silence. The dust swallowed my footsteps, and the door opened on oiled hinges.

The light coming in the small windows on either side of the altar illuminated a narrow strip of space. Before and beyond lay darkness, the Tonantzin/Virgin statue a black shadow against the lighter wall.

I had my pocketknife out and opened to the largest blade by the time I reached the statue. I put the knife on the altar and placed my right hand on the outstretched arm of the figure, my left around the base. I pulled the form forward, surprised at how light it was, and when the base had half cleared the *sillar* block pedestal on which it rested, I slid my left hand underneath and lifted the statue off the block and set it gently onto the floor in the shaft of moonlight. I eased it onto its back, reached for my knife, and knelt at the base, feeling with my fingers for the same plug of wood that Irene had discovered in the base of the small version. Outside the thunder rumbled again, much closer this time.

I thought—imagined?—that I felt a slight line in the smooth wood. I held the knife carefully and pushed until the tip seemed to move into the wood without force.

I worked the tip rhythmically around the line in the base. It was like trying to open a tin can with a pocketknife. When I had reached the point of my beginning, I worked the blade straight in, and lifted. I repeated this at four more points around the plug until I detected a slight give and, shoving the knife in to the hilt—about four inches—I felt the wood give. One more movement of the knife and the plug popped out like a cork.

I rested on my heels for a moment, half afraid the hollow I now knew was there, carved out of the long center of the nearly life-size statue as it had been out of the small, would be empty. My hand trembled as I tentatively reached in, felt paper that tore in my hand, and then...something, a package of some kind bound up with paper and tied with twine.

I tugged, felt the roll give, tugged again, pulled hard and fell backward onto my fanny as whatever it was came loose. I rolled over and on hands and knees cut the twine at both ends of the long bundle, found the edge of the paper wrap and flipped it open. The skins had been rolled up hide-side in. I turned them over. Whoever had skinned the dead animals had been an expert—the hides were perfect. I touched a trembling hand to the top skin and felt beneath the thick, coarse fur a gritty texture, the way Phobe felt after she rolled in the sand. I rubbed my fingers across the fur. A faint scent rose. I imagined sunlight and jungle, but the skins smelled of chemicals and death.

"I knew you'd lead me to the skins."

Only my eyes moved. In the edge of the moonlight, I saw the toes of a pair of boots.

I put my hand over the knife where I'd dropped it beside the skins, clasped it against the palm of my hand, and got to my feet.

"Why were you so sure I'd do that, Josh?"

"'Cause you remind me of a nosy schoolteacher I knew once who couldn't leave anything alone."

He reached out for the skins. In a icy wave of fury, I drove the blade of the pocket knife through his hand.

Stupid move, I reflected in the two seconds it took him to backhand me hard with the other hand. Over the ringing in my ears, I could hear him cursing me as I hit the near-wall and half fell, half slid down to the floor.

I watched as he stood in the moonlight, yanked the knife out of his hand, and dropped it onto the altar. I could see blood drops hit and splatter against the floor. He wrapped the stab wound tightly with a handkerchief. His eyes glinted with pleasure as he picked up the knife and came toward me. I scrambled out of reach and made it halfway around the stone altar. From in front of me a hand reached out of the dark, gripped my upper arm, and pulled me clear of the altar and into the black shadows before letting go.

I heard quick footsteps, a grunt, then two figures danced together around the altar, like a macabre black-and-white movie, one held in a backward grip, wriggling and kicking its feet, trying to get away. A half-cry, a choking sound like nothing I'd ever heard, and the kicking feet stilled, one figure slumped in the arms of the other. The arms let go and the figure fell in a heap on the floor, a black pool spreading around it, enveloping the moonlight.

Father Jack would have to perform a second exorcism.

"You can get up, now, Señora Jones."

I did. Mata wiped off the long blade of his knife on Josh's blond hair, retracted it into the sheath and slipped it into his pocket. He looked around, picked up my pocket-knife from where Josh had tossed it, and came close enough to hand it to me. The bright moonlight shone into his eyes, and what I saw there reminded me of what I had seen in the eyes of the rattlesnake that had bitten Pete's son. No emotion. Only deadly instinct.

"The Mennonite had no respect," Mata said. "He actually called to say he expected to be compensated for not informing El Señor about my little sideline. That was foolish. When El Señor wished the smuggling of skins to be stopped, I obeyed. This boy should have taken notice. I trust you will not be so foolish. I prefer not to kill an American and draw unwelcome attention to this area. El Señor would not approve."

He walked around to the far side of the altar, picked up

the skins, rolled them up, put them under his arm, and moved toward the door.

"Buenos noches," he said, and stepped through the doorway.

I leaned against the wall—it was the only thing holding me upright—and slowly followed it to the door. Beyond my pickup, I could see only one other vehicle parked and no sign of Mata.

Then the gentlest of voices said, "Do not be afraid, Señora. It is I."

Antun.

I went out. The Maya stood on the bottom step looking up at me. There was a bundle under his arm. The roll of skins.

"You have them," I whispered.

"I have them. Thanks to you."

"How did you…"

"I follow to watch over you. The skins put you in danger."

"But where, what…"

"The *mestizo* forgets, if he ever knew, that my people are warriors. We fight longer and kill more Spaniards than any other peoples."

He spoke as if the Conquest continued. And in racial memory, I guess it did.

"My life is full of lost dreams." He held up the roll of skins. "With these, one is redeemed."

I sighed.

He said, "You go now."

I gestured toward the chapel. "There's a dead man inside…"

"The desert hides many things. Death most easily of all. Go now, before they look for you."

I went, climbed into the pickup, backed and turned. As

I drove past the second vehicle I saw a long, too-still shape stretched out on the ground next to it.

I reached the village and managed to walk to the porch and sit down as if nothing had happened. I looked for Clay, but though the chess pieces still rested on the table, there was no sign of my husband or Hector. I suspected that somewhere in the dark, they were setting up the fireworks. The guitar player strummed *Cielito Linda,* the villagers sat in bunches, talking, arms wrapped around one another in inebriate goodwill. The lanterns burned low, and the dogs fought one another for food scraps.

The first Roman candle burst into the sky and banished the moon in its red glow. Voices hushed. Upturned faces reflected the falling stars of light. Another burst, white this time. Red. Yellow. White again. I sat and watched and felt tears streaking my face.

A hand touched my arm and the woman sitting next to me said, "You are unwell?"

I shook my head.

"Please, be happy. This is fiesta."

I managed a smile and wiped my face. "Don't worry," I told her. "It's the fireworks. Fireworks always make me cry."

Too polite to look puzzled, she patted my arm and went back to watching the dazzling display, but I could almost hear her thought: Poor, foolish *gringa.*

I wiped my face with my hands.

Foolish *gringa* indeed.

The final starburst shot up and out and slowly fell and vanished as if it had never been, leaving us sitting in the dark.

EPILOGUE

THREE WEEKS LATER to the day, a glossy pickup I had never seen before stopped in front of the trading post. The man who got out and filled up the dual tanks wore jeans pressed to a military crease, a well-made western shirt, exotic leather boots and matching belt.

When he came in to pay, he carried with both hands a deep mahogany box that he placed ceremoniously on the counter before me.

"You are Señora Jones?"

"Yes."

"This is yours. Please open it."

I did. And sniffed the aroma of fine cigars. A thick, cream-colored card rested on top of the smoky, dark layers. In its center, boldly written, the single letter *G*.

The vaquero clicked his heels, dropped four twenties on the counter, and strode out the door, waving off my cry of, "You have change coming."

I put the cash away, picked up the card, and turned it over. Blank. I put it aside, took out a cigar, found the matches under the counter, and lit up.

I decided I'd keep a few for myself and send the rest to my father. Thinking of my own close relationship with my father reminded me of the devotion to her father I had witnessed in the idealistic Julia, and Ghee's obvious delight and pride in her. No one better to break a father's heart than a daughter. No one more judgmental of a parent than a child. When the inevitable moment came in which Julia realized what her father was, what would she feel? Repugnance at his occupation? Would she turn away from him in condemnation or try to separate her love for him from the corruption of his occupation? Or would the cosseted lifestyle of luxury and power prove the strongest hold? I put down the cigar and went to light a candle for Julia.

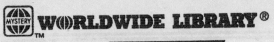